**Dangerous Consequences**

'God Rachel,' said Luke, 'do you normally dress like this or are you wearing this stuff just for tonight?'

'Just for tonight,' she replied, adjusting the lace cups of her basque.

'If I'd have thought you were wearing something like this when I first met you,' he continued, 'I think I would have taken you down to the basement and made love to you right there and then.'

'In the library?' she asked.

'Yes. And I don't think I'd have cared who was watching.'

# Dangerous Consequences
Pamela Rochford

BLACK LACE

Black Lace books contain sexual fantasies.
In real life, always practise safe sex.

This edition published in 2006 by
Black Lace
Thames Wharf Studios
Rainville Road
London W6 9HA

Originally published 1997

Typeset by SetSystems Ltd, Saffron Walden, Essex
Printed and bound by Mackays of Chatham PLC

ISBN 0 352 33185 2
ISBN 9 780352 331854

For Gerard, with all my love

# Chapter One

Rachel half-wished that she lectured in chemistry. Then she'd know exactly what to put into Colin Gilson's coffee to give him a lingering and extremely painful death, but to leave no trace of the cause of death afterwards. Or if Jennifer, her best friend, had been a crime writer, then she would have had a book on poison for research, and Rachel could have borrowed it. Rachel knew that arsenic and strychnine were too traceable, but she was sure that she'd read something, somewhere, about certain fungi interacting with alcohol and becoming poisonous. Maybe she could suggest having dinner, cook a mushroom stroganoff with a very special selection of mushrooms and serve him red wine while she drank mineral water. And then, a few hours later, Colin Gilson would be no more.

She rolled her eyes. It was a fantasy – and a pathetic one, at that. Apart from the fact that she wasn't really cut out to be a murderer, no way would she want to have dinner with Gilson. She could only just force herself to put up with him at work, by reminding herself that there were only a few short months to go before she got her PhD. Then she could find herself a job as far away as possible from the University of London and Colin bloody Gilson.

If Gilson didn't wreck her thesis completely beforehand.

It was just the luck of the draw, she thought, trying to be positive. Except that it was bloody difficult to stay positive where Gilson was concerned. Most of her friends who'd stayed on to do their doctorates had ended up with good supervisors: ones who had a sense of humour, at least, and ones you could talk to about almost anything. It was just Rachel's bad luck that she'd been assigned to Colin Gilson, Professor of the English department and specialist in Victorian studies.

Gilson had no sense of humour, no personality – and he wasn't even remotely attractive. He had a thick jowly face, a fleshy nose and ears, and tiny piggy brown eyes which would have looked better if they'd been hidden behind small round glasses. His hair was grey, greasy and slightly frizzy; and he had thin, cruel lips. Rachel couldn't imagine that Gilson had ever been attractive, even when he'd been in his twenties.

If only he'd been like Paul Bailey, the lecturer who had overseen her second-year undergraduate thesis. Paul had looked like Jeremy Irons in his Brideshead role, and had had a sweet personality to boot. But Colin Gilson was just an arrogant pig-headed bastard, who'd driven her almost to the point of throwing the whole thing in. Though she was too stubborn to take the final step and give up on her future. She wasn't going to give him that satisfaction.

She pulled a face at the coffee machine, and selected black coffee with two sugars. She could do with the caffeine to help her concentrate; and although she didn't usually take sugar, maybe the sucrose would do something to her blood-sugar levels and sweeten her mood. She took a swig of the hot steaming liquid, grimaced and headed back to her cubby-hole, her mind returning to her thesis rather than Gilson.

The next moment, she was shockingly aware of a surprised 'Hey!' Then she realised that she'd collided with someone – and that her coffee had been emptied over his papers.

'Oh, God, I'm so sorry,' she said, flushing. The sheaf of notes he was holding had been written in ink, rather than ball-point, and the neat pale-blue handwriting of a few seconds before had been reduced to a series of illegible coffee-and-blue coloured smudges.

Her flush deepened as she looked up into a pair of greeny-grey eyes, framed by small oval wire-rimmed glasses. She'd never seen him before, though there was something familiar about him. She couldn't place it, but he was utterly gorgeous. He was about six foot tall, she guessed, with dark hair swept back from his forehead, pale skin, those beautiful eyes, and a wounded puppy-dog mouth. He was wearing the almost regulation university clothing of a black polo-neck sweater and faded jeans, teamed with suede desert boots, and Rachel was overcome by a bad case of instant lust.

If she hadn't been so bloody careless, she thought, maybe she could have got to know him properly. As it was, there was no way that he'd even want to talk to her, let alone anything else. Not after the way she'd ruined his notes. If he was a student, he'd be very pissed off with her indeed; and if he was a fellow lecturer from a different department, or even a visiting writer . . . Well, she'd blown it, completely and utterly.

'I'm sorry,' she said again, biting her lip. 'I was miles away – I should have been looking where I was going.'

'Yes.' He looked ruefully at his notes. 'But that'll teach me to be a poseur and write in ink. I think I'll stick to ball-point in future.'

'Look, if there's anything I can do – I dunno, dry them out and type them up for you or something?' The words were out before Rachel could stop them. She cursed herself inwardly; God, now he'd think that she was trying to pick him up. And she wasn't – was she?

To her surprise, he smiled. 'Actually, there is some-

3

thing you can do. I'll accept an apology in caffeine; and I don't mean the muck in the library vending machine.'

It took a moment for his words to sink in. He was telling her that she could take him for a coffee? Rachel was stunned, then elated. If there was a God, it looked like he was trying to make up for Gilson. And how. 'Well, there's a café just over the road,' she said. 'We could go there, if you like.'

'Sounds good to me.' He smiled at her. 'I'll just leave these to dry over my desk. Shall I meet you by the bottom of the stairs in ten minutes?'

'OK.'

He gave her a lop-sided grin. 'Try not to drown anyone else in coffee beforehand, hm?'

'Yeah.' She couldn't help smiling back at him.

She watched him walk away; even the way he walked was attractive, a half-lope which showed off his long legs to perfection. She shivered. She hadn't felt like this about anyone for a long time; she'd spent her time and energies concentrating on her career. Although she'd had the odd affair, including one very wild one-night stand which still made her quim flex when she remembered it, there had never been anything really serious. And she certainly hadn't had a bad case of lust like this before.

She shook herself. An apology in caffeine. That was the way he saw it; so she should do the same. Act cool, Kemp, she told herself fiercely. You've just got your second chance. Don't blow it by going too fast. At the same time, she couldn't help wishing herself a slender five feet eight with long dark hair, blue eyes and long legs. The extra five inches would have made a lot of difference, she was sure. If only she were an elegant businesswoman, dressed in a tailored suit, rather than a short and faintly chubby lecturer with unruly fair hair, boring hazel eyes, an ordinary face and a bad habit of scruffing around in leggings or jeans and baggy sweaters. But she wasn't; so there was no point in thinking of might-have-beens.

4

Ten minutes later he joined her at the foot of the stairs. They walked in silence across the road to the small café.

'What would you like?' Rachel asked as they reached the serving desk.

'Espresso.' He gave her a sidelong look. 'There's not so much of it to spill.'

'Yeah, you have a point.' She smiled wryly back at him. 'The pastries here are good.'

He nodded. 'I'll go with whatever you recommend.'

'Two double espressos, please,' she said to the waiter. 'And two *pains au chocolat*.'

'Coming up. Take a seat,' he said, smiling back at her.

Rachel walked over to a corner table by the window; her nameless companion joined her. 'I really am sorry about your notes,' she said. She held out her hand. 'Anyway, I'm Rachel Kemp.'

'Luke Holloway,' he said, taking her hand and shaking it.

The touch of his skin against hers made her palms tingle. She could so easily imagine him touching her a little more intimately, his hands stroking her skin as he undressed –

She stopped herself short and coughed, to cover her confusion. 'I hope your notes survive. I meant it about typing them up for you. I've got a computer in my office.'

'So you're a lecturer, then?' He tipped his head to one side, looking at her. 'I had you pegged as a student.'

'Not exactly.' She wrinkled her nose. 'I'm thirty, and at the tail end of my PhD. I took a couple of years out after my first degree, but I wasn't really cut out to be an accountant.'

'So you don't teach maths, then.'

Again, that quirky smile. Rachel felt her nipples start to harden. To borrow one of her friend Jennifer's phrases, Luke was 'sex on legs'. Completely gorgeous. But she couldn't allow herself to start fantasising: the coffee was merely an apology for wrecking his notes. There was nothing more to it than that. This wasn't a date, and it wasn't likely to lead to one. 'English,' she supplied. 'Specialising in nineteenth-century fiction and the odd bit of poetry. How about you?'

'Economic history.'

A department which had no real connection with Rachel's own; no wonder that she hadn't met him before. 'Student?' she guessed.

He grinned. *'Touché.* No, I teach.'

She nodded. 'Right.'

The waiter came over to their table, placing the coffees and pastries in front of them; Rachel smiled her thanks at him and took a sip of the dark bitter liquid. 'God, I needed that,' she said, revived by the coffee.

He added sugar to his own. 'That sort of a day, is it?'

'Something like that.' She didn't want to think about Gilson; she took another swig of coffee and changed the subject. 'I'm trying – and failing – to place your accent.'

'Home counties. Though I've spent the past three years working in America; someone told me recently that I've got a bit of a transatlantic drawl.' He laughed. 'It'll wear off, now I'm back – given a couple of months.'

'Probably.' Rachel suddenly realised whom he reminded her of: an American actor in a cult science-fiction series, whose pictures had been culled from the *Radio Times* and *Time Out* and pinned on virtually every woman's office pin-board in her corridor. She was only surprised that no one else had seen the resemblance and talked about it with friends. Gossip travelled very fast through the university, particularly where attractive men like Luke were concerned.

He smiled at her. 'So, Rachel, what was so interesting that you forgot to look where you were going?'

She winced. 'It wasn't that interesting. I was working on my thesis.'

'Oh?' he prompted.

'It's on the role of women in the Victorian novel. The conventional ones end up marrying; the unconventional ones end up dead, or as good as. Mrs Dombey, Maggie Tulliver, Sue Bridehead . . .' She grimaced as she heard herself switch into lecturer mode. 'And I'll shut up now, because I could bore for England on the subject.'

'Seriously, I'm interested.' His eyes flickered.

'Yeah, well.' She spread her hands. 'I'm just having a few problems with it, at the moment.'

'Writing it up?'

She shook her head. 'I'm sure that you've got a hundred and one better things to do than to listen to a junior lecturer whinging.'

'Not until my notes have dried out.'

She flushed. 'I did say that I was sorry.'

'And I shouldn't tease you,' he agreed. He took her hand. 'Rachel, it sounds to me like you need someone to talk to.'

'I don't think that talking is going to help.' Particularly if Luke was going to keep touching her like that. It made her want more – much more. It made her want to be completely alone with him, skin to skin, using her hands and her mouth to explore him properly. Letting him explore her, too, discovering how her body could react to his touch.

'Try it.'

His voice broke into her thoughts; she drained her coffee, trying to preserve her calm, and hoped that her voice wasn't shaking. 'Let's get another coffee, first.'

'My shout.'

'No. It's the least I can do, after what I did to your notes.'

He grinned. 'I forgave you for that quite a while ago.'

'Well.' She caught the waiter's eye, and ordered two more espressos.

Luke took a bite of his *pain au chocolat*. 'Mm, you're right, these are very good.'

'Especially when you've had a bad day,' Rachel said wryly. The pastries were fast becoming a habit, with the way Gilson had been acting towards her all term.

'So tell me, Ms Kemp,' Luke said, in his best impression of a New York shrink, 'what seems to be the problem?'

'In a word, Gilson.' She sighed. 'I shouldn't be talking to you about this. It's unprofessional.'

'But it's better to talk about it than to keep it bottled up,' he said.

'Maybe.' She wrinkled her nose. 'Basically, I don't get on with the guy who's supervising my PhD – the professor of our department. It's a major personality clash; we disagree on just about everything. Politics, music, art – we even disagree on our views of nineteenth-century literature. He loves Dickens and Austen, whom I hate; and I adore Hardy and George Eliot, whom he doesn't.'

'Ouch.'

'Yeah. Luckily we don't have any of the same tutorial groups or have to mark each other's papers, or we'd be in real trouble. We really don't like each other; but I suppose that we're stuck with each other. There's absolutely nothing that I can do about it. He's made me rewrite my thesis six times already – and I don't mean just work on it to improve it, I mean nit-picking over the most tiny details, and then changing it back to the original version six months later.' She grimaced. 'When I crashed into you, I was thinking of ways to murder him. Very slowly.'

'Right.' His mouth twitched. 'Pity that I'm not a chemist.'

'Yeah. My sentiments exactly.'

'What you need,' he said, 'is something to take your mind off it.'

'Mm.' Rachel couldn't meet his eyes. She could think of something that would take her mind off her problems; but how could she tell him? Excuse me, Luke, I wondered if you fancied catching the tube back to my place and spending the next forty-eight hours making love with me? Hardly.

8

'I don't have any answers,' Luke said, oblivious to the lascivious look that Rachel was sure was passing over her face, 'but how about dinner?'

'Pardon?' Rachel couldn't quite believe what she'd just heard.

He shrugged. 'Sorry, I got it wrong.'

She frowned. 'I'm not with you.'

'Asking you out to dinner. I should have checked first. Maybe your boyfriend won't like it.'

She shook her head. 'There's no boyfriend. I just wasn't sure that I'd heard you properly.'

'You're really in training for the absent-minded professor bit, aren't you?' he teased.

'Something like that.'

'Well, I don't know many people in London since coming back from the States, and if you're not already busy, it'd be nice to have dinner with you. An evening of good food, good wine and good conversation.'

'I'd like that. Thanks. Though we go Dutch,' she warned.

'Sure. I like Dutch food. There's a place just round the corner from me, in Holborn.'

She rolled her eyes. 'That isn't what I meant and you know it.'

He grinned. 'OK. We'll split the bill. Is Italian all right with you?'

'Italian would be lovely.'

'Right.' He smiled at her. 'What time?'

'Half seven?'

He nodded. 'I'll pick you up. Where do you live?' Rachel gave him her address; he smiled. 'I should have guessed that a Victorian specialist would live in Walthamstow. William Morris country.'

'I like the area,' Rachel said. 'OK, so it's not Regent's Park or St John's Wood, but Vallentin Road's not that far from the station, and it's a quiet road.'

'OK. I'll see you there at half seven, then.' He finished

his coffee. 'And I suppose we'd both better get back to work.'

Rachel flushed. 'I really do feel bad about your notes.'

'These things happen.' He gave her another of those lop-sided grins. 'See you tonight, then.'

'OK.' She watched him leave, then finished her coffee. She still couldn't quite believe this. The most attractive man she'd met in months had asked her out to dinner, even though she'd ruined his work by throwing coffee over him. And it had happened when she was at a low ebb, even considering giving up her doctorate. She smiled. These things happen, he'd said. Well. Who knew what the evening was going to bring?

In the end, Rachel didn't bother doing any more work in the library. She simply picked up her notes, checked out a couple of books and went back to her small Victorian terrace. She caught sight of herself in the mirror as she closed the door and grimaced. 'Luke must have been bloody lonely or incredibly bored,' she told her reflection. Why else would someone as gorgeous as he was ask someone like her to have dinner with him?

She dropped her soft leather briefcase in the hall and walked over to the mirror, studying herself. Her fair hair was an acceptable colour, and if she kept it pulled back from her face with an Alice band, it looked reasonable. Her face was heart-shaped; she didn't have a big nose or big teeth, but she wasn't stunningly pretty either. Just average, she thought. Ordinary eyes, a warm hazel that turned gold when she was happy and orange when she was in a temper; a rose-bud mouth; and even, white teeth. She was definitely too short for her weight, though. If the extra couple of stone had been stretched through another four or five inches, she'd have looked good; at five feet three, she was unfashionably curvy. Though at least she was in proportion, she supposed.

On impulse – and knowing that no one could see her through the solid wooden door – she peeled off her sweater and looked critically at herself. Her breasts were good. 38D, the underwiring of her white lacy bra deepening her cleavage. Soft, pale skin. She pushed down the cup of one bra; rosy nipples, which were so responsive to the touch. She traced her areolae, and her nipple hardened immediately.

'Mm,' she murmured. The thought of Luke doing that to her made her stomach lurch with pleasure. He'd barely touched her – just stroked her hand – and that had turned her on. Supposing that dinner led to coffee at his place, and he touched her more intimately?

She kicked off her ankle boots and removed her leggings. Licking her lower lip, she pushed down the other cup of her bra, so that both her breasts were exposed lewdly. Her cheeks were flushed slightly, her eyes glittering, and she looked completely wanton, she thought. And lush. She was all curves, her waist narrowing in. Her previous lovers had grown hard just at the sight of her breasts, imagining what it would be like to slide their cock between the soft lush globes. Would Luke do that, later that evening?

She licked her forefingers and thumbs and began to rub her nipples, pulling gently at the hard peaks of flesh. She loved her breasts being touched like that; and she could imagine Luke's long slender fingers working on her, teasing her until her nipples were so hard that they hurt. And then he'd use his mouth on her, sucking hard, using his teeth but keeping it just the right side of pain, until she was writhing beneath him and begging him to touch her more intimately.

And then he'd let one hand drift over her abdomen. Rachel closed her eyes and her right hand slid down over her belly, her fingers dipping beneath the lace edge of her knickers. She let her hand drift lower, extending her middle finger and letting it glide between her labia. She was already warm and moist, ready for him; in her mind, she pictured him touching her, his hand burrowed

11

between her thighs and his fingers stroking her quim, exploring her folds and crevices.

She gave a small moan of pleasure as she touched her clitoris; the little bud of flesh was already swollen, responding sharply to her touch. Pleasure lanced through her; she altered her stance slightly to give herself easier access, and pushed her finger deep inside, scooping out the nectar. She slicked it over her clitoris, and began to rub in earnest, her finger moving in a rapid figure-of-eight pattern.

'Oh, yes,' she breathed, rubbing herself harder; with her other hand, she continued to squeeze her nipples, pulling on the hard peaks of flesh and imagining Luke's mouth there. Or even better, kneeling in front of her with his tongue deep into her vulva or his mouth sucking hard on her clitoris, while his fingers slid along her quim, dabbling in her moistness and spreading it over her perineum, caressing the rosy puckered hole of her anus and finally penetrating her.

Pleasure lanced through her at the thought; she wanted to be filled, but her own right hand wasn't good enough. She couldn't possibly make it up the stairs to grab the vibrator from her bedside cabinet: she needed it now, right now. She couldn't wait. 'Oh God, oh God,' she moaned, continuing to rub herself hard and wondering what the hell she had near at hand to ease the ache.

A smile spread across her face. Of course. She paused long enough to extract the hairbrush from her briefcase, then pushed the gusset of her knickers to one side and fitted the end of the brush to the entrance of her sex. She pushed gently and sighed with relief as the thick handle slid into her, filling her; then she began to use it, pulling it almost out of her, then pushing it back in hard, as though Luke were really there with her and fucking her as they stood in the hall.

'Oh God, yes,' she moaned; she dropped her other hand from her breasts, and began to rub her clitoris again, stimulating the bundle of nerves in the same rhythm as she used the brush. It felt so good, so very, very good; she could feel the pleasure starting in the soles of her feet, growing warm, making her flesh tingle as it crept up over her calves, through her thighs, finally coiling in the pit of her stomach and exploding. She tipped her head back, crying out as she came, her quim flexing hard round the thick handle of the brush.

Then she was still, letting herself float, her body drifting in the pleasure as her breathing slowed. When the final aftershocks of her climax died down, she opened her eyes and smiled wryly at the sight in the mirror. If anything, she looked even more wanton, the hairbrush lodged between her legs, her bra lewdly positioned and her creamy flesh mottled with the rosy shadow of her orgasm.

'This one's for you, Luke,' she said softly. And if things went well enough that evening, she'd have something much, much better than a hairbrush to pleasure her.

# Chapter Two

*A*t seven-thirty precisely, Rachel's doorbell rang. Her
eyes widened. She'd been half-expecting Luke to
stand her up, once he'd had time to think about his offer
of dinner and to regret it.

She, on the other hand, had thought of nothing else
that afternoon. She'd intended to work on her disserta-
tion, but she'd been unable to concentrate, thinking of
Luke. In the end, she'd given in, spending the afternoon
lying curled up on her bed with a good novel and a glass
of wine. Half the time, she hadn't been paying attention
to the book, either: she been imagining what it would be
like to make love with Luke, and had spent more time
masturbating than anything else, hoping to get it out of
her system before she met him for dinner. Except that, if
anything, it had made things worse. She wanted him
even more badly than before.

She shook herself and answered the doorbell.

'Hi.' He smiled down at her. He was dressed casually,
in stone-coloured chinos, another black cotton poloneck
sweater and suede boots, topped with a long black
cashmere coat. He looked completely gorgeous.

'Hi.' She smiled back, glad that she'd gone for the
semi-casual look of tailored black trousers, a black chif-

fon shirt patterned with small beige and blue flowers and court shoes. Not too dressy; but not scruffy, either. She'd managed to hit the right note for once.

'Ready?'

She nodded.

'Come on, then.'

Rachel grabbed her coat, locked the door behind her and followed him out to his car. Her eyes widened as she realised that he was driving a black MG roadster – one that was twenty years old, admittedly, but she'd never met anyone who drove a sports car before.

'Meet Bess,' he said languidly as he opened the passenger door for her.

'Bess.' She suddenly clicked what he meant, and grinned. 'See yourself as Mr Turpin, do you?'

'No. It was just a very feeble joke at the time and it stuck,' he answered, climbing into the driving seat.

Rachel settled back into the surprisingly comfortable seat. 'So where are we going?'

'Italian, we agreed. There's a nice place I know in Islington.'

'Wouldn't it be easier to go by tube?'

He grinned. 'Probably, but I happen to like driving. Like I said, I haven't been back in the country for that long, and I can't get enough of driving – especially where Bess is concerned.'

'Fair enough.' Rachel wasn't a car aficionado but she could understand what he meant. Driving the MG would be a pleasure rather than a chore.

They lapsed into a companionable silence on the way to the restaurant. The journey took less time than she expected and they were soon at Islington. Luke parked round the corner from the restaurant and ushered her out of the car. To her faint disappointment, he made no attempt to take her hand; but it was early days, she reminded herself. They'd barely met. Don't rush it, she told herself silently. If it happens, it happens.

The restaurant turned out to be a small and very cosy

15

bistro-style place, with bare wooden floors, terracotta-coloured marbled walls and small scrubbed wooden tables with candles stuck in old raffia Chianti bottles. There was a jazz band playing softly in the corner and a huge blackboard testified to a wide range of specials. A proper Italian restaurant, Rachel thought with pleasure as she glanced over the board, not just a pizza and pasta place.

A smiling waiter greeted them at the door. 'Good evening, Mr Holloway.'

'Hello, Roberto.' Luke smiled back.

'Your table's ready for you.' The waiter took their coats and ushered them over to a table in the corner. 'Can I get you a drink while you're choosing?'

Luke gestured to Rachel. 'What would you like?'

'Um – red wine, please.'

'And a mineral water for me, please.'

'Certainly.' The waiter made a note on his pad and handed them a menu each.

Rachel looked at Luke, her head tipped slightly to one side. 'You know this place pretty well, then.'

'Mm.' He flushed, slightly shame-faced. 'They also sell take-out and I hate cooking.'

That had to be an understatement, Rachel thought: Islington was hardly next door to Holborn, and if he was prepared to drive here for a take-out, just to avoid cooking ... 'I see.' She paused. 'Do you recommend anything in particular?'

'The crab-stuffed ravioli's very good,' he said. 'And their steak with blue cheese sauce is excellent – if you're not a vegetarian, that is.'

'I'm not. So that's nice and easy, then,' she said with a smile, folding her menu.

'We'll make that two, with a bottle of red wine.' His lips twitched. 'If you're like most of the women I know, I think you'll like the Carrigano del Sulcis Riserva.' Rachel waited for him to make some kind of sexist comment about the wine being light enough for women to cope with it, and was pleasantly surprised when he merely informed her, 'Because it has a finish of pure chocolate. I thought that it was just sales patter until I tried it.'

'Chocolate,' she said, her disbelief obvious. 'A red wine that tastes of chocolate.'

'Seriously. It's Sicilian, and this is the only place I know that sells it. I've asked in all the local wine merchants and they don't have any; I'm trying to talk Roberto into selling me a case.'

'Right.'

The waiter returned with their drinks and took their order. Rachel was amused to notice that Luke ordered their meal in perfect Italian, rather than relying on the English translation. And yet there was no hint of showing-off: it seemed natural, just the way he was.

The meal turned out to be as good as Luke had promised and the wine did indeed taste of chocolate. Rachel found herself relaxing more and more in his company; Luke was fun to be with, his sense of humour similar to her own. There was a serious side to him, too, and the more she got to know him, the more she liked him.

And the more attractive she found him.

Whether it was due to the fact that she'd drunk a lot more wine than he had, the ambience of the restaurant, or pure and simple pheromones, she wasn't sure, but it was so tempting to slip her shoe off and let her foot stroke his ankle. She only just managed to hold herself back, though she was sure that Luke could tell exactly what she was thinking. Rachel was very much a 'what you see is what you get' kind of person, her feelings written over her face. No doubt she was a picture of slavering lust. Calm down, Kemp, she told herself crossly. Don't come on too strong. This is a first date; don't blow it.

But if Luke noticed, he was too kind to say anything; he continued chatting easily to her, finding out more about her tastes in books and music and art, and discovering that they both loved blues rock, bawdy Renaissance drama and cult science fiction. He was going to become a good friend, Rachel thought. They had so much in common. And, with luck, they'd be more than just good friends. Much more.

When they'd finished their espressos, Luke paid the bill. Rachel protested, reminding him that they'd agreed to go Dutch, and he smiled. 'Let's make it your shout next time, then.'

'Deal. Though next time, neither of us drives. I'm going to have one hell of a hangover in the morning.'

He chuckled. 'Well, you couldn't waste the bottle, could you?'

'Especially a wine as nice as that one.'

'I'm glad you liked it.' He took their coats from the waiter and helped her on with hers, shrugging his own over his shoulders.

'I did, very much. I've really enjoyed this evening.'

'Me, too.'

And it doesn't have to end just yet, Rachel thought to herself as he drove them back to Walthamstow. 'Would you like to come in for a coffee?' she asked, when he parked outside her house.

'Thanks, that'd be nice.' He locked the car and followed her into the house. His lips twitched as he looked round.

'What?'

'I should have guessed that you'd have a nineteenth-century place.'

'Aren't most London terraces Victorian?' she asked lightly.

'Mm. But I bet not all of them have been as lovingly restored as this one.' He nodded at the tiles on the hall floor. 'Reclamation, right?'

She was surprised and impressed. 'How did you know?'

'Because my sister's an interior designer. Most of her

work's to do with period restoration, rather than modern places, and she always says that you can tell original materials a mile off.'

'Probably. I just – oh, I dunno. I suppose I just wanted to do it properly.' Rachel kicked her shoes off and hung her coat on the bentwood stand. She avoided looking in the mirror, flushing as she remembered her behaviour earlier that afternoon, and padded into the kitchen. Luke followed and leant against the worktop, watching her as she made the coffee.

'Better carry it yourself,' she said with a grin, handing him a mug. 'You don't have any notes to protect you this time, and I think that this would make a hell of a mess of your chinos.'

He chuckled. 'True.'

'The sitting room's the second door on the right,' she said.

He nodded and walked back down the hall. Rachel hadn't drawn the curtains before she'd left that evening, so the room was lit with the orange glow of the street-lamp, enough to show him where the light-switch was. Rachel closed the curtains as he turned on the light, then smiled at him. 'Shall I put some music on?'

'Sure.'

She balanced her mug on the mantelpiece and flicked deftly through the rack of CDs, finally picking an old Free compilation. As the first notes flooded into the air, Luke smiled approvingly. 'I love this one.'

'Me, too.'

He set his mug down on the mantelpiece. 'Mind if I . . .?' He gestured towards her bookshelves.

'Help yourself.' She retrieved her coffee and curled up on the sofa, watching Luke as he scanned the shelves. Even from the back, he was attractive: broad shoulders, a nice bum. She would have bet serious money that he looked even better without the chinos and sweater.

Then she noticed which particular shelf he was scanning. She took a gulp of coffee. This was definitely make or break time. Either he'd be interested or he'd make an excuse to leave, and fast.

To her relief, it was the former. He turned round, holding a book. 'You're a Jude Devereaux fan, then?'

'She's a good friend of mine, actually.'

'And that's why you have her books on your shelves?'

Rachel grinned. 'And because I like reading them.'

'Right.'

'She lives in Yorkshire. I'll introduce you next time she comes down to London for the weekend, if you like.'

'Yes, I would. Very much.'

Jennifer and Luke would hit it off immediately, Rachel thought. 'So how come you're familiar with her work, then?'

'She's very popular in the States, too.'

However broad-minded Luke was, Rachel couldn't quite see him breezing into a bookshop and buying women's erotica. 'And?'

'All right, an ex-girlfriend introduced me to her books. This particular one was responsible for one hell of a night.' He grinned back and replaced the book on the shelves, continuing to scan the spines on that particular shelf. 'You've got quite a collection here. Is the Victorian stuff original?'

'Reprints. I couldn't afford the original stuff – even if it wasn't near-impossible to track down.'

'Work or pleasure?'

'Work,' she said. 'I don't have a taste for Victorian porn. It's too samey and I get bored reading about blushing virgins being deflowered by huge Negroes. Actually, it's part of my thesis – or rather it was. Gilson made me remove that particular section.'

'Why?'

'I think that it embarrassed him.'

'And you, of course, didn't have that at all in mind when you wrote it?' he teased.

Rachel chuckled. 'I suppose there was a bit of that in it. But it was genuinely part of my thesis. In Victorian times, women were seen as the "angel in the house" – but also as the sinner. I just chose to contrast the two different views of women by using erotica.' Her lips twitched. 'I admit most of it's pretty hackneyed stuff – but at least the women aren't quite as annoying as Esther Summerson.'

'*Bleak House*.' Luke grimaced. 'I was forced to do that for A-level. I hated every minute of it.'

'Mm. I refuse to teach it.'

'Which I bet goes down a bundle with Gilson.'

'He's a real Dickens fan,' she said wryly. 'So yes, it doesn't exactly help my cause.' She pulled a face. 'Anyway, I don't want to think about Gilson tonight.'

'Fair enough.' He came to sit beside her. 'How did you get to know Jude Devereaux, then?'

'We met at a conference, would you believe? We were sitting next to each other and we started chatting. We hit it off straightaway, and we found out that we've got so much in common. We like the same kind of music, the same kind of art and books and films.' They found the same kind of men attractive, too, though Rachel decided not to tell Luke that. She and Jennifer didn't share men. Just fantasies. 'If she has to come to London on business, she usually stays with me; and I've got a standing invite to the Yorkshire moors whenever things get too much for me, here. I suppose, really, I count her as my best friend.'

Luke gave her a sidelong look. 'And is she anything like I imagine?'

'That depends on what you imagine.'

'Tall, curvy, lots of red hair – a bit pre-Raphaelite – and quite glam?'

'Dark hair; otherwise you're spot on. Except when she's got a hangover – then she scruffs around in faded leggings, a T-shirt and a baggy old cardie that's seen better days, looking pale and drawn and saying that she's never going to drink again.' Her lips twitched.

21

'Though she's not the type to vamp people. She doesn't actually live out her books.'

'I don't think she'd be able to sit down if she did.'

'So you really have read some of her stuff.' The words were out before Rachel could stop them.

He grinned. 'Did you think that it was an excuse to start talking about sex?'

'No.' She flushed. 'It's just . . . well, Jude's audience is primarily female.'

'With the odd male,' Luke agreed. 'I like her style. And, like I said, an ex-girlfriend introduced me to her books. I've probably read most of them since.' His eyes caught hers. 'Rachel. I suggested dinner tonight because I wanted to get to know you better. But if I stay here for much longer and we continue discussing this particular subject, I think that I'll outstay my welcome.'

Rachel was still feeling faintly tipsy and the look in his eyes made her take the risk. She smiled. 'Who says?'

In answer, he cupped her face, drawing it closer to his, and touched his mouth lightly to hers; she tipped her head back slightly, her lips parting, and he nibbled at her lower lip. He slid one hand down to cup the nape of her neck and the other stroked gently down her spine, coming to rest at the soft swell of her buttocks.

Rachel slid her arms round his waist, pressing against him; he nudged her thighs apart with one knee, sliding one leg between hers. She murmured slightly and he kissed her properly, his tongue flickering against hers. 'Mm, Rachel. I want you,' he told her hoarsely as he broke the kiss. 'I've been thinking about you all afternoon. I didn't get any work done.'

'Ditto,' she admitted.

'Because you were thinking about me?' She nodded, and he smiled. 'I wasn't sure. That's why I drove.'

She frowned, not understanding.

'Because it meant that I'd have to concentrate on the road and I wouldn't make a fool of myself, trying to rush you.'

She smiled wryly. 'I was having the same thoug[ht],
believe me. I nearly kicked my shoes off and starte[d]
playing footsie with you in the restaurant.'

'If you had, I think we'd have had to get a taxi back
here – or to my place,' he told her. 'And fast.' He looked
at her for a moment, as if considering something, then
bent his head again, kissing her hard. Rachel responded,
tugging at his sweater and sliding her hands underneath
it, smoothing the skin of his back.

He broke the kiss again. 'I want to make love with
you, Rachel. Right now. I want to touch you, to stroke
you all over – and then do it again, with my mouth. I
want to make you shiver in my arms and I want to make
you come, over and over and over again, until you're
crying out my name.'

His words sent a thrill through her. 'Then what are
you waiting for?' she asked softly.

'You, to lead me to your bedroom,' came the pragmatic
answer. 'I could make love to you here – but I think that
it'd be better for both of us in comfort.'

She chuckled. 'And who says that I don't sleep in a
single bed?'

'A woman with a collection like that' – he indicated
her bookcase – 'doesn't just sleep in bed. She reads as
well; and that means, she likes to read in comfort.' He
rubbed the tip of his nose against hers. 'Particularly as
that kind of book usually leads to something else.'

She flushed. 'Oh?'

'Don't be bashful, Rachel. The sight of an attractive
woman pleasuring herself is one that . . .' He shivered at
the thought. 'Let's just say that it's one that most men
enjoy. I certainly do.' He smiled at her. 'And some time
soon, I'm going to read one of Jude's books to you – and
watch the effect it has on you. Because I guarantee that
you'll have your hands between your legs within fifteen
minutes.'

She lifted her chin. 'Is that a challenge?'

He nodded. 'But not for tonight. Tonight I want to

yself. I want to make love with you, skin to
ood up and drew her to her feet. Rachel led
, not bothering to turn off the light in the
sitting room on the way; she wanted to feel Luke's
mouth on hers again and then feel him carry out his
promise to kiss her all over.

She loosed her hand from his as they reached her
bedroom, then walked over to draw the curtains and
switch on the bedside light before coming back to stand
before him. He smiled at her, and removed the black
velvet Alice band which held her hair back from her
face, letting her curls fall down to her jawline. 'I love
your hair,' he told her, burying his face in it and
breathing in her scent. 'Coconut,' he pronounced; then
he held her at arm's length, and slowly began unbuttoning her shirt, keeping his eyes fixed on hers.

Rachel shivered as she felt his fingers brush against
her breasts; her nipples hardened immediately. God, she
wanted him. She wanted him now. She tipped her head
back slightly, pushing her breasts towards him; he
smiled.

'Patience is a virtue.'

'Not one that I possess,' she informed him huskily.

'Indeed.' Then he allowed himself to look down and
his eyes widened as he realised what she was wearing.
A black basque, underwired to emphasise her cleavage;
her skin was creamy through the lace of the garment,
and he could see the darkness of her nipples. He drew
one finger through her cleavage, making her moan, and
then pulled her to him again.

He kissed the curve of her throat, nibbling at the
hollows of her collarbone, then rubbed his face against
her breasts, taking in her perfume. The hard peaks of her
nipples thrust at him through the silk and lace; he didn't
bother trying to undo the hooks at the back of her
basque, but slid his fingers under the cups, pushing
them down to free her breasts.

Rachel moaned, and he began to tease her nipples,

24

rolling them between thumb and forefinger and pulling them gently so that they were distended. She arched against him, wanting more, and tugged at the hem of his sweater. 'Skin to skin, you said.'

He smiled wryly, releasing her for a moment while he removed his sweater. His torso was lean and firm and his chest well-developed with a light sprinkling of dark hair; Rachel couldn't help licking her suddenly dry lips. He looked as good as she'd imagined: and this was going to be more than a pleasure for both of them, she knew.

Gently, he cupped her chin in both hands, drawing her face towards his; he nibbled softly at her lower lip, running his tongue along it before kissing her deeply. His hands slipped down to her waist and he slowly undid the zip of her trousers, eased the material down to her knees and slid one hand between her thighs to cup her mons veneris. The heat of her quim pulsed against his fingers through the thin silk of her knickers; she flexed her internal muscles, wanting to feel him inside her.

'I want to taste you, Rachel,' he told her huskily. 'Properly.'

She shivered, and he knelt before her, sliding her trousers down to her ankles as he did so; she stepped out of them, and his eyes widened as he took in the picture of the woman before him, wearing the lewdly positioned basque, matching knickers and hold-up black stockings with lacy welts. 'God, Rachel. Do you normally dress like this or was this just for tonight?'

'Just for tonight,' she confirmed.

'Mm. Because if I'd dreamt that you were wearing something like this when I first met you, I don't think that I'd have arranged to go to the café with you. I think I'd have taken you down to the basement and made love to you right then and there.'

She flushed. 'In the library?'

'Mm-hm. And I don't think I'd have cared who was watching.' Slowly, he eased her knickers over her but-

25

tocks, revealing soft globes of creamy flesh and let the thin silk drift to the floor. 'Rachel. You're utterly, utterly desirable.' He rubbed his face against her thighs, breathing in her musky scent. 'And I want you. I can't wait.'

Rachel felt herself grow wet at the thought of what he was about to do; she murmured softly, shifting her position slightly to give him easier access. She felt him smile against the soft skin of her inner thigh, and then at last she felt the slow stroke of his tongue as he parted her labia, searching through her intimate folds and crevices until he found her clitoris.

He teased it out of its hood, his tongue flicking rapidly across it and then he drew the small hard bud into his mouth, sucking gently at first, and then harder. Rachel moaned softly, sliding her hands into his hair and digging the pads of her fingers into his scalp. Luke, tasting how much pleasure she was receiving, continued to lick and suck at her until his mouth was full of her musky juices and he could feel her sex-flesh quivering against his mouth.

He dropped a kiss against her quim, then slowly got to his feet again, caressing her cheek. 'OK?'

She nodded, opening her eyes and looking at him. Her pupils had expanded until her eyes looked almost black. 'Definitely OK,' she said. Her voice was husky still, her breathing slightly ragged. She traced his lower lip with a fingertip. 'Thank you.'

'The pleasure was mine, believe me.' He drew her finger into his mouth, sucking the tip in a way that made her shiver. 'And I haven't finished, not by a long way.' He removed his trousers, pulling off his cotton boxer shorts. Then he took her hand and curled it round his erect cock. 'Feel what you do to me,' he told her huskily.

Rachel couldn't help moving her hand slightly, caressing his cock; he moaned, then picked her up to carry her over to the bed. 'I know this is macho, but it isn't meant to be. I just can't wait any longer,' he told her. He kicked the duvet aside and placed her gently on top of the mattress. 'And I'm bloody glad that you've got a double bed.'

He moved to lie next to her, tracing the soft curves of her body with the palm of his hand. 'You're one beautiful woman, Rachel Kemp,' he said softly, pulling her closer to him. 'I want you, very badly.' He shifted, rolling over and pulling her with him so that she was straddling him, the ends of her hair brushing his face as she tipped her head down slightly. He could feel the moist heat of her quim against his cock and opened his mouth in a wordless sigh of longing.

The sight sent a thrill down her. The fact that she could make a man as gorgeous as Luke react like that to her was the biggest boost her confidence had ever had. She lifted herself slightly and slid her hand between their bodies, guiding the tip of his cock to the entrance of her sex. Then, slowly, she lowered herself onto the rigid muscle. Luke groaned as his flesh was encased in warm liquid velvet.

His hands spanned her waist and he lifted his upper body from the bed so that he could kiss the soft creamy flesh of her breasts, drawing the tip of his nose down her cleavage. 'You taste beautiful,' he said, licking her skin until she shivered. The tip of his tongue traced the veins of her breasts until he reached the darker pimply skin of the areolae; she arched backwards as he took each nipple into his mouth in turn, sucking on the sensitive flesh. 'And later,' he said, his mouth still full of her nipple, 'I'm going to lick you all over like a cat. But first I want you to fuck me. Hard.'

Her eyes sparkled. 'Is that a request or an order?'

'I'll beg if you want me to.' He pushed up, tilting his pelvis so that his cock slid more deeply into her. 'Rachel. I want you. Make love with me. Please?'

She nodded, began to move over him in small circles, lifting up from him until he was at the point of slipping out of her, then pushing back down hard until her pubis ground against him. Luke tipped his head back, squeez-

27

ing his eyes shut tight and opening his mouth as his orgasm grew nearer.

She began to pant, still moving over him. She could imagine how they looked together: the big, muscular man spread out naked on her bed and herself straddling him, still wearing her stockings and the basque. It was a scene that could have graced one of Jennifer's books, she thought; and grinned to herself. Thanks to Jennifer, this was happening a lot sooner than she'd hoped. Because Luke had read some of her books, too, and they turned him on as much as they turned her on.

And his threat-cum-promise of reading to her while she lay on the bed, until she was so turned on that she had to pleasure herself, was a delicious thought. Normally, she regarded masturbation as a private habit, something she didn't do in front of her lovers: but she had a feeling that with Luke it was going to be different. Very different. She could imagine Luke suggesting playing out some of Jennifer's wilder scenarios; and she knew that she would do it. Something about Luke unleashed something deep and primitive inside her.

She bent down to kiss him; his mouth opened under hers and she slid her tongue into his mouth, exploring him. He still tasted of her, honey and seashore and vanilla; the thought made her start using her internal muscles on him, playing along his cock as she rode him. Luke groaned and eased his hand between their bodies so that he could rub her clitoris. She gasped and rode him harder, delighting in the action of his probing, questing fingers.

Pleasure bubbled through her veins, pooling in her solar plexus; as it exploded, she felt his cock throbbing inside her and the warm wet gush of his seed filling her. She cried out and heard his answering moan; neither of them could talk coherently.

Luke wrapped his arms round her, drawing her down on his chest and stroking her hair.

28

'What a beginning,' he said softly, when his breathing had slowed enough for him to talk again.

'What a beginning,' she echoed, smiling.

'I wondered if I might have the rest of that coffee for breakfast,' he murmured into her ear. 'Because there's an awful lot I want to do with you, and even the first part's going to take all night.'

'Promises, promises,' she teased.

'Mm.' He bit her earlobe gently. 'Starting right now.' He rolled her on to her back, then knelt between her thighs, rolling her stockings down and then picking up one leg, licking her instep and the hollows of her ankle. 'Like I said, I want to touch and kiss you all over.'

Rachel smiled and closed her eyes, giving herself up to pleasure.

# Chapter Three

*R*achel stretched luxuriously in bed. It had been one hell of a weekend. Luke had lived up to his promise, making her come time and time and time again, using his mouth and his hands and his cock until she was shaking with pleasure. She didn't think that she had ever met such a good lover.

He'd stayed for most of the following day, too; they'd made a half-hearted attempt to get up, but had ended up making love in Rachel's shower and headed back to bed again. Luke had finally left just after six o'clock on the Sunday evening, saying that he had a pile of essays to mark before a tutorial the next morning, and promising that he would be in touch.

She smiled to herself. The best thing was, she could tell that he meant it.

Luke parked his car, then let himself back into his flat. He really hadn't wanted to leave Rachel. After her initial awkwardness with him had dispelled, she had been as warm and promising as he'd hoped. He found her incredibly desirable and it had taken a real effort to drag himself away from her. Only he had work to do. Not quite the work he'd told her he had to do; he felt bad about lying to her but, in the circumstances, there was nothing else he could have said. He wasn't ready to tell her the whole truth – not yet.

He made himself a cup of coffee, then sprawled on his sofa, picking up the phone and dialling a familiar number. The line rang once, twice; and then there was a click as the receiver was picked up.

'Hello?' A well-spoken and precise voice: exactly who Luke had hoped it would be.

'Hello, Max.'

'Luke.' The elder man sounded genuinely pleased to hear him. 'How are you?'

'Fine, fine.' Luke paused. 'I have some news for you.'

'I'm all ears.'

Luke grinned. 'That's one way of describing you, I suppose.'

'Less of your cheek.' The rebuke was tempered with affection. 'What have you got to tell me then?'

'I may have found someone to work on the diaries.'

'Really?'

'Mm. Someone at the university.' Luke smiled. 'We met over coffee. Literally. Anyway, her name's Rachel Kemp and she's specialising in the right subject and the right era.'

'We need something a little more than that, Luke. Bear in mind what the material is,' Max reminded him.

Luke chuckled. 'I don't think that we're going to have any problems on that score. She's pretty broad-minded.'

'I see. I don't think that I'd better ask just how you know that.'

Luke grinned. 'You're guessing in the right direction.'

'Indeed.' Max paused. 'We have to be sure, though.'

'I know.'

'Draw her out a little more,' Max advised. 'Then we'll decide if she's right for the job.'

'You want to meet her, then?'

'Yes. But not until you're absolutely sure.' Max paused. 'Have you mentioned the job to her?'

'No, of course not. Not without talking to you, first.'

'Keep it that way.'

'All right.'

There was another pause. 'What about the other matter?'

Luke sighed. 'I'm not ready to discuss that. Not now.'

'But?'

He smiled wryly. Max was incredibly sharp, his ear attuned to every nuance. 'Let's just say that I think I'm getting near to finding out the truth.'

'Be careful.'

'Oh, yes. I'm being that, all right.' Luke coughed. 'I'll talk to you later in the week then.' He replaced the receiver thoughtfully. Rachel was perfect for the job. She hated what she was doing now, she had an interest in the period – and, judging by the weekend they'd just spent together, she had the right kind of attitude. He had a feeling that she and Max would get on very well. All he had to do was spend a little more time with Rachel, take things a little further between them – and then arrange a meeting.

The next morning, Rachel was starting to mark a pile of essays when her computer bleeped. She ignored it until she'd finished the essay she was marking – knowing that if she broke off, she would have to redo a lot of the work she'd already done on it – and then flicked into her electronic mail program.

She smiled as she saw the ID. Following university convention, it was the first five letters of the surname, followed by the initials. HOLLOLJ. It could be only one person. She selected the message and began to read it.

'Rachel. I've been thinking about you all night. Thinking about what I want to do with you; and I can't keep it to myself any longer. Tonight, I'll meet you at six, outside the building, and we'll go back to my place. Once we're there, I'll put some music on and open a bottle of wine. Pink champagne, I think.'

Rachel chuckled. Very *Hotel California*.

'And then I'm going to take your clothes off, so very slowly. I'm going to peel off your sweater and leggings; then I'll push down the cups of your bra, so that your beautiful breasts are bared but still pushed together and up by your bra, deepening your cleavage. Have I told you how much I love your breasts? They're so soft, so warm. I could drown in your breasts, Rachel. Even thinking about them makes me hard. Believe me, my cock's going to be like a ramrod by the time I've finished undressing you – but I think that I'll leave your bra on. It'll make you look more lewd and wanton. I'll kiss every inch of skin as I reveal it. And then I'll pick you up and carry you to my bed.'

Mr Macho, Rachel thought wryly.

'Did I tell you that I have a big brass bed, Rachel? King-size, for comfort, with lots of goose-down pillows. I'm going to lower you very gently on to the sheets – they're white silk, soft and warm, like your skin. And then I'm going to take four black silk scarves and tie your wrists and ankles to the bedstead – not too tightly, it won't hurt, but tightly enough so that you can't move. Then you'll be at my disposal and I can do anything I like with you. And what I'd like to do, I think you'll like, too. Very much.'

Rachel pressed the 'page down' button, intrigued.

'I'm going to take an artist's brush, a brush of pure sable. Then I'm going to sit next to you on the bed and draw the brush very slowly down your quim. I'm going to keep doing it until the brush is soaked with your juices and your cunt's wet and glistening for me. Then I'm going to paint your nipples and your lips, so that they're glistening with your nectar, too. And I'm going to kiss you, hard, to give me a taste of what's going to happen later when I go down on you and bring you to a climax with my mouth.'

Rachel shivered with delighted anticipation.

'But before I do that, I'm going to make you come. I'm

going to continue brushing your beautiful cunt, so very slowly, working on your clitoris until you're writhing and almost begging me to fuck you – although you won't be able to move very far, as you're still tied to the bed. I'm not going to slide my cock into you, not yet. I'm going to continue brushing you, teasing you with the soft sable bristles until you come. And then I'm going to turn the brush round and slide it into you, while your internal muscles are still contracting. I'm going to pump it back and forth, like a slim and rigid cock, and I'm going to lean over your body and work on your breasts at the same time. I'm going to suck one nipple and roll the other between my finger and thumb, until you're pushing up to my mouth and my hand. And all the while, I'm going to use the brush like a dildo on you, back and forth, until you're coming again.'

She could imagine the scene, and she felt her sex grow moist and puffy at the thought. Whether Luke was fantasising or making a statement of his intentions, she was none too sure; either way, it thrilled her.

'Then I'm going to use my mouth on you. I'm going to kneel between your legs, and put my palms flat on your thighs, opening you as widely as I can. I'm going to kiss all the way up your thighs, stopping just short of your beautiful quim – so you can feel my breath against you and know what I'm going to do next. But I won't do it until you're shivering with anticipation, Rachel. I won't do it until you beg me to, your voice husky with desire. Then, and only then, I'll lower my mouth to you and draw my tongue along you, from the top to the bottom of your slit. I'll taste you, the honeyed nectar of your arousal. Your flesh will be warm and wet and soft under my mouth, and the scent and taste of you will be so good, so very good. Like honey and vanilla and musk and seashore, all mixed in together.

'Then I'm going to make my tongue into a sharp point and work your clitoris, moving my tongue back and forth until you're almost screaming with pleasure. I'm going to suck it, then, drawing it hard into my mouth. And then you'll be coming, flooding my mouth with your juices. You'll taste so good, Rachel, so very good. It makes my cock throb even thinking about the way you taste. I can't get enough of you. I want to lick you and lick you and lick you.'

Rachel closed her eyes for a second, almost feeling his mouth on her there and then.

'And then I'm going to take my clothes off. My cock's going to be so hard for you, hard and hot – and I'm going to slide it into your warm wet flesh. I'm going to fill you to the hilt. I'll stay there for a moment, feeling the aftershocks of your orgasm ripple round me – and then I'll start to move, pushing deep into you. I'll be kissing you, Rachel, so you can taste yourself on my mouth. I'll take you to another orgasm, Rachel, and another. And then I'll untie you and withdraw from you just long enough to turn you over. You'll be shaking still, but I'll guide you on to your hands and knees – and then I'll use my mouth on you again. I'll kiss all the way down your spine, nuzzling your skin and breathing in your scent.

'I'll move lower, then, nuzzling your buttocks; and I'll gently put my tongue against your beautiful puckered rose, licking you until you're shivering again. Then I'll straighten up and push my cock back into your cunt, filling you; and I'll push my finger against your pretty little *cul*, sliding into you so that I can feel my cock inside you too. Then I'll start to move again, filling you and fucking you until you're moaning with pleasure. And when you come this time, it's going to be so strong that it's going to tip me into my own orgasm.'

Rachel swallowed. God. One or two of her past lovers had indulged in erotic phone calls, when they'd been away on business and drunk too much over dinner, going back to their hotel rooms and feeling like making love, then masturbating while indulging in faintly risqué calls with her, but this ... this was even more explicit.

Enough to make her want to masturbate, then and there, to relieve the sudden surge of desire.

She slid her hand between her legs, pressing her crotch through her leggings. She could imagine Luke doing all those things to her – and more. The idea excited her. And the fact that she could print his email and re-read it as often as she liked, use it as bedtime reading and a way of relaxing herself after a hard day: the thought made her shudder with pleasure.

She began to rub herself through her clothes, thinking of Luke and what they were going to do together that night. It was going to be so good, so good. Her nipples hardened, rubbing against the lace of her bra, and she gave a small moan of pleasure. If this was his imagination, the real thing was going to be unbelievably good. She pressed harder, feeling her clitoris throb beneath her fingers, and closed her eyes. Yes. It was going to be –

A knock on the door distracted her; she swore under her breath and opened her eyes, glancing at her watch. Her tutorial group already. Shit. She straightened her clothes, closed Luke's email, and removed the Alice band from her hair, raking her hands through her fair curls and replacing the band again. Her sex felt wet and puffy, ready for a man; no doubt the air smelled of her arousal, she thought. Christ. Well, hopefully her students wouldn't twig what had been going on.

'Come in,' she called.

Four students trooped in. She gave them a smile that she didn't quite feel and reached over for her coffee pot. Right at that moment, she could have done with a few more minutes to herself, to finish what Luke's email had started; but then again, this was her only tutorial of the morning. In an hour, she could re-read his words and do something about it.

The tutorial passed relatively quickly; with relief, she closed the door behind her last student and turned back to her computer. So Luke liked indulging in kinky emails, did he? Well, she'd give him something to think about.

Rapidly, she opened a new file and began to type.

'Tomorrow night, I'll meet you at six, outside the library. We'll go back to your place – again we'll open a bottle of wine. Sparkling Australian Chardonnay. We'll listen to some music, maybe talk a little – but all the time, you'll be thinking about what I'm going to do to you in a few minutes' time. You'll know exactly what I'm going to do, because I'm telling you now – and the anticipation will make it all the sweeter when it happens.'

Grinning, she added a page-break, then continued typing. 'We'll go into your bedroom. While you close the curtains, I'll light half a dozen scented candles – vanilla-scented candles, I think. Candle-light has this amazing effect on bare skin, don't you think? All soft and sensual. And then I'm going to kiss you, hard. I'm going to make all the running and you'll be completely in my hands. That's a promise, not a threat.

'I'll unbutton your shirt, stroking your skin as I reveal it. I'll let the shirt fall on to the floor and then I'll let my hands drift down to your belt, unbuckling it. I'll undo the button and zip of your jeans and slide the soft denim down over your hips. Your cock will already be rigid, clearly outlined through your underpants, and I'll curl my fingers round it, squeezing gently and teasing you, so that you close your eyes and tip your head back, your mouth opening in invitation.

'And then you'll help me remove your jeans properly and the rest of your clothes. I'll kiss you again, my tongue sliding into your mouth to explore you, and I'll walk you backwards to your bed. This time, the sheets will be pure crisp cotton, not silk, cool and soothing against your skin – but I have nothing pure in mind, believe me. The silk scarves are still attached to the head and foot of your bed, from when you tied me up; this time, it's my turn to tie you up. You submit willingly, letting me tie your wrists and ankles; you're spread out like a starfish, and you can't move.

'You look beautiful like that, your skin gleaming in the candle-light and your cock so hard and ready for me. I want to paint you or sculpt you, though I'm no artist: you look so good. You lick your lips and look at me expectantly, waiting; but I'm not going to touch you. Not yet. First, I want to give you something to think about.

'You have a CD player in your bedroom; I've picked a couple of tracks out. Slow, bluesy rock, perfect for dancing to. I put the music on; then, when I'm sure that you're watching me, I start to undress. I dressed very carefully, that morning, putting on something I think you'll appreciate. To the outside world, I'm just mousy Rachel Kemp, in a sweater and jeans: but underneath . . .'

Again, she put a page-break in. 'I take off my sweater and you can see that I'm wearing a basque. But it's not just any basque: it's made of the softest green leather, a deep jade green that emphasises the creaminess of my skin. The cups are little more than a shelf for my breasts and you can see my nipples peeping over the edge of the cups. Next, I take down my jeans and I'm wearing a lace G-string, exactly matching the colour of my basque. It doesn't hide anything. I'm also wearing the lace-topped hold-up stockings you like so much, and a pair of high-heeled black patent-leather shoes. I kick off my shoes for a moment, so I can take off my jeans properly; then I turn round, putting my shoes back on, and bend over.

'You can see everything, as I slowly roll down my stockings. You can see how excited I am already, the wet patch on the gusset of my G-string obvious as you look at me. I kick off my shoes again, remove my stockings and then my G-string. I turn back to face you and start swaying to the music. You're not quite sure what I'm going to do until I close my eyes and slide my hands down my body. The leather basque is so smooth, so soft; my nipples are hard, a sharp contrast to it, and I lick my lips as I begin to stroke my nipples, pulling at them and pushing my breasts together.

'You give a small moan of appreciation, and I let one hand slide down lower, over my abdomen. The heel of my palm rests on my mons veneris, and you know what I'm going to do. I'm going to pleasure myself, make myself come, while you're watching. Slowly, I push one finger between my labia; I'm already wet, excited. I start to rub my clitoris, and my breath hisses from me as I work the little bud of flesh, pressing harder, harder. It feels so good. Then I push my middle finger deep inside me, pistoning my hand in and out; every time I withdraw my finger, I rub against my clitoris and rub again as I push my finger back in. It's so good, so good, warming me up for your cock, a little later.

'My nipples are so hard, they almost hurt. I ache to feel your mouth on them – but not yet, not yet. I'm near the edge, so very near. My hand's almost a blur, it's working so fast; and then I cry out as my orgasm splinters through me.

'I'm still panting as I walk over to the bed. I climb on to the bed, and you wait, almost breathless with anticipation. I straddle you, facing away from you, and you can smell my recent climax, a spicy musky scent that makes you want to taste me. I push backwards, so that my quim is just within your reach, and you stretch out your tongue, licking me.

'Then I bend my head. Your cock's incredibly hard by now, and there's a tiny bead of clear fluid at its tip. I stretch out my tongue to lap it up, savouring its muskiness, and you groan, wanting more. I haven't finished yet, not by a long way. I've barely started. Gently, I open my mouth and slide the tip of your cock between my lips. You moan again and start to lap me in earnest; I use a slower rhythm, though, as I begin to suck you. Slow, long strokes, which make you moan and writhe beneath me.

'I make my tongue into a sharp point, teasing your

frenum in a way that drives you wild. Then I resume sucking you again, taking you deep into my mouth. I can feel how near you are to coming and I want to make this last. So I take your cock out of my mouth, squeezing just below the head – not hard enough to hurt, but hard enough to hold back your climax. You moan, then continue licking me; I can feel the ripples of orgasm starting at the soles of my feet again, moving up through my legs, and finally exploding in my solar plexus. My internal muscles contract sharply, and I cry out your name.

'You've distracted me for a moment – but only for a moment. When my pulse slows down, I shift position, so that I'm kneeling between your thighs. This time you can see everything I'm going to do to you, as well as feel it. I begin to masturbate you, using long, slow strokes: ten long, spaced about a second apart, and then ten quick. Ten slow, ten quick. Ten slow, ten quick. You're losing count and you're losing control; again, I squeeze just below the head of your cock, delaying your climax.

'You want to come so badly. But I'm not ready yet. I want to bring you to a higher peak, so you almost see stars when you come. I wet my finger and look up at you; you know immediately what I'm going to do, and even the idea of it turns you on. I start to stroke your perineum and you moan, spreading your legs for me. Then I gently push against the puckered rosy hole of your anus, my finger sliding into you. With my other hand, I pick up the bottle of wine and take a swig. I offer you some, and then take another swig – though what you don't realise is that I'm holding the wine in my mouth.

'I put the bottle back on the floor and then I ring your cock with my free thumb and forefinger. Then I bend my head again, taking you into my mouth and letting the sparkling wine swirl over your glans. It prickles and teases and you cry out; I swallow the wine, and smooth your skin with my tongue, soothing you. Then I start to suck you properly, still penetrating you with my finger.

40

I use the same rhythm, pushing into you and rubbing you and sucking you, until you're almost delirious. This time, when I feel your balls lift and tighten and hear you moaning my name, I don't hold you back; I feel your cock jerk in my mouth and then my mouth is filled with warm salty liquid. I swallow every last drop, then gently move my hand; you're lying there, unable to move even if I hadn't kept you tied up. And then I crawl up the bed to kiss you, so you can taste yourself on my mouth. And then I untie you and pick up the wine again.'

She grinned and typed her initial, followed by a row of kisses. Then she quickly typed Luke's ID at the top of the message and pressed the enter key; the computer bleeped, signalling that it had sent the message. 'Let's see what you make of that, Mr Holloway,' she said softly, and picked up her red pen, ready to continue marking the pile of essays.

Several minutes later, the phone rang. Rachel glanced at her screen and grinned. Her email had just been selected. Well, Luke, let's hear what you have to say for yourself, she thought, picking up the receiver. 'Hello. Rachel Kemp.'

'This is Leonard Hollis.'

Shit, Rachel thought. This was the last thing she'd been expecting. She'd thought that it would be Luke. 'Hello. What can I do for you?'

'Will you come over to my office?' His voice was cool and clipped.

Just what did the head of the library want with her, she wondered. 'When?'

'Now.' His tone brooked no argument.

Trouble, Rachel thought. Shit, shit, shit. The last thing she needed was a row with the head of the library. Trouble which would no doubt be reported to Gilson. 'All right. I'll be with you in ten minutes.'

'Good.'

The line went dead; Rachel replaced the receiver, frowning. Why did Leonard Hollis want to see her? She hadn't made any special requests through the library for months, so it couldn't be anything to do with that. But he hadn't sounded as if he wanted to discuss business with her. He'd sounded as if he was only just keeping his temper in check. The only thing she could think of was that one of her students had upset him – probably by not returning books on time or not paying library fines. It was standard procedure for the librarian to have a quiet word with the tutor in those cases, and get the problem sorted out quickly.

Ah well, she thought, better go and unruffle his feathers. She hadn't had that much to do with Leonard Hollis, but she knew that he was friendly with Gilson, so it was best to keep on his good side. She couldn't afford to have him complaining to Gilson about her – not the way things were between her and Gilson. That would be just the excuse that Gilson needed to have another go at her.

She stood up, stretched and made her way over to the library. Hollis's door was closed; he didn't subscribe to an open door policy, let alone the open plan office common to libraries in other universities. Here we go, Rachel thought, knocking on the door.

'Come in.'

She walked into his office, and closed the door behind her.

'Sit down.'

Hollis was unsmiling, his grey eyes hard.

'What can I do for you, Mr Hollis?' Rachel asked. She didn't dare call him 'Leonard', and judged it best not to take the coward's route of not mentioning his name. Leonard Hollis was one of the old school, believing that his position demanded respect. She hoped that she'd struck the right note.

'I believe that your email ID is KEMPRS?'

'Ye-es.' She frowned, not understanding.

'And you sent this to me, this morning.' He turned his computer to face her, and Rachel's face whitened as she saw what was on the screen. Her email to Luke.

42

# Chapter Four

*R*achel sat in silence, stunned. Christ. She had been so sure that she'd sent it to Luke. What was it doing in Hollis's mailbox?

'Perhaps you'd care to explain yourself, Miss Kemp.'

'I . . . Look, I'm sorry. There's been some kind of mistake.' She bit her lip. 'It wasn't meant for you.'

His eyes glittered. 'But you sent it to me.'

'In error.' She looked at the top of the screen. Hollis's ID was very clear: HOLLILJ. One letter away from Luke's ID; one slip of a finger on the keyboard. A slip that had been so very easy to make, and so very hard to spot. 'I'm sorry, Mr Hollis.'

'You've been caught abusing university property, and you're sorry.' His voice was very quiet, very measured, very precise. There was an undercurrent of danger in it. Rachel wasn't sure whether she felt like a naughty schoolgirl, called in to see the headmaster after being caught playing a childish prank, or whether she really was frightened. Hollis could cause a lot of trouble for her if he decided to take the matter further.

She swallowed. 'Like I said, Mr Hollis, it wasn't meant for you.'

'And you think that it's perfectly all right to send this

kind of filth across the university network, using university equipment and university time?'

Rachel closed her eyes. Of all the people she could have sent the email to by mistake, Hollis just had to be the worst possible one. Except, maybe, for Gilson. If it had arrived with someone younger, more open-minded – well, they might have called her to tease her about it, but they certainly wouldn't have reacted this badly. She closed her eyes again, hoping that Hollis would see the penitence in her face and let her go. 'I'm sorry, Mr Hollis.'

'You're sorry,' he repeated.

Guilt and embarrassment made her snappy. She opened her eyes and glared at him. 'What else do you want me to say?'

He stroked his jaw. 'Well, I think that maybe I ought to call in your head of department to make him aware of just what his staff do when they're supposed to be teaching.'

Her eyes widened. Surely he wasn't going to involve Gilson? 'Look, I didn't type it during tutorial time or during a time when I was supposed to be working on a lecture. It was in my own free time.' Time when she should really have been marking essays, she knew; but she'd often worked at home in her own time, which more than made up for the few short minutes she'd spent on typing that email.

'The fact remains, Miss Kemp, that you sent it. Whether you sent it by mistake or not, you're the one who sent what I can only describe as a pornographic message – using university equipment.'

She sighed. 'Look, I don't want any trouble. I really don't think that Mr Gilson needs to be involved.'

'Well, I disagree. I think that he should know just what kind of staff he has.'

'Please, Mr Hollis. It was a genuine mistake. I'm sorry if I've offended you. But please, don't bring my head of department into it. I promise you that it won't happen again.' She looked beseechingly at him.

Hollis nodded. 'All right. Stand up.'

She frowned, but did as he asked.

'Take off your sweater.'

Her eyes widened in shock. Had she just heard him tell her to take off her sweater? 'You what?'

'If you want me to keep this just between us,' Hollis said, his voice still very cool and measured, 'then I suggest that you do exactly what I tell you.'

She flushed. 'I . . .'

'It's up to you.' He shrugged. 'I can quite easily send a copy of your email to your head of department and ask him to deal with you himself, if that's what you prefer.'

Ask Colin Gilson to deal with her – Gilson, who'd use it as an excuse to throw her out of the university. She knew that. She couldn't afford to lose her job; and getting another, with the kind of reference that Gilson would give her, would be almost impossible. At the same time, she was damned if she was going to strip off for Hollis, titillate him.

Maybe he was bluffing. Two could play at that game. She lifted her jaw. 'And if I say, go ahead? Publish and be damned?'

'Clichés don't suit you.'

'All right. If I say that I don't care what you do?'

He shrugged and replaced Rachel's ID at the top of the page with Gilson's. 'It's your choice, Miss Kemp. Either I can send this to your head of department right now – or you take off your sweater.'

She swallowed. He really meant it. 'If you're thinking that I'm really wearing that green basque, you'll be disappointed. It was just a fantasy.'

'Which you intended to send to whom precisely?'

Her flush deepened. 'Does it matter?'

'Yes.'

'It's private.'

45

'Not any more. I suggest that you tell me, Miss Kemp.' His voice was very cool, and very dangerous.

She sighed. 'All right. I meant to send it to Luke Holloway.'

'The American.'

'He's English, actually. He's just worked in America for the past couple of years, and it's affected his accent slightly.'

Hollis put his hands behind his head, leaning back against his chair. 'It amazes me how defiant you are, Miss Kemp, considering your position. If I show this email to Colin Gilson, he could have you dismissed – not just for abusing university time and property, but for obscenity, behaviour not fitting your position as a lecturer.'

Her lips thinned. 'What do you expect me to do?'

'I've already told you. Take off your sweater.'

Rachel was shocked to discover another feeling flooding through the pit of her stomach. Not just anger and fear at Hollis's high-handed attitude and shame that her private fantasy had gone to completely the wrong person; she was also aroused by Hollis's stern headmasterish stance. There was a tell-tale pulse beating heavily between her legs and her sex felt warm and puffy. Christ, she thought, I don't believe this. I can't possibly be turned on by him – can I?

'You have ten seconds, Miss Kemp, to make your decision.'

There was only one decision she could take, whether she liked it or not. Slowly, she took hold of the hem of her sweater and pulled it upwards, crossing her arms as she pulled the garment over her head.

'Hm. As you so rightly said, you're not wearing this green basque.'

She bit her lip. Anyone could walk in and see her – anyone. The gossip would be unbearable. 'Mr Hollis – '

'Shut up,' he cut in sharply. 'I didn't give you per-

46

mission to speak. Now, pull the cups of your bra down, as if it really were like the green basque you described.'

She swallowed. 'I . . .'

'Just do it.'

Part of Rachel was furious. Who the hell did he think he was, ordering her about? On the other hand, she couldn't afford him to carry out his threat of telling Gilson – and part of her was ashamed to realise that she was actually enjoying this. She liked the idea of exposing herself to Hollis.

It was crazy. He wasn't her type. He was a good twenty years older than she was and he wasn't particularly attractive, in the way that Sean Connery and Al Pacino were attractive older men. At the same time, he wasn't exactly ugly: more unexceptional, she supposed. Leonard Hollis gave the impression of being a very precise and fastidious man, his grey eyes shrewd and calculating, and his fair hair cut neatly. He was dressed neatly, too, in a dark grey serge suit, with a white shirt and an understated tie. Rachel would have bet money that his shoes were black and highly polished, and that his socks were grey. He was a typical stereotype of a librarian: the only thing missing was a pair of small round gold-rimmed spectacles, or maybe he wore contact lenses.

And yet despite his unremarkable appearance, he had a certain kind of attraction. Rachel presumed that it was the kind of attraction of a dormant volcano – cold and forbidding on the outside and a seething hot mass on the inside. The idea of bringing this cold and precise man to a raging sexual heat was . . . She shivered in anticipation.

'I said, do it, Rachel.'

The fact that he used her first name shocked her into obeying. She pulled the cups of her bra down, so that the garment still supported her bare breasts, but everything was exposed to his gaze.

'Now, your jeans. Unzip them.'

Almost as if in a dream, Rachel did so.

'Take them off.'

'I . . .'

'Take them off,' he repeated coldly, his eyes still fixed on her.

She pushed the soft denims over her hips, wriggling out of them, and unzipped her ankle boots so that she could remove her jeans properly. She removed her socks at the same time, thinking that Hollis would hardly appreciate the Ermintrude socks that a friend had once bought her as a joke.

'Now your knickers.'

Rachel's eyes widened. What was he intending her to do? Did he want her to display herself, to masturbate in front of him? Or was he intending to shed his own clothes and take her over his desk? Either way, a shiver ran down her spine, a shiver of mingled fear and shame and excitement.

'Your knickers, Rachel. Take them off. Now.'

Slowly, she tugged at the sides of her knickers, sliding them down. There was a damp patch on the gusset from when she'd read Luke's email and written him a fantasy of her own.

'Give them to me.'

She flushed. 'I – I can't.'

'Give them to me, Rachel.' He took them from her shaking fingers and inspected the gusset, fingering the damp patch thoughtfully. 'So this is what happens when you start writing your fantasies to a man. You cream your knickers.'

Rachel flushed with shame as he raised her knickers to his face and breathed in her scent. 'You were very aroused, I'd say. Did you masturbate at your desk to get yourself into this sort of state? Or was merely writing it enough to make your juices flow like that?'

She didn't answer, too ashamed to admit that she'd considered masturbating – that she'd even started to rub herself through her clothes when she'd read Luke's email.

48

'This turns you on, too, doesn't it? Standing like this, in front of me, displaying yourself?'

'No,' she muttered.

'Liar.' His voice was cold, yet almost caressing, at the same time. 'There are ways of dealing with people who lie.'

She swallowed. 'What – what are you going to do?'

'With you?' His smile held no mirth, no warmth. 'Well, I think that I need to teach you a lesson, Rachel. I'll have to teach you not to abuse university property. Now, put your hands on the edge of my desk and bend over.'

'Bend over?' she repeated stupidly.

'That's what I said, Rachel. You're supposed to be an English graduate. Surely you can understand monosyllables?'

Her skin heated again. 'I . . .'

'Do it, Rachel. Before I change my mind and send your little missive to Gilson.'

Rachel swallowed and did what he told her to do. His light oak desk was almost completely clear; she held on to the edge of it, her knuckles white, and bent over.

'Now, let's see.' He took a ruler from his desk drawer and stood up, walking round to the other side of his desk.

Rachel tensed with horror. Christ, he was going to smack her with the ruler, give her six of the best, like a naughty schoolgirl!

'Close your eyes, Rachel.'

She swallowed. 'I can't – I can't see you, anyway.'

'Close your eyes. Unless you want me to blindfold you.' He paused, thoughtful. 'Maybe I should gag you. Maybe I should use your knickers to gag you, Rachel – you'd like that, wouldn't you? Tasting your own arousal, while I'm busy teaching you a lesson.'

'No!' She almost shouted the denial, but she was horrified to realise that a part of her, a very little part of her, was extremely excited by the idea. Christ, what was

49

happening to her? She was plain, ordinary, boring Rachel Kemp; although she enjoyed the exotic tales written by her friend Jennifer, she'd never actually wanted to live them out. And today, she'd written a steamy email to her lover, sent it to the wrong man, and was standing virtually naked in front of him, her quim flexing with excitement as he described more sophisticated pleasures than she was used to.

'I think that you're lying to me again, Rachel.' Still his voice was cool and calm.

'I . . .' She could hardly speak.

'Then perhaps I won't gag you. Perhaps you'd enjoy it too much. And, like I said, this is supposed to be a lesson. Close your eyes.'

Rachel squeezed her eyes tightly shut.

'Now.' She felt his hand smooth over her buttocks, and tensed. Any minute now, she was going to hear the swish of the ruler and feel it land like a line of fire across her flesh.

'So soft, so smooth,' he whispered. 'Spread your legs.'

'I . . .'

'Spread your legs,' he insisted. 'Show yourself to me.'

Rachel knew that she had no choice, and yet she was almost weeping with shame. The moment she exposed herself to him, he'd see just how aroused she was, her labia puffy and her sex glistening. Keeping her eyes tightly shut, she widened her stance, sticking her bottom up into the air.

He gave a sharp intake of breath as he saw her. 'I see. So much for this being a lesson. You're enjoying yourself, aren't you, Rachel?'

She was silent.

'I asked you a question. I advise you to answer me.'

'I . . .'

'You're enjoying it, aren't you? Exposing yourself to me like a slut. You're really enjoying it.'

Still she was silent.

'Rachel.' He used her name as a caress and as a warning, at the same time.

'I – yes,' she muttered.

'Louder.'

'Yes.'

'Yes, what?'

'What do you want me to say?' she whispered.

'Yes, I'm enjoying displaying myself to you,' he prompted. 'Sir.'

Rachel squirmed inwardly; but at the same time, she knew that it was true. 'Yes, I'm enjoying displaying myself to you – sir,' she murmured.

'I can't hear you.'

'Yes, I'm enjoying displaying myself to you, sir.'

'That's better. Easy, wasn't it?' She felt something smooth and hard resting against her buttocks, and flinched. It was the ruler. 'I'm in two minds, Rachel. You need to be taught a lesson, that much is obvious. But if I thrash you with this' – he tapped her lightly on the bottom with the ruler – 'I think that you'll enjoy it far too much.' He paused. 'I have proof.' She felt him slide a finger down the crease of her buttocks, pressing in lightly against her anus, and then down across her perineum. His finger inserted itself easily into her warm wet channel, and he laughed shortly, removing his hand. 'Proof, indeed.'

The next thing she knew, his hand was by her face, his finger by her mouth. 'Clean me,' he demanded.

'Clean you?' she repeated, not understanding.

'I'm sticky from you, Rachel. Your juices are running down my finger. Now, lick them off.'

Still with her eyes closed, Rachel opened her mouth, stretching out her tongue so that she could lick his finger clean. He tasted sweet-salt, a taste she knew was her own arousal, and her face burned. Christ, how long was this humiliation going to go on?

'Until I choose to stop.'

51

Her flush deepened as she realised that she'd spoken aloud. 'I . . .'

'Just stay there, Rachel.'

Her eyes widened. 'Where are you going?'

'Your place isn't to ask questions,' came the swift rebuke. 'And if I find that you've moved when I return, you'll be in very serious trouble.' He leant across the desk; from the rapid clicking, Rachel guessed that he was logging off the computer system. He didn't trust her not to delete the offending email while he was out of the room. 'Now, stay where you are,' he directed, and she heard the door click behind her.

She opened her eyes again. If only she could hack into systems. She'd probably have enough time to go into his mailbox, remove the email, and then dress and leave his office, before he returned. Unfortunately, she couldn't. If she left his office, he'd send the email to Gilson, and she'd be in a hell of a lot more trouble. If she stayed . . . Apart from the fact that anyone could walk in and see her, exposing herself lewdly, Hollis intended to 'teach her a lesson'. But if he wasn't going to smack her, just what was he going to do to her?

She flexed her shoulders. Her position was extremely uncomfortable – not to mention the fact that her quim felt hot and wet, in need of a man or her own right hand to ease the ache. But she didn't dare slide a hand between her legs and bring herself off: she had no idea when Hollis was going to return, and she didn't think that he'd appreciate it if he walked back into the room and saw her masturbating.

In the end, she did nothing; she stayed still, until she heard the door open and close again.

'Good girl,' Hollis said approvingly. 'I wondered if you'd still be here.'

'And if I wasn't, you'd have sent the email to Gilson.'

'Yes.' He paused. 'So, do you repent of your behaviour, Miss Kemp?'

She swallowed, relieved. It was over. He was going to let her go. 'Yes.'

'I don't believe you.'

Shocked, she fell back into silence.

'This tells me otherwise, Rachel. You don't regret a moment of it.' Again, he slid his finger along her quim, pausing to rub her clitoris. 'And this ... You've been thinking, Rachel. Fantasising. Thinking about who could walk into my office and see you like this, and what they'd do when they saw you. How they'd touch you.'

'No.' Her voice was hoarse.

'Really?' He gave a mirthless chuckle. 'Or were you just thinking how hot you feel, how you want to feel something filling you and stretching you? Were you thinking about touching yourself, Rachel, to give me a pleasant little sight on my return?'

'I . . .' How could he read her mind like that?

Again, he chuckled. 'Yes, I thought you were. Well, like I said, you need to be taught a lesson, Rachel.' He stroked her bottom. 'Very much so.'

She tensed. 'If you're going to hit me – '

'I'm not,' he cut in. 'And you don't speak until you're spoken to, Rachel. Remember that.'

She swallowed.

'The answer is, "yes, sir",' he prompted.

'Yes, sir,' she muttered.

'Say it as if you mean it.'

'Yes, sir.'

'And keep your eyes closed.'

She heard the clink of a buckle, then the soft hissing of a zip being undone, and her eyes widened as she realised just what Hollis's intentions were. Then she heard a soft tearing sound and then a snapping sound; as paper skidded across the desk, she opened her eyes briefly and looked at whatever had made the noise. As she'd half-guessed, it was an empty condom wrapper. So that's what Hollis had been doing when he left his office.

Buying a packet of condoms from the machine in the toilets.

'Now, Rachel.' His voice was almost a caress, and she felt the tip of his cock pushing against the entrance of her sex. 'Let this be a lesson to you – teach you what happens when you send pornographic emails to the wrong person.'

She realised with shock just how big his cock was as he pushed into her, up to the hilt. Impressively long and thick, enough to make many men of her own age jealous.

'It's not much of a lesson, though,' Hollis continued, staying completely still inside her. 'Because you're enjoying this, Rachel. I can feel your cunt flexing round me, so hot and wet.' He slid his hands round to cup her breasts and rolled her nipples between his thumbs and forefingers. 'And these . . . They're so hard, I bet they almost hurt. You need to be touched, Rachel, don't you?'

'Yes – sir.'

'Then I think you'd better tell me what I'm doing to you, don't you?' His voice was silky, soft – and completely in control.

'You're penetrating me, sir.'

'Very different language from the text in your email,' he mused. 'I wonder, have you learned your lesson, Rachel?'

She swallowed. 'I – what do you want me to say?'

'Sir,' he prompted.

'Sir.'

He chuckled. 'At the moment, nothing.' He continued rubbing her nipples, sensitising them until Rachel was almost writhing beneath him; then he moved one hand, slapping her lightly across the bottom. 'And I didn't give you permission to move. Stay still.'

Rachel swallowed. This was a new, very refined, game. One she'd never played before – and one whose rules she didn't really know. What the hell's wrong with me? she asked herself, almost panicking. I'm letting a man I barely know do what the hell he likes with me, fucking me and keeping me completely under his control. I ought to tell him where to get off, but . . . I can't. I like what he's doing to me too much. I need him to give me an orgasm.

'That's better,' he said approvingly, as she stopped wriggling. 'Silent and still. That's how you should be while you're learning a lesson.'

Rachel tensed as he slid his hand across her abdomen, then cupped her mons veneris. He parted her labia, seeking and finding her clitoris, and began to rub the small nub of flesh. Rachel bit her lip, trying desperately not to make a noise; as if he sensed her discomfort, Hollis chuckled, then began to thrust.

She swallowed hard; the combined movements of his finger on his clitoris and his cock thrusting into her were almost too much to bear. She flexed her internal muscles round him and he leaned forward to whisper in her ear, licking her earlobe in a way that made her shiver. 'Rachel. I told you to stay absolutely still. And I meant it.'

'Sorry.'

'Your phrase of the day, I think. Sorry. Only it's not quite good enough, Rachel.'

She clenched her jaw. What was he going to do now? Was he going to tell Gilson after all?

To her shock, she felt him straighten up again, and then one finger slid down the crease of her buttocks. He pressed lightly against the puckered rosy hole of her anus; she bit back a moan as his finger slid into her, up to the second joint. If she'd found it hard to stay still while he was merely rubbing her clitoris and thrusting into her, this made it nearly impossible – particularly when he began to move his finger in and out, massaging her.

She tensed her body, trying to remain completely still; and she had to bite her lip hard, drawing blood, to stop herself crying out as Hollis continued to work on her, rubbing and thrusting and stroking. She felt the familiar rippling of her orgasm begin in her calves, sliding insidiously up her legs, a rolling and sparkling sensation which increased in strength as it gathered momentum, finally coiling in her gut and exploding with a force that shocked her. Almost at the same time as her internal muscles contracted sharply round his cock, she felt Hollis's cock twitch deep inside her, and he exhaled sharply.

He withdrew from her, then she heard a snapping sound as he removed the condom. She heard him wipe himself, and then the soft hiss of something else skidding along the table. She risked a peep and nearly gasped as she saw her knickers. He'd cleaned himself on her knickers. Then there was the rasp of his zip and the clink of his buckle; a few moments later, he was sitting back in front of his desk.

'Stand up, Rachel. Open your eyes,' he commanded.

She did so. Hollis looked as pristine as the moment that she'd first walked into his office. No one, looking at him, would possibly have guessed what he'd just been doing with her. In sharp contrast, she felt as though she'd been dragged through a hurricane.

'Get dressed,' he said softly.

She shook her head. 'Not until you tell me what you're going to do with that email.'

'Get dressed, Rachel. You're in no position to make a bargain.' He gave her a wry smile. 'And how would you explain it, if someone walked into my office right now and saw you?'

Rachel swallowed. 'I don't know.'

'You'd better get dressed, then, hadn't you?'

She grabbed her knickers from his desk, putting them on and restoring order to her bra. He watched her intently as she pulled her sweater back on, then her jeans, and finally her socks and ankle boots.

'So what happens now?'

'I think that you've learned your lesson – for now,' he said quietly. He logged on to the computer system and turned the screen to face her. He selected her email, then deleted it.

'Thank you,' she said.

'Don't mention it.' He rubbed his jaw. 'And stay away from Holloway.'

'What?' The command was so unexpected that it shocked her.

'I said,' he repeated quietly, a note of steel in his voice, 'stay away from Holloway. He's out to cause trouble – and it won't do you any good to be seen in his company.'

Rachel's temper flared. 'What gives you the right to tell me who I can and can't see?'

'I'm merely giving you some advice, Miss Kemp.' Hollis, back in his position behind his desk, had retreated into formality. Rachel could hardly believe that, only a few minutes ago, he'd been touching her so intimately. 'If you're at all concerned with your career in this university – or any other, come to that – then you'll stay away from Holloway.'

'But why? What's he done?'

'Let's just say that if you don't, you'll reap the consequences. And they won't be pleasant.'

'But what's he done?' Rachel repeated.

Hollis shook his head. 'It's not your place to ask questions, remember?'

Rachel swallowed. 'All right. May I go now?'

He nodded. 'And remember what I said.'

'Yes.' Rachel couldn't bear to be there for one minute longer. She dearly wanted to argue with him about Luke – Luke wasn't trouble, and she knew it – but her need to be away from there was greater. She left his office, clicking the door shut behind her, and leant against the wall, closing her eyes. What had just happened had been unbelievable – the more so, because she'd allowed it to happen. Hot shame washed over her. And the worst thing was, she'd enjoyed it. She'd actually enjoyed the way he'd ordered her about, the way he'd

57

made her display herself so lewdly for him before he violated her body.

'What's happening to me?' she asked softly. 'Just what the hell is happening to me?'

# Chapter Five

*L*ater that afternoon, Rachel was in the basement of the library, looking up some source material for her thesis. She was completely absorbed in her task, thumbing through the documents; suddenly, she was shockingly aware of hands sliding across her eyes.

'What the – ?' she began.

'Hello, Rachel.' She relaxed as she recognised Luke's voice and felt a light kiss against her earlobe. 'I've been looking for you, all afternoon,' he said quietly. 'I rang your extension, but there was no answer, and eventually it switched through to the departmental secretary. She didn't seem to know where you were; all she said was that you didn't have any lectures or tutorials, so if you weren't in your room, you could be in the library or you could even have gone home for the day.'

She pulled his hands from her eyes. 'I don't have to account to you for every movement I make, you know.'

'I know.' He spun her round to face him. 'Rachel. Is something wrong?'

'Wrong? What should be wrong?'

He sighed. 'It's that bloody email, isn't it?'

She flushed deeply. The email. The reason why she'd ended up in Hollis's office, acting like a slut that morning.

'Oh, Rachel.' He stroked her face. 'I'm sorry if I've offended you. That really wasn't my intention, believe me.'

'You haven't offended me.'

'Are you sure? You're acting very wary.'

'I'm fine, Luke.' She remembered Hollis's warning to stay away from Luke, and shivered. Would Hollis know that she was already defying him – and if he did, what would he do about it? Although he didn't have the email, Gilson would probably be happy to take Hollis's word about the contents. God. It was all such a mess.

'Rachel.' Luke took the book from her hands, closing it and placing it on a nearby shelf. 'Rachel.' He cupped her face in his hands, bending his head and brushing his lips lightly against her own.

She pulled back. 'Luke – not here.'

'No one's going to see us. Hardly anyone comes down here.'

'Luke, I – '

'Sh.' He bent his head again, nibbling at her lower lip; this time, she couldn't help responding, opening her mouth and sliding her hands round his neck. Encouraged, Luke burrowed under the edge of her sweater, stroking her back and unclipping her bra; he eased one hand round to her front, pushing her bra away and squeezing her breast, massaging it gently. Rachel arched against him, and he began to tease her hardening nipple with his thumb and forefinger, sensitising it.

His kiss deepened, his tongue slipping into her mouth; Rachel suddenly stopped caring that they were in a semi-public place. It didn't matter that the basement echoed slightly and anyone could hear them kissing. Or that they'd be reported to Hollis if they were caught. It wasn't important: what mattered was the effect that Luke was having on her body, the way her quim heated and softened, growing ready for him.

'Mm, Rachel,' he murmured against her ear, licking the sensitive spot at the side of her neck. 'Rachel. I've been thinking about you all day. Remembering how we made love, the way your body moved against mine. Feel what you do to me, Rachel.' Gently, he disentangled one of her hands from his hair, sliding it down his body and pressing it against his groin so that she could feel his erection. 'I want you, Rachel. Here and now.'

'But – '

'But nothing,' he cut in. 'Like I said, hardly anyone comes down here. We're not going to be caught.'

'But supposing someone does come?'

'Doesn't that make it even more exciting?' he asked. 'The fact that someone could catch us? The fact that someone could just walk down here, looking for some musty old tome or other – and see us, with my cock buried deep inside you and your face flushed with pleasure?'

Rachel swallowed, embarrassed and turned on at the same time.

He smiled, rubbing his nose affectionately against hers. 'You worry too much, Rachel. No one's going to catch us. And I want you so badly. I want to feel your beautiful warm wet cunt wrapped round my cock. I can't wait, Rachel. I can't wait for tonight, until we're back at my flat. I need you, right now.' Before she could protest any more, he kissed her again, his lips warm and soft and coaxing. The next thing Rachel knew, Luke was easing her sweater over her head. A couple of seconds later, her bra dropped to the floor next to it, and Luke was cupping her breasts, pushing them up and together.

'Mm.' He dipped his head, nuzzling the soft globes. 'Did I ever tell you how beautiful you smell, Rachel? I don't know if it's your perfume, your shower gel, or what, but it's beautiful. French vanilla and jasmine. And it turns me on in a big way.'

She closed her eyes as his mouth closed over one nipple; he drew fiercely on it, making her gasp and arch against him. Then he transferred his attentions to her other breast. The feeling of cool air against her spit-slicked skin made her shiver with pleasure; she slid her hands into his hair again, urging him on.

'Rachel, Rachel. I can't resist you, do you know that?' he murmured against her skin. 'You're adorable. I love the way you curve, the way you feel.'

She felt him undo the button and zip of her jeans, slowly pulling them downwards.

'Hold on.'

He stopped and looked at her, surprised. 'What?'

'You're wearing a hell of a lot more than I am,' she reminded him. It made her feel cheap – and reminded her of the way Hollis had fucked her across his desk: fully clothed, while she was almost naked, with just her bra pushed into a lewd position.

He grinned. 'If that's all you're worrying about, it's easily remedied.' He stripped off his cotton polo-necked sweater. 'Better?'

She shook her head. 'Not quite.'

'Then do something about it, Rachel,' he urged her quietly. 'How do you want me? Show me.'

She unzipped his jeans, pushing his boxer shorts down at the same time as the faded denims. His cock sprang up, large and erect; for a moment, Rachel was tempted to drop to her knees, taking him into her mouth. Then the pulse beating between her legs reminded her: she needed her own satisfaction, now that Luke had aroused her. She wasn't in the mood to be generous. She wanted mutual pleasure, skin to skin, belly to belly and cock to cunt.

'Not all the way,' Luke said softly, stilling her hands.

'What's sauce for the goose,' she quipped.

'Not in this case. If you were wearing a skirt, then you could leave it on, because all I'd have to do is push it up a bit,' he pointed out. 'But for what I've got in mind – your jeans are going to have to come off, Rachel. They're too much of a constriction for me.'

'If someone walks in – '

'They won't. Stop worrying.' Luke slid a hand between

her thighs, using the hard base of his thumb to rub her quim through her knickers.

Rachel gasped as desire kicked through her. 'Luke . . .'

'I know. I want this, too.' He kissed the tip of her nose. 'I'll leave your knickers on, if it makes you feel any better. Actually, the extra friction will feel good.'

She smiled, despite herself. 'Oh, Luke.'

'That's better.' He licked his lower lip. 'God, I can't resist you, Rachel. I don't normally behave like this, believe me – but when I'm with you, my hormones just take over. All I can think about is touching you and tasting you and making love with you. Nothing else seems important.' He resumed his task of removing her jeans, stooping down and nuzzling her midriff. Rachel felt another kick of desire in her loins, and lifted first one foot and then the other so he could remove her boots and jeans.

'God, you're so lovely,' he said, stroking her legs. 'So very lovely.' He bent his head, kissing his way up her leg; Rachel closed her eyes, tipping her head back. She could still remember how good his mouth had felt against her sex the previous night; the thought that he was going to do that again thrilled her.

'Rachel.' He pushed the gusset of her knickers to one side; she widened her stance, giving him the access he needed, and he slowly drew his tongue across her quim, tasting her arousal. She murmured encouragement and he began to lap at her in earnest, making his tongue into a sharp point to tease her clitoris from its hood, rapidly flicking across the hard bud of flesh until she was shaking.

If someone caught them . . . But then again, she'd taken just as big a risk in Hollis's office that morning. Probably more of a risk – it was far more likely that someone would knock on the door of the head of the library's office, than that someone would come searching for some obscure Victorian source material in the basement. Rachel made an effort to forget where she was and abandoned herself to Luke's mouth, to the way he coaxed her body inexorably towards its climax.

She couldn't help a soft moan as her orgasm took her by surprise, snaking through her gut and making her internal muscles flex sharply. Luke stood up, a grin on his face, and kissed her thoroughly, letting her taste herself on his mouth. Then he took her hand, leading her deeper into the recess between the shelves, and turning her round so that her back was to the wall.

The painted plaster was cold against her back and she stifled a yelp; but she made no protest when Luke lifted her slightly, balancing her against the wall, still keeping the gusset of her knickers pushed to one side. He entered her easily, and she wrapped her legs round his waist. He felt good inside her, long and thick and hard; as he began to move, pushing deeply into her, she kissed him, pushing her tongue into his mouth.

He began to thrust rapidly and she felt her desire rise again, a warm shivery feeling that started somewhere in her gut, connected to her nipples and her clitoris, and built to a rapid crescendo. She moaned into his mouth as her quim contracted hard around the thick rod of his cock; and she felt rather than heard his answering cry as he, too, reached his climax, his cock throbbing inside her.

He held her close for a moment, still kissing her; then he withdrew, lowering her gently until her feet were back on the floor. He kissed the tip of her nose, then pulled his jeans back up, zipping them, and went to retrieve the rest of their clothes. He dressed her in silence, stroking her skin and covering her reluctantly; then, when she was fully clothed, he pulled his sweater on again.

'Sorry about that,' he said, not looking in the least bit contrite.

Rachel grinned. 'Liar.'

'Yeah, well. You have this effect on me. You've turned

me into whatever the male equivalent of a nympho-maniac is.'

'A sex maniac, I think.'

He wrinkled his nose. 'That makes me sound like a dirty old man. And believe me, I don't feel anything dirty about you.'

'No?'

'No. Lustful, yes. Licentious, even.'

She groaned. 'Why do I get the nasty feeling that you're going to start quoting poetry at me?'

'Wrong. I just wanted to tell you that there's nothing dirty about the way I feel about you. It's very pure.'

'Pure?' she scoffed. 'You're telling me that what we just did was pure?'

He chuckled. 'Pure sex. The best kind – mutual pleasure. Don't tell me that you didn't enjoy it.'

'Well.' She bit her lip. 'We took a hell of a risk.'

'A calculated one – and I only gamble when I know that I'm going to win.' He took her hands, curling his fingers round them and lifting them in turn to his lips. 'Now, are you going to tell me what that was all about earlier?'

Rachel frowned. 'I don't follow you.'

'It was almost like you were avoiding me. When you selected my email, I was expecting you to call me.'

'I couldn't. I had a tutorial.'

'OK. When your tutorial had finished then. You could have called me.' He paused. 'Unless I shocked you?'

She shook her head. 'No.'

'So I didn't upset you?'

'No.'

He frowned. 'So why were you avoiding me, then?'

She sighed. 'All right, you might as well know. I sent you an email back.'

'An email?'

'Pretty much like yours, in fact.'

'Well, I didn't get it.'

'I know.'

He frowned. 'You sent me something, I didn't receive it – and you tell me that you know that I didn't receive it. What's going on, Rachel?'

She sighed. 'When I typed your ID at the top of the mail, my finger slipped. I sent it to the wrong person.'

Luke stared at her, then chuckled. 'You're kidding! Why didn't you just recall it?'

'Because,' she said softly, 'I didn't realise that I'd sent it to the wrong person. Then the phone rang, and I thought it was you.'

'And?'

She bit her lip. 'I don't think I want to talk about it.'

'No, come on. You have to tell me now. You can't just let me guess.' He paused. 'Who did you send it to?'

She closed her eyes. 'Leonard Hollis.'

'Leonard Hollis? As in the head of the library?' Luke whistled. 'Shit. When you make a mistake, you make it big time, Rachel. Did he read it?'

'Yes. He wasn't very impressed,' Rachel said. 'In fact, he was furious. He called me into his office to give me a dressing-down.' And something more – though she wasn't going to tell Luke about that. She couldn't possibly tell him how Hollis had humiliated her, dominated her – and how she'd enjoyed it, deep inside. Even now, the memory aroused conflicting emotions in her. Anger and shame and pleasure, all mixed together.

'What did you write exactly?' Luke asked.

'Just a couple of pages' worth.'

'Tell me.'

She shook her head.

He pulled her close. 'Whisper it, then.'

'No.'

'Tell me.' He licked her earlobe. 'Unless you want me to call Hollis and ask him to pass my property over to me.'

'No!'

'Tell me then.'

Rachel didn't think that Luke's threat was serious, but

she wasn't taking any chances. Besides, the idea appealed to her: it was like the erotic phone calls she'd had with past lovers, late at night, only better – because Luke was with her and she could feel his reactions. 'All right. I outlined a little scenario where we were back at your place. In your bedroom, to be precise, with some music and some candles and some sparkling wine.'

'That's a good start. What happens next?'

'I undress you. Then I walk you backwards to your bed, and tie you to the bedframe.'

'Kinky,' he teased.

'You started it,' she reminded him. 'You're the one who wrote me an email about how you were going to tie me up and do all sorts of things to me with a brush. Which is very Anaïs Nin, by the way.'

'Are you accusing me of talking in clichés?'

'No. Plagiarism,' was the swift retort.

He grinned. 'It wasn't a fantasy, Rachel. It was a statement of fact. And when you're coming so hard that you're almost screaming, I'll remind you of your little comment about plagiarism and see what you have to say for yourself then.' He bit her earlobe. 'You'll have to apologise before I continue.'

'Oh, yes?'

'Yes.' He rubbed his nose against hers. 'But you were telling me what you wrote to me. What happens next?'

'You're lying there on the bed, waiting for me, and I decide to entertain you. I strip, very slowly, to the music: and I'm wearing some underwear especially for you. A soft green leather basque, very low cut, a lace G-string and lace-topped hold-up stockings. Oh, and high heels. Black patent leather.'

'Mm. I might just hold you to this. I love women in high-heeled shoes – I love watching the way their bodies shimmer as they walk.' He stroked her buttocks, pulling her against him; she could feel his cock stirring again, becoming erect as she talked to him. 'What then?'

'Then I masturbate in front of you. I touch my breasts,

working on my nipples, and you can see exactly what I'm doing to myself. It turns you on, watching me touch myself. Then I slide one hand between my legs. I make myself come while you're watching. Then I climb on to the bed and straddle you.'

'Mm.' He nuzzled her cheek. 'And I get to sink my cock into your lovely warm wet depths.'

'Nope.' She grinned. 'I'm facing away from you, Luke.'

He sighed with pleasure. 'Oh, yes. What a view.'

'I push backwards and you start licking me. Your cock's hard and it looks so tempting; I take it into my mouth and suck you.'

'Oh, yes,' he sighed, slipping one hand under her sweater again, undoing the button of her jeans. 'I love the idea of your beautiful mouth wrapped round my cock.'

'Luke,' she hissed as he lowered her zip. 'Stop it.'

'I just want to touch you,' he said, burrowing inside her jeans and sliding his hand down the front of her knickers.

She parted her legs, letting him cup her mons veneris. 'And then,' she said, 'I use a delaying tactic on you. You make me come, distracting me for a moment.'

'Like I am now?'

She grinned. 'Do you want to hear this or not?'

'Yes,' he said, sliding a finger into her wetness. 'But I want to touch you as well.'

'Well, then I move between your thighs, facing you, so you can see what I'm doing. I start masturbating you, using slow strokes and then speeding up, then slowing down again. Just as you're losing control, I delay your climax again. And then I wet my finger, pushing it between the crease of your buttocks and deep into you, massaging you until you're writhing beneath me – as much as you can, in the scope of your bonds.'

'Mm,' Luke said, rubbing her clitoris with his thumb.

'And at the same time, I give you a champagne blow-job.'

'Oh, my God,' he said. 'I don't know if I can handle all that at the same time!'

'You don't. You come, pretty deliriously,' she informed him.

'Mm. I like the idea, Rachel. I like it a lot,' he said. 'In fact, I think I'll buy us some champagne on the way home.'

'Indeed.'

Luke continued working on her. 'And Hollis read all that, thinking that you meant it for him?'

She flushed. 'Not exactly.'

'Then what?'

'He guessed that I'd sent it to him by mistake. He threatened to tell Gilson.'

'Ouch.' Luke rubbed her clitoris, hard. 'But he won't, will he?'

'No.'

'I bet I know what he's going to do tonight,' Luke said. 'He's going to print that out – then he's going to go home and wank himself silly over it.'

'I doubt it.'

'I dunno, Rachel. He's the quiet, austere type. They're usually the ones with the more . . . let's say, sophisticated tastes.'

Rachel flushed. How right he was – though she couldn't possibly tell him.

'He'll have been thinking about it all afternoon. All through budget meetings and the like – all he can think about is your email and how turned on he is by it. Imagining you doing all those things to him. Imagining watching you stripping for him and warming yourself up for him. He won't be able to pay attention to anything until he gets home.'

'Stop it, Luke.'

He ignored her. 'All the way home, his cock's going to be rigid. Neat, prissy Mr Hollis is going to have one hell of a hard-on. And when he gets indoors, he won't be able to wait to undress and do something about it.'

'He might be married for all you know.'

Luke shrugged. 'Even so. Imagine that he's on his own when he gets home. He has the whole evening to himself. He could just go upstairs and strip and wank himself silly, but he can't even wait that long. He'll just go into his sitting room, draw the curtains, switch on the light and take your email from his briefcase. He'll be lying there on the sofa, reading what you wrote, and imagining every last detail. The way you look, the way your nipples grow hard as you touch yourself, the scent of your beautiful quim as you grow more and more turned on. The whole room smelling of sex.' Luke continued to push his finger in and out of her increasingly wet channel. 'He won't even be able to wait to undress. He'll just undo his suit trousers and take his cock in his hand. He'll be so hard, it'll almost hurt. And he'll want you. He'll think of the way you said you'd suck his cock and he'll start pumping his hand up and down, bringing himself closer and closer to the edge. Then he'll squeeze his cock, just below the head, to delay himself – because he's enjoying it, fantasising about you.'

'Luke,' she murmured.

'Mm. Touch yourself, Rachel. Do it,' he said softly.

Rachel pushed her hands under her sweater, rubbing her hardening nipples through the lace of her bra. The way that Luke was describing Hollis's reaction turned her on even more because she could imagine it so easily. From her experience with Hollis, that morning, she was sure that he'd know exactly how to prolong his pleasure.

Luke continued to rub her quim. 'Mm. He might even copy the way you said you'd masturbate him – slow, teasingly slow, then speeding up again, then slow. He won't be able to simulate your champagne blow-job, but he'll imagine it. He'll imagine the way the bubbles would burst against his prick, tingling and teasing him: and the way you'd swallow the wine, soothe his skin with your tongue. He might even lick his palms, pretending that the wetness wrapped round his cock is your mouth, not his hand.'

'Oh.' Rachel shivered as she felt her orgasm begin to build.

'He'll work himself harder and harder, faster and faster. His mouth will be open and he'll be shouting out your name as he wanks himself into a frenzy – and then he'll come, all over his prissy white shirt.'

It was enough to push Rachel over the edge, and she moaned softly as she climaxed.

Luke stilled his hand until the aftershocks of her orgasm had died down; then he removed his hand from her knickers and licked every scrap of juice from his fingers. Rachel shivered as she watched him, remembering how Hollis had made her clean her juices from his fingers in such a similar way.

'Well.' He smiled at her. 'Think of that, next time you see Hollis.'

Her colour flared. 'Luke!'

'I bet he starts thinking about it, the next time he sees you.'

And more, Rachel thought. He'll be thinking about a lot more. How he had me over his desk, displaying myself and calling him 'Sir'. How he fucked me, making me stay perfectly still while he invaded my arse and rubbed my clitoris and thrust his cock into me. She swallowed hard, not wanting to remember it, and changed the subject, zipping up her jeans.

'Hollis doesn't like you, Luke.'

'How do you mean?'

'He told me to stay away from you for my own good. He said that you were trouble.'

Luke laughed. 'Yeah, we've crossed swords.'

'And that's why he doesn't like you?'

'Sort of.' He wrinkled his nose. 'A benefactor at the university I was with in America wants to buy some original records, a few documents which happen to be held here in the university library. You know as well as

I do how badly this place needs cash – and no, I'm not going to give you a lecture on politics. I'm just stating a fact.'

'And you think that we should sell the records?'

'Maybe. Anyway, Hollis doesn't approve of the documents leaving Britain.' Luke rolled his eyes. 'And because I worked there, he's convinced that I'm in league with them somehow and I'm plotting to go above his head and do some kind of deal.'

'But that's crazy.'

'You know that and I know that.' Luke shrugged. 'Anyway, that's why he doesn't like me.'

'I see.'

'Rachel, this is a free country. You can see whoever you like, whenever you like. So if you're worrying that Hollis is going to know that you're still with me – don't. Because he can't do anything to you.'

'He can tell Gilson about the email.'

'True.' He paused. 'Did Hollis delete it?'

'Eventually.'

'Well then. He doesn't have a record of it.'

'But supposing he printed it off?'

Luke grinned. 'If he did, it was to do exactly what I've just described to you. Stop worrying, Rachel.' He glanced at his watch. 'Anyway, I need to be going.'

'Going?' she repeated stupidly.

'Yes. I have a bottle of champagne to buy – and a sable brush.' He gave her a wicked grin. 'So you go back to whatever you were doing – and I'll see you outside this building at half past five, OK?'

She smiled at him. 'OK.'

# Chapter Six

'Well, hello there, stranger. So I've caught you in at last.'

Rachel smiled as she recognised the voice on the other end of the line. 'Hi, Jen. Sorry, I did get your answerphone message the other day – I just haven't been in to return it. How are you?'

'Fine. Look, I was planning on coming up to London in a couple of weeks. Is it all right to stay at your place?'

'Of course it is,' Rachel said warmly. 'You don't have to ask, you know that.'

'Well, you might have been busy. You've been out every night for the past week.'

Rachel grinned, catching the sub-text of her friend's comment. 'Stop fishing, Jen.'

'All right, all right. How's the thesis coming along?'

'Painfully. You know, the other day, I was really wishing that you were a crime writer – so you could tell me what kind of poison's untraceable and I could doctor Gilson's coffee or something.'

Jennifer chuckled. 'Rach, he's a bastard and I sympathise with you a hundred per cent – but he's just not worth it.'

'Yeah, I know. I was fantasising, that's all.'

'There are better things to fantasise about,' Jennifer said.

'Too right.'

'Oh? Something you want to tell me, is there? What's his name?'

Rachel sighed. 'I swear, you've got some kind of radar. You know the minute that I've met someone.'

'No, I just know you fairly well. Spill the beans then. I want to know all about him.'

'His name's Luke Holloway, he's a couple of years older than me, and he lectures in economic history. I bumped into him – literally – in the library.'

'Knocked his books flying?'

'Worse. I spilled my entire cup of coffee over him.'

'Way to go, Rach,' Jennifer teased. 'So what did you do? Offer to mop him up?'

'His notes took the worst of it. I apologised and he suggested that I buy him a cup of coffee. I think he was lonely actually – he said he's just come back from the States and he doesn't know many people in London.'

'Nice chat-up line,' Jennifer said. 'Looks?'

'Tall, dark hair, greeny-grey eyes – very, very nice. He looks a bit like that actor you've had a thing about for months.'

'Hm. Well, if you get bored with him, send him up to Yorkshire. I'm sure I could keep him busy.'

Rachel chuckled. 'I should think so. He's a fan of yours.'

'He's what?' Jennifer was surprised.

'He came back to my place and saw the half-shelf of Jude Devereaux novels. It turns out that his last girl-friend read all your stuff. So he read it, too – and he liked it.'

'Thanks for the ego-boost.'

'Seriously.' Rachel grinned. 'I think you two would get on pretty well. He has an interesting line in emails. I might send a copy to you, actually – it'd make good background reading for you.'

'Tut, tut. And I thought you were slaving away in your office, not indulging in erotic email conversations,' Jennifer teased.

'I wish I had been.'

'What happened? Did Gilson walk in and read it over your shoulder? Or catch you doing something that you should have been doing in private, rather than in the middle of your office?'

'No. I sent Luke an email back – and mistyped his ID.'

'You mean you sent it to someone else?'

'By mistake. Yep.'

Jennifer whistled. 'I hope he appreciated it.'

Rachel coughed. 'Sort of. He called me into his office to give me a bollocking.' She paused. 'And he's pretty friendly with Gilson.'

'Shit. I hope you don't get into trouble over it, Rach.'

'I don't think I will, somehow.' Rachel, who'd felt too ashamed to tell Luke what had happened, felt no such embarrassment with Jennifer. And she needed to tell someone what had happened. It would make her feel better about it. 'Actually, you'd never believe what happened.'

'Tell me.'

Rachel suddenly remembered what her friend did for a living. 'I dunno, Jen.'

'I'm not going to use it in a plot, I promise. Tell me.'

Rachel sighed. 'All right. I asked him – very nicely – not to tell Gilson. And he told me to take my clothes off.'

'You're kidding!'

'Straight up.'

'And did you?'

Rachel coughed. 'Yes.'

'What happened then?'

'He made me bend over his desk. He had a ruler in his hand and I thought that he was going to use it on me.'

'You mean, discipline you?'

'He was considering it – but, in the end, he didn't. He

told me to stay where I was and disappeared. I was panicking, in case someone walked into his office and saw me like that.'

'You could have just got dressed and left.'

'And have him send that bloody email to Gilson? I couldn't risk it, Jen.'

'So what happened then?'

'It turned out that he'd just gone out to get some condoms. He took me, over his desk.' Rachel paused. 'It was weird, Jen. All the time, I hated what he was doing – and I loved it, at the same time. He was cool and commanding and demanding. He humiliated me, Jen, and it really turned me on. I didn't think that I was into that sort of thing. Not in real life, anyway.'

'Maybe you're just discovering something about yourself,' Jennifer said. 'Have you told Luke about it?'

'No. How could I?'

'If he's the kind to write you a raunchy email, he'll probably like the story,' Jennifer said.

'Even so. I couldn't, Jen. I feel – well, ashamed, I suppose. Embarrassed. I just did everything Hollis told me to do; I didn't argue, I didn't tell him to go fuck himself or anything like that. I just let him do whatever he liked to me.'

'But you can talk to me about it.'

'That's different.'

Jennifer paused. 'Was he good?'

Rachel swallowed. 'Yes. That's what makes me feel so bad about it. I mean, I've just started this thing with Luke – and I've let another bloke treat me in the most obscene way. Literally.'

'These things happen.' Jennifer coughed. 'Look, let's discuss this properly over a bottle of wine when I'm down in London.'

'Mm.'

'And I want you to point this mystery man out to me – and to meet Luke.' Jennifer's amusement filtered

76

through her voice. 'I think that it's going to be rather an interesting meeting.'

'Jen, you're not going to say anything to him, are you?'

'About this Hollis guy? No, of course not. That's up to you to decide if you want to tell him what happened.'

'He knows that I was hauled in for a bollocking, but that's all,' Rachel said. 'He found it quite amusing. In fact, he reckons that Hollis was probably going to take a copy of my email home and spend the night masturbating over it.'

'You could probably get away with telling him then,' Jennifer said. 'But it's up to you. Anyway, I'd better let you go. See you in a fortnight.'

'Let me know what time your train gets in and I'll meet you at the station,' Rachel said.

'OK. Take care.'

Rachel replaced the receiver, feeling better now that she'd told someone about what had really happened with Hollis. She only hoped that Gilson knew nothing about it. And as for telling Luke ... Maybe she'd tell him. But not just yet.

The following day, Rachel was in her office, working on her thesis. The phone rang; she saved the file she was working on, then picked up the receiver. 'Hello. Rachel Kemp speaking.'

'Gilson.'

Rachel closed her eyes. Shit. Just what she didn't need. 'What can I do for you?'

'In my office, please. Now.'

'I'm on my way.' She replaced the receiver. 'Shit, shit, shit. Now what?' Had Hollis broken his word to her and said something to Gilson? Or had Gilson looked at the latest section of her thesis and decided to reduce it to shreds again? On balance, she thought, it was probably the latter. Rachel pulled a face and headed for her supervisor's office.

She rapped on the door. 'Come in,' he called. When he saw her, he nodded. 'Sit down, Rachel.'

He didn't often use her name; Rachel was immediately on her guard. 'Is there a problem with my thesis?' she asked.

He shook his head. 'It's not your thesis. There's no easy way to say this, Rachel.'

'To say what?'

'I've had a memo from the chancellor of the university. We have to make cuts.' He paused. 'You're not one of our doctorate employees, so I'm afraid that we'll have to let you go at the end of term.'

'What?' She was shocked. 'But – '

'This isn't up for discussion. All the departments have had to make cuts, Rachel. You're one of the unlucky ones.'

Not even a 'sorry', for politeness' sake, she noticed. 'But – I'm not the last one who joined the department.'

'Even so, you don't have a doctorate.'

Yes, Rachel thought, and if you get your way, I'll never bloody get one. 'So that's it? I'm out?'

'I'm afraid so.'

Rachel stared at him in disbelief. She was popular with the students and she'd worked well with them, encouraging several of the less able ones and bringing them up to standard. Despite the fact that Gilson always shredded her work, she knew that her thesis was sound. They weren't letting her go because she was useless at her job: Gilson was simply using the chancellor's memo as an excuse to get rid of her because he didn't like her. He couldn't even be bothered with the usual managerial platitudes of being sorry to see her leave and regretting that he had to make her redundant – because he wasn't sorry in the slightest. He was pleased, in that snide little way of his. 'I see.'

'We will, of course, make sure that none of the students are affected by this,' he added. 'We'll make sure that there's a proper handover procedure.'

78

Rachel nodded. 'And I have a seminar shortly. If you'll excuse me, I'd like to make sure that I'm properly prepared for it.'

'Of course.'

She left the room in silence; only when she'd slammed the door to her own office, very hard, did she give vent to her feelings. 'You fucking, fucking bastard, Gilson!' And everything that had happened in Hollis's office had all been for nothing. Gilson had been planning to get rid of her anyway. She'd just lost her job – and her chance of finishing her PhD.

'Oh, Christ,' she said softly, sinking into her chair and propping her elbows on her desk, resting her face in her hands. 'Oh, Christ.' She wasn't usually given to emotional outbursts but she couldn't help the tears rolling down her face. Her future lay in ruins, and there was nothing she could do about it.

She wasn't sure how long she'd been sitting there in tears, when there was a knock at her door.

She scrubbed at her face, hoping that the fact that she'd been crying didn't show too much. 'Yes?'

Luke stuck his head round the door. 'Can I come in?'

'If you like.'

He closed the door behind him, then and frowned. 'Rachel, what's wrong?'

'Nothing.'

'It doesn't look like nothing to me.' He sat on the edge of her desk, taking one of her hands and stroking it. 'You've been crying.'

'Yeah, well.' Rachel made a vain attempt to shrug it off.

'What's happened?'

She sighed. 'I may as well tell you now. It's not going to change anything. Gilson's had a memo from the powers-that-be. He has to lose some staff – so he's getting rid of me.'

'He's what? Oh, no.'

She shrugged. 'Nothing I can do about it.'

79

'Rachel, I'm so sorry. So very sorry.'

'He's not. Do you know, Luke, he didn't even say that he was sorry? He enjoyed telling me that he had to get rid of me,' she said bitterly.

'Don't worry. You'll soon find another job.'

'English lecturers are ten a penny – especially because this isn't the only place that's had to make cuts. Do you know how hard you have to fight to get a job in the arts faculties?'

He nodded. 'History's an arts subject, too.'

'Yeah. I know. Sorry.'

'Hey, it's all right. In your shoes, I'd be just as upset.'

'He said that he was letting me go because I don't have a doctorate.' She laughed shortly. 'I'm so bloody near to it too. If he hadn't messed me about last year, I would have had my doctorate by now. He's probably been planning this all along. And I bet he doesn't have to get rid of non-doctorate staff either. He was just saying that, using it as an excuse to get rid of me – because he hates me, Luke. He really, really hates me.'

'Well, you'll get a better job, somewhere that deserves you,' Luke said. 'Oh, Rachel.'

'It's not fair, Luke. It's not bloody fair.'

'I know.' He drew her to her feet, holding her close and stroking her hair. Rachel bit back the tears and he nuzzled her neck, sympathy radiating from him. She closed her eyes, relaxing into his arms: at least Luke understood how she was feeling. He cared – unlike her bastard of a boss.

Luke was kissing her neck, gentle soothing kisses which started just below her ear and trailed round to her face. Instinctively, Rachel turned her face to his and his lips met hers. His kiss was sweet and gentle; suddenly, Rachel felt a fierce flood of desire for him. Her world had crashed apart: but there was one thing that would make her feel better. Making love with Luke. And if Gilson walked in on them – well, tough. She was going anyway. So she could do what the hell she liked. She didn't care if she offended Gilson or not. And the best thing was, on her last day she could tell him exactly what she thought of him. Using extremely choice language. She smiled bitterly to herself. Yes. And she'd do it in front of the whole department for maximum impact.

Her seminar forgotten, she slid her hands into Luke's hair, drawing him closer. He smoothed his hands down her back, cupping her buttocks and pressing her against him so that she could feel his erection throbbing against her pubis.

'Oh, Rachel,' he said softly. 'This isn't going to change anything.'

'I know. But it's going to make me feel better. Please, Luke. Make love with me.'

'Here? Are you sure?'

'Absolutely.'

He nodded and undid the buttons of her loose tunic shirt very gently, pushing the material from her shoulders. He gave a sharp intake of breath as he saw her breasts, the burgundy lace of her bra contrasting with the creaminess of her skin. 'Rachel, you're adorable.' He stooped down to bury his face between her breasts, nuzzling them and breathing in her scent. 'I love the way you feel. Your skin's so soft, so smooth.'

Rachel felt a pulse kick between her legs. She gave a small sigh of pleasure as Luke undid her bra, dropping the burgundy lace garment to the floor, then cupped her breasts, lifting them up and together slightly to deepen her cleavage. He bent his head again, his tongue tracing the outline of her areolae; he blew gently on the skin he'd just wetted and Rachel gasped, her nipples hardening immediately. Then he drew one nipple into his mouth and began to suck, very gently. She tipped her head back, closing her eyes. God, it felt so good. So very, very good.

'Rachel.' He murmured her name against her skin and transferred the attentions of his mouth to her other

81

breast, licking and sucking the nipple and rolling its twin between his thumb and forefinger, extending it gently but firmly, until she was pushing against him. 'Oh, yes, Rachel,' he said, dropping to his knees before her.

She was wearing a pair of black jersey leggings; he made short work of sliding them down, unzipping her boots and removing her socks at the same time, so that she was left wearing only a pair of burgundy lace knickers. 'Christ, Rachel, you look so good. I want to wallpaper my room with pictures of you like that.'

She smiled wryly. 'That'd be two of us out of a job then.'

'I meant my bedroom. That, or make love with you in a room full of mirrors, so I that could see you everywhere I looked.'

'Mirrors on the ceiling, hm?' she teased.

'Yes. Mirrors everywhere. Reflecting you, reflecting my cock sliding in and out of your delectable cunt.' He stroked her thighs and she shivered, automatically widening her stance. He smiled. 'I love the way you respond to me. I can't get enough of you, Rachel. I want you so badly.'

'It's the same for me. Since that first meeting.' She stroked his hair. 'Did you know, I went home and I ended up masturbating with a hairbrush in my hall, because I couldn't wait long enough to go upstairs and find a vibrator?'

'Wicked girl,' he breathed, his voice husky. 'And you'd only just met me.'

'I spent the afternoon reading one of Jen's books, my hand between my legs. I thought it might get it out of my system, so I'd behave myself when I went out to dinner with you.'

'Didn't work, though, did it?'

She smiled. 'No.'

'I'm glad. I'm glad that you ruined my notes, too – because it was worth it, for this.' Gently, he eased his finger under the leg of her knickers, sliding his finger down to part her labia. She shivered and he let his finger explore her folds and crevices, finally sliding his finger deep into her vagina. She flexed her internal muscles around his finger, and he smiled. 'Rachel. Look at me.'

She did. He withdrew his hand, then put his finger into his mouth, sucking every last drop of her juices from it. Then he peeled down her knickers, drawing the lacy material over her hips and down to her ankles. She stepped daintily out of her knickers and widened her stance again. Luke crouched between her thighs, parting her labia and sighing happily. 'I love this. I love the scent of you when you're starting to become aroused. I love the way you taste, all seashore and honey and musk. I could eat you for ever.'

She could feel his breath against her quim and it made her shiver in anticipation. Luke stretched out his tongue, licking from the top to the bottom of her slit in one slow, easy movement which made her stomach kick. 'Oh yes,' she said softly. 'Yes. Please. Do it.' She slid her hands down to tangle in his hair, urging him on, and he began to lap at her in earnest, his tongue exploring her and flickering quickly across her clitoris and then sliding down her quim and pushing deep into her vagina.

Rachel felt her orgasm coil in her gut, then suddenly explode. She shivered and Luke held her close, continuing to nuzzle her until the aftershocks of her orgasm had died away. Then he got to his feet, taking her into his arms and kissing her hard. When he broke the kiss, she leant against him. 'Thank you, Luke.'

'I haven't finished yet.' He kissed the tip of her nose. 'Undress me, Rachel,' he invited huskily. 'Let's go all the way.'

She smiled and cupped his face, drawing his mouth down to hers again. Still kissing him, she bunched up the hem of his sweater. She broke the kiss and he held up his arms, letting her remove his sweater completely. She drew her hands over his chest, feeling his flat button

83

nipples harden as she touched him, then let her hands drift slowly over his abdomen, down to the button of his jeans. He gave a soft murmur of pleasure as she undid the button, then slid the zipper downwards. She eased the soft faded denim over his hips; he kicked off his shoes and she removed his jeans completely, taking off his socks at the same time. Then she rocked back on her haunches and looked up at him, a question in her eyes.

He shook his head and sank to the floor beside her. 'Not this time, Rachel,' he said. 'This isn't for me. It's for you.'

'For both of us,' she amended.

'Mm.' Somehow, he manoeuvred their positions so that he was lying on the floor of her office, and she was straddling him. He was still wearing his boxer shorts, but she could feel the length and girth of his hard cock pressing against her. She hooked her thumbs into the waistband of his boxer shorts and slowly drew the garment down. He lifted his bottom, so that she could remove the shorts, then sank back down again. She rested her hands on his shoulders and slowly rubbed her quim against his cock, letting the hard muscle glide over her warm wet furrow.

He shivered. 'Rachel. I want to be inside you.'

'I want it too,' she said huskily.

'Then let's do something about it.'

She nodded and sat up straighter, lifting herself slightly and curling her fingers round his shaft. She fitted the tip of his cock to the entrance of her sex and slowly sank down on him, loving the way he filled her, stretching her. Luke licked his lips, tipping his head back and opening his mouth in pleasure as he felt her warm, wet depths encompass his cock. He tilted his hips and she began to move over him, lifting and lowering herself and moving her body in tiny circles. He looked at her, then licked his thumb and forefingers and began to tease her nipples again, pinching them slightly.

Rachel groaned and slid her hands over his, linking

84

their fingers together and helping him to rub her nipples. God, this felt so good, she thought. So very good. It was just what she needed to take her mind off her problems.

'Touch yourself,' he urged. She continued massaging her breasts, squeezing them and kneading them and rubbing her nipples. Luke smiled at her, easing one hand between their bodies, and began to rub her clitoris. She moaned softly and quickened the rhythm, still moving over his cock in small circles. She tossed her hair back and shuddered again as his fingertip teased her clitoris, pressing the sensitive nub of flesh.

'Don't stop,' he urged, continuing to massage her clitoris.

She moaned, slamming down harder on to his cock and squeezing her internal muscles round him as she lifted herself up again. She ground her pubis against his, her movements wild. Then, at last, she felt orgasm wash through her again, her internal muscles convulsing sharply round him. Almost at the same moment, Luke gave a groan and she felt his cock throb deep inside her. She collapsed on to him and he wrapped his arms round her, holding her close and stroking her hair.

Some time later, when their breathing had slowed, she sat up again. 'Luke.'

'Yeah, I know.' He traced her lower lip with his forefinger. 'You've got a tutorial.'

'A seminar.'

'Cancel it.'

She shook her head. 'I can't, Luke. It isn't fair. I can't take it out on my students, just because Gilson's decided to get rid of me.'

'No.' He stroked her buttocks. 'You'll find something, Rachel. Believe me. There's an opportunity waiting for you just round the corner.'

'Mystic Luke knows everything, hm?'

'Trust me.'

'Yeah.'

'In the meantime ... I don't feel like letting you get up.'

'Tough. I have work to do.'

'I'm comfortable.'

Rachel eyed the cheap cord carpet in disbelief. 'On that?'

'With my cock buried in you, my sweet.' His eyes glittered. 'Rachel. Let's stay here all day.'

'You'll have stripes on your bum.'

He grinned. 'Is that a threat?'

She rocked against him. 'Not quite how you think. I'm talking about the pattern of the carpet.'

Whatever he was about to say next was forestalled by a knock at the door. Rachel froze. 'Shit. Whoever it is, they're early.'

'Tell them to go away,' Luke said.

'Just a minute,' Rachel called as the door began to open. 'I'll be with you in a second.'

To her relief, the door closed again. Hastily, she lifted herself off Luke and dressed. He moved in a much more leisurely fashion; she frowned at him. 'Hurry up,' she whispered. 'My students are waiting outside.'

'All right.' He pulled her to him, kissing her hard.

She pulled away. 'Luke! I don't want them thinking that I'm some kind of lush!'

He kissed the tip of her nose. 'You look beautiful. Your eyes are shining and your skin's radiant.'

'You mean I look as I've just been screwing?'

'To me, yes; to them, they probably won't even notice. They're probably worrying that you're going to set them a difficult essay with a short deadline.' He bit her earlobe. 'Apart from your male students, that is. They're probably all fantasising about doing what I just did.'

'Making love with me, you mean?'

'On the floor of your office.' He stroked her face. 'And on that note, I'd better leave. I'll see you later.' He grinned. 'I'll even cook dinner for you tonight.'

She chuckled. 'And this is the man who hates cooking.'

He pulled a face. 'Well, I didn't mean "cool" literal sense. I'll order us a pizza. And then we'll s action plan to get you a new job.'

She smiled at him. 'Thanks, Luke. I appreciate it.'

'I know. And you can thank me properly later – skin to skin.' He gave her a mock-leer and left her office, letting in the half-a-dozen students who were waiting outside.

Rachel turned away to fix some coffee, her face burning: no doubt they could all smell sex in the air and guessed exactly what she'd been doing with the good-looking dark-haired man who'd just left her office. But she was leaving in a few weeks; so what the hell did it matter, anyway?

# Chapter Seven

*T*he soft *burr-burr* on the line continued; Luke swore softly. Trust Max to be out when he needed to talk to him – and have his answerphone switched off too. Luke was just about to clear the line when the receiver was snatched up. 'Hello?'

'Max. It's Luke.'

'Hello.' Max caught the urgency of the younger man's tone. 'Developments?'

'You could say that.' Luke quickly outlined what had just happened between Rachel and Gilson. 'So I think that the position has changed.'

Max sighed. 'All right. Arrange a meeting. But no promises until I've met her, all right?'

'Thanks, Max. I promise you, I wouldn't have suggested her if I didn't think she could do it.'

'I know.' Max paused. 'Lunch, I think. Somewhere discreet, next Thursday.'

'Fine. Leave it to me.'

Max chuckled. 'And yes, before you ask, I'll pick up the bill. I just hope that she's worth it.'

'Believe me, she is,' Luke said.


That evening, Luke arrived at Rachel's house, bearing three large shallow boxes and a large bunch of red roses.

He rang the doorbell; a few moments later she answered, looking slightly flustered.

'Delivery for you, ma'am,' he drawled, his accent at its most transatlantic, and handed the flowers to her.

'Roses? Oh, Luke.'

'Well, I thought that you could do with something nice to cheer you up. Hence the flowers – and these.'

She looked at the boxes and smiled, despite herself. 'Pizza.'

'Well, I promised you that I'd sort dinner tonight – and this is the nearest I get to cooking.'

'Roberto's special, is it?' she asked as she ushered him inside.

'Mm. They do the best pizzas in London,' he said. 'And their garlic dough-sticks are wonderful.'

'All right, I'll believe you.' She led him into the dining room. 'Can you clear that lot to one side while I put the roses in water and get some plates and cutlery?'

'Sure.' Luke put the boxes on the table and started stacking the papers to one side. He glanced through them as he gathered them together: Rachel's CV, neatly typed, with handwritten amendments; the jobs pages of various professional publications with the corners of some pages turned down: obviously pages with jobs that interested her, he thought. He knew of something better – and Max would be a good boss, leaving her to get on with the job and giving her all the support she needed. He was tempted to tell her about it there and then; but he'd promised Max not to say anything. Not yet.

Rachel returned with the plates, the cutlery, a bottle of wine and two glasses. Luke smiled at her and served up the pizza, putting the dough sticks on a separate plate. Rachel poured the wine and handed him a glass. 'Cheers,' Luke said. 'To you – and may you get the job you deserve.'

Her expression was bleak. 'That depends a lot on Gilson's reference, doesn't it?'

'Not necessarily.' Luke took a sip of wine. 'Write a

good enough letter and you'll get an interview. Your CV's impressive; they'll want to know more. Then, once they meet you, they'll like you – and you can explain that you had a personality clash with the head of your department so you're not expecting a good reference from him. You'll have two other references which will back you up – one personal and one professional – so whatever Gilson says about you, it doesn't matter a stuff.'

Rachel didn't share his optimism, but said nothing, concentrating on the pizza.

Luke decided to change the subject. 'What do you think of the pizza?' he asked.

'It's good. Very good.'

'Try these.' He cut a piece from the dough sticks, leaning over the table and holding it to Rachel's lips.

She ate the morsel and nodded in satisfaction. 'Mm. You're right. Gorgeous.'

He smiled at her. 'One day,' he said softly, 'I'm going to feed you like that. Bite by bite.'

'Very *Nine and a Half Weeks*,' she said acerbically.

He grinned. 'Try it – then tell me that.'

'Hm.' She continued eating her pizza.

'Rachel – there was something I wanted to ask you.'

'Oh?'

'Are you busy next Thursday lunchtime?'

She frowned. 'Why?'

'Because I'd like to take you out to lunch.'

'Why next Thursday?'

'Why not?' he fenced. 'So may I?'

'All right.'

'Good.' He smiled at her. 'I happen to have a free afternoon – that's why I suggested next Thursday. I'd like to take you out somewhere really nice, for lunch.'

She wrinkled her nose. 'It's really sweet of you to want to cheer me up but I'll survive, Luke. Really. A couple of days of sulking – and then I'll find myself another job, stick two fingers up at Gilson and be back to my normal self,' she said. 'You don't have to do this.'

'I want to,' he told her. He also wanted her to meet someone – but he didn't think that now was a good time to bring that up. The kind of mood she was in, he had a feeling that she'd refuse.

'All right.'

'And, Rachel . . .'

'Mm?'

He crossed his fingers beneath the table, hoping that he wouldn't blow it. 'Would you wear a skirt?'

'A skirt?'

'Or a dress. Whatever.'

She frowned. 'Why?'

'Because I've never seen you in a skirt and I'd like you to indulge me,' he said, giving her a winning look.

She smiled, despite herself. 'Oh, Luke. You're crazy.'

'So, will you?'

'All right. Though I'm not really a skirt person,' she warned.

He smile at her. 'Thanks. I appreciate it. And it'll be a really good lunch.'

'A sandwich would have done, you know.'

He shook his head. 'Having lunch out, properly, feels incredibly decadent. And get someone else to take your lectures that afternoon – because you won't be going back to work afterwards.'

Rachel thought about it. 'In the circumstances, there's not a lot that Gilson could do about it. He can't sack me – because he's already given me my notice.'

'Exactly. Play him at his own game.'

'Mm.' The thought of Gilson and her job plunged Rachel back into gloom; she ate the rest of her pizza in silence. Luke watched her, noting the way that she was knocking back the wine. She was incredibly upset – and who wouldn't be in her circumstances?

As she pushed her empty plate away, he took her hand. 'Rachel.'

'Mm?'

'Do you want me to go?'

'Yes – no. Oh, I don't know. I'm just not very good company, right now.'

'You're stressed out,' he said. 'And it's not surprising. Anyone would be, in your shoes.'

'I suppose so.'

'When I was in the States,' he said, 'I was introduced to neck massages. They really help when you've had the day from hell, and you're really tense.'

She gave him an old-fashioned look. 'Are you trying to tell me that you're an expert masseur?'

'No – but I'm not bad. If you'd like me to, I'd be more than happy to give you a massage.'

She couldn't help smiling back at him. 'With no ulterior motive?'

He grinned. 'That's an unfair question and I'm not going to answer it.'

Her lips twitched. 'Oh, Luke.'

'Give it a try,' he urged.

'OK.'

'Up you get.' Luke moved his chair, and turned her chair to face his. 'You'll probably find it more comfortable if you rest your arms on the back of the chair and put your head forward.'

Rachel did as he asked, sitting with her back to him. 'And I suppose you want me to take off my sweater,' she said.

'Well, it's going to be difficult to massage you through your clothes. I don't do Shiatsu.'

'Then what are you going to do?'

'Aromatherapy.' He paused. 'Assuming that you have some oils, that is?'

'Yes. Actually, a friend gave me an oil-burner for my birthday; I haven't used it yet. She bought me some oils to go with it.' She nodded at the dresser by the wall. 'It's all in the second cupboard, middle shelf.'

92

'I'll need some carrier oil, too – otherwise it'll be too strong. Do you have any olive oil?'

'In the kitchen, in the cupboard below the kettle.'

While Luke fetched the olive oil, she removed her sweater, discarding it on the floor. He rummaged in her dresser and crowed with delight as he found the oil-burner. 'Brilliant. You've got a relaxing blend; that saves me trying to remember which oils do which,' he said.

'Are you sure you know what you're doing?'

'Trust me,' he said, anointing his hands. 'Close your eyes and relax. If I'm working you too hard, tell me, won't you?'

'I will.' Rachel closed her eyes and rested her head on her arms, and Luke began to rub the tension out of her shoulders.

He had nice hands, she thought. Firm and yet sensitive. And he knew exactly what he was doing, his fingers digging into the knots of tension in her neck and shoulders, loosening them.

'Good?' he asked.

'Mm. Very.'

He said nothing, but continued to massage her, pausing occasionally to pour some more oil into his palms, then stroking her skin again. Rachel felt herself relax under his ministrations, the stresses of her day fading away.

As Luke felt her tension dissolve, he smiled, pushing her hair away from the nape of her neck and putting his lips to the sensitive spot, kissing her lightly. Rachel gave a small murmur of pleasure and he smiled, sliding one hand down her back to undo the clasp of her bra and pushing the garment off her shoulders. When she made no protest, he continued rubbing her skin, his hands sliding with practised ease down her spine. Eventually, he curved his hands over her ribcage to touch the underside of her breasts and Rachel sighed, shifting slightly and straightening up.

'OK?' he asked softly.

'Mm.'

'Good.' He continued to caress and stroke her skin, cupping her breasts and pushing them up and together slightly; she tipped her head back, arching her body. Luke's fingers splayed over her breasts, letting her nipples peep out between his middle and ring fingers; then he squeezed his fingers together again, gently pinching her nipples.

At the same time, he bent his head again to kiss the curve between her neck and shoulders, making Rachel shiver with pleasure. His lips travelled up the side of her neck, concentrating on the sensitive spot just below her ear. He nipped gently at her earlobe and she shivered again. Her nipples were hard and taut, needing release: she wanted him to kiss them, to lick them and suck them. She wanted him to lick her in more intimate places, too – to use his mouth on her until she came, her eyes wild and her hair mussed, her sex flexing under his tongue. And then she wanted him inside her, filling her and stretching her.

'Luke,' she said, her voice a hoarse whisper. 'I think I need this as much as you do. Let's go to bed.'

He took her hand, drawing her to her feet, and then picked her up, carrying her up the stairs to her bedroom.

'Mr Macho,' she teased.

He set her on her feet and went over to draw the curtains. 'Well, if you'd rather play it another way . . .'

'Mm.' She tugged at the hem of his sweater; he lifted his hands, letting her remove the garment. His jeans followed next, together with the rest of his clothes; he was already erect. Rachel smiled to herself. That little interlude downstairs had aroused him just as much as it had aroused her.

He pushed the duvet back, then finished undressing her, stripping off her jeans and the remainder of her underclothes. Then he sat on the bed, drawing Rachel down beside him, and shifted their positions so that she was lying in his arms, cuddled into him. Rachel closed

94

her eyes, resting her head on his chest and running the pads of her fingertips across his belly, taking pleasure in the contrast between the softness of his skin and his silky hair. His body was perfect, she thought, absolutely perfect. Not skinny: and not overdeveloped, either. Just perfect.

She let her hand drift down, curling her fingers round his penis and making a small sound of satisfaction in her throat: he felt so good, so very good. Gently, she began rubbing his foreskin back and forth, letting her fingers play over his cock; eventually Luke murmured, arching his back and putting his hand over hers to still it.

'Rachel.'

'Mm?'

'I thought I was supposed to be indulging you – not the other way round.' Gently, he removed her hand from his cock and moved her so that she was lying on her back. He knelt beside her, just running the pads of his fingertips over her body.

Rachel shivered and arched up towards him.

Luke smiled, stroking her ribcage, and letting his hands drift up to caress the soft undersides of her breasts. 'Rachel. You're so beautiful,' he said huskily, brushing her breasts with the flat of his palms; then he cupped her breasts, bringing them up and together to deepen the vee of her cleavage. He rubbed the pad of his thumb over her areolae, smiling as the rosy tissue hardened and darkened beneath his touch. 'I don't know whether I want to touch you or taste you, more,' he mused.

'Why not both?'

He chuckled. 'What a good idea.' He bent his head, licking each nipple in turn and sucking hard on one while he rubbed the other.

Rachel willed him to go down on her. He'd already teased her, under the guise of making her relax; her sex felt wet and puffy and she wanted him badly. She wanted to feel him kiss his way down her body, rubbing

95

the tip of his nose against her belly and breathing in the musky scent of her arousal as he finally buried his face between her thighs.

Now, now, do it now, she thought, squeezing her eyes shut and concentrating. At last, he began to drop a trail of kisses down over her abdomen. She pushed her thighs wider apart, wanting him to lick her until she was at screaming point; Luke laughed against her skin, and teased her again, licking his way down one leg, pausing to kiss the soft skin at the back of her knees and in the hollows of her ankles, then nibbling his way back up the other leg.

'Luke – please. I need this.'

'You need what?' he asked, his breath warm against her inner thigh.

'You know what I want.'

'Tell me,' he invited.

'I want you to go down on me. I want you to use your mouth on me.'

'You only had to say,' he teased; then, at long, long last, she felt the stroke of his tongue on her quim. He drew it along the full length of her sex, parting her labia and exploring the soft folds and hollows of the intimate topography under his mouth. Rachel was moaning softly, pushing herself up to meet his mouth, when he finally made his tongue into a point, sliding it deep inside her. She gave a small cry of satisfaction, letting her head rest back against the pillows, and slid her hands into his hair, urging him on.

Luke smiled and began to lap in earnest. He caught her clitoris between his lips and sucked hard on the erect nub of flesh until she whimpered, her fingers digging into his scalp. He continued to lick and suck until he felt the familiar fluttering of her flesh under his mouth; then, when the tremors of her orgasm subsided, he reached up to kiss her so that she could taste her juices on his mouth.

'I haven't finished yet,' he informed her, the huskiness in his voice betraying his arousal.

Rachel looked up at him, drowsy-eyed, her pupils a luminous gold. 'What did you have in mind, Luke?'

'Just this.' He knelt between her thighs, positioning his cock at her entrance; then he slid slowly inside her, up to the hilt.

Rachel closed her eyes in bliss. He felt so good, the way he filled her and stretched her. Just when she expected him to start thrusting, he leant back on his haunches, lifting her up so that her buttocks were lifted clear of the bed and her thighs were draped over his, her feet flat against the mattress.

She opened her eyes, staring at him. 'Luke?'

'I think you're going to enjoy this,' he promised. He eased one hand between their bodies and started rubbing her clitoris with the pad of his thumb; Rachel groaned and reached behind her to grip the rails of the headboard, her knuckles whitening as her grip tightened. She pushed against him, wanting to feel him make love with her properly, but he refused flatly to start thrusting; he merely lay there, inside her, while he rubbed her clitoris.

She reached another sobbing orgasm, her internal muscles spasming wildly round his cock; he smiled then, rolling over on to his back without withdrawing from her. 'We have some unfinished business,' he said softly.

'You bet.' Somehow he'd pulled her with him so that she was already kneeling comfortably astride him. She smiled and leant back slightly, changing the angle of his penetration to give them both the most pleasure. Then she began to move, lifting herself up until his cock was almost out of her, then slamming back down again on to him, so that the root of his cock rubbed hard against her clitoris.

'Oh,' she said, closing her eyes and swallowing hard.

'Touch yourself,' Luke urged softly, taking her hands and placing them on her breasts.

She began to massage her breasts, rubbing them

gently, and then harder as her movements over Luke
grew more and more wild. She rubbed her nipples
between thumb and forefinger, tipping her head back
and opening her mouth in a silent wail of pleasure; and
suddenly the familiar rush of ecstasy was there as she
came, rippling through her quim and seeming to explode
in her solar plexus.

Her internal muscles quivered along Luke's cock; it
was enough to tip him over the edge into his own
orgasm and he pushed upwards as he came, his cock
throbbing and discharging the warm salty spurts of his
semen.

Rachel collapsed on to him and buried her face in his
neck.

'Better?' he asked, stroking her hair.

'Better,' she confirmed. 'Though it hasn't solved my
job problem.'

He kissed the curve of her shoulder. 'One thing at a
time, sweetheart,' he told her softly. 'One thing at a
time.'


The following Thursday, Luke rapped on Rachel's office
door, opened it, then leant against the door-jamb.
'Ready?'

She nodded, saving the file on her screen and switch-
ing off her computer. 'Ready.'

'You look lovely.' He appraised her briefly as she
stood up. She was wearing the dark patterned chiffon
shirt she'd been wearing when they'd first gone out to
dinner, teamed with a black pleated ankle-length skirt,
which fell in soft silky folds and rustled when she
walked. She was also wearing black stockings – at least,
Luke assumed that they were stockings – and black
polished leather court shoes with a higher heel than she
normally wore. She'd tamed her hair with an Alice band
as usual, and was wearing very light make-up, a neutral
eyeshadow and mascara which widened her eyes and a

98

neutral lipstick which emphasised the perfect cupid's-bow shape of her mouth.

'Thanks.' She smiled at him. 'You don't look so bad yourself.'

'I like this.' He walked over to her and ran his hand down her back, smoothing over her buttocks and taking the material of her skirt between his fingertips, rubbing it lightly. 'Maybe you should wear skirts more often.'

She grinned. 'I think not. All my students have been asking me if I've got an interview this afternoon – and you look like you're going to one too.'

He wrinkled his nose. 'The grapevine's spread the news that you're going then?'

'Yeah.' Her lips twitched. 'Some of them have been threatening to get up a petition and to boycott Gilson's lectures. But there's no point. A petition won't work and they'll only hurt themselves by skipping his lectures. It won't bother him but they'll lose out on what he can teach them.' She shrugged. 'It's time for me to move on anyway.'

'I suppose so.' Luke took her hand. She'd adjusted well to the circumstances; after that brief spell of tears in her office and her black mood of that evening, she'd been remarkably cheerful, even writing letters on speculation. He smiled to himself. Did she but know it, lunch was going to be a kind of job interview. But not, knowing Max, a conventional one. 'Let's go then.'

She grabbed her coat. 'So where are we going?'

He tapped his nose. 'Wait and see.'

She groaned. 'You sound like my parents when I was a kid. My father used to love telling me that we were going "there and back, to see how far it is". It used to annoy the hell out of me.'

'All right, we're going to Mayfair.'

'Mayfair? We're having lunch in Mayfair?' Her eyes widened. 'Luke, you're talking expensive.'

He shrugged. 'So?'

'I told you, just a sandwich would have done me.'

'Well, I fancy eating somewhere nice. Humour me?'

'Hm. Though I still think we should – '

'Go Dutch?' he interrupted. 'Not this time, sweetheart. Humour me.'

She sighed. 'All right.'

'Come on, then.'

# Chapter Eight

*A*fter Rachel had locked her office door, they left the building and walked to Luke's car. They drove to Mayfair in companionable silence; Luke parked the car and led her to the restaurant.

'Um – Rachel,' he said, pausing by the door.

'Yes?'

'I – er – there's someone I want you to meet.'

Rachel's eyes narrowed as she took in the guilty look on his face. 'When?'

'In about thirty seconds.'

She frowned. 'I thought that lunch was meant to be just you and me?'

'Mm, well.' He winced. 'It's going to be lunch for three actually.'

'I see.' She tipped her head on one side. 'Why didn't you say anything to me before?'

'Because . . .' He pulled a face. 'Oh, it's complicated.'

'Try me.'

He winced and glanced at his watch. 'Not now, Rachel.'

'So whoever you want me to meet is waiting for us here?'

Luke nodded.

'I see.'

'Rachel – this isn't a set-up or anything like that.'

'Isn't it?' She gave him an old-fashioned look. 'It's the reason why you wanted me to wear a skirt, isn't it?'

'Yes,' he admitted, flushing. 'Look, Rachel, you trust me, don't you?'

'I'm not sure now.'

'I know I shouldn't have sprung this on you. Look, I can't tell you the whole story just now; but, believe me, it's nothing bad.'

She considered it for a moment, before nodding. 'All right. Do I get to know anything about this person, before we meet?'

'His name's Max.'

'Thanks, Luke.' She rolled her eyes. 'That tells me a lot.'

'Look – let's have lunch now and have a fight afterwards, hm?'

She smiled, despite herself. 'I ought to walk out on you right now. Why didn't you tell me anything before?'

'Because I can't.'

'What is this, MI5?' she asked caustically.

'No.' He sighed. 'Rachel, I'm hungry. And Max is waiting.'

'All right. But I want to know what's going on, Luke.'

'I promise I'll tell you everything. Just not right now.' He opened the door. 'Come on.'

Rachel walked into the restaurant and her eyes widened. This was a very expensive place indeed, she thought. It wasn't just the quiet operatic arias which filled the air or the starched damask tablecloths or even the fact that the glasses on the table were obviously best crystal and the cutlery was silver: the whole place simply exuded exclusivity.

For all that, it was full, so the food was obviously good. Various groups of people sitting at the tables were conversing quietly and intently, as though continuing a business meeting over lunch. Rachel watched them suddenly glad that Luke had pushed her into wearing a skirt. Her usual clothes wouldn't have gone down too well among the Savile Row suits, designer dresses and expensive watches.

An unobtrusive waiter came up to Luke and Rachel, taking their coats.

'We're with Max Houghton,' Luke said.

'This way, please.' The waiter ushered them over to a secluded table in the corner. The man who was sitting there, sipping mineral water, stood up, holding out his hand in greeting.

He was in his early forties, Rachel judged: about the same height and build as Luke, with greying dark hair brushed back from his face and very blue eyes behind small round gold-rimmed glasses. Designer glasses, she thought, stylish and very expensive. He was wearing a dark grey suit, slightly darker than Luke's and made of an obviously expensive material; it looked hand-tailored. No doubt his shoes were also hand-made, highly polished Italian leather. His white shirt was pure silk, as was his colourful tie – which was the only flamboyant thing about him. Everything else was expensively understated.

He was an attractive man, with high cheekbones and a strong jaw; he reminded Rachel of an older version of Charlie Sheen. He had the same intense, sensual look about him. He also reminded her faintly of Luke – but that was crazy. Luke hadn't said that Max was related to him. Then again, she remembered, Luke hadn't said very much about Max Houghton at all.

'You must be Rachel.' He smiled at her.

She nodded. 'And you're Max?'

'Yes.' His handshake was firm. 'Pleased to meet you, Rachel.'

'And you.' Her smile was slightly tight, betraying her doubts.

'Hello, Luke.' Max smiled at the younger man.

'Max.' Luke nodded back, looking slightly shame-faced.

'Do sit down.' Max patted the chair next to him. Rachel did as she was told, fixing a polite smile on her face; all the time, her mind was whirring with unanswered – and unanswerable – questions. Just who was Max Houghton? Why had Luke been so secretive about this meeting? Why hadn't Luke simply said that he wanted her to meet a friend of his, over lunch? And why exactly did Luke want her to meet Max anyway?

'What would you like to drink?' Max asked.

'I'm driving,' Luke reminded him.

Max grinned. 'Bess. She'll be the death of your social life, you know. Mineral water for you then. Rachel?'

'I – er – dry white wine, please.'

'Chablis?' Max asked.

Rachel nodded. 'Thank you.'

'Good.' He caught a waiter's attention, ordered the wine and mineral water and smiled at her. 'I was led to believe that you had a little more to say for yourself.'

Her eyes widened. 'You and Luke have discussed me?'

Luke winced. 'Rachel – I'm sorry.'

'You discussed me.' Rachel shook her head, annoyed. 'Luke, I don't believe you could do that.'

'He hasn't said anything at all to you about me, has he?' Max asked ruefully. 'I'm afraid that it's all my fault.'

'Oh?'

The wine arrived; Max poured Luke some water, and Rachel and himself a glass of Chablis. 'Rachel. Let's drink to the beginning of a good friendship.'

Her eyes narrowed. 'I don't know you.'

'Yet. But I know that we're going to be friends. Very good friends.'

'Just what is this?' Rachel asked.

'Let me explain. But first, drink your wine.'

Rachel took a sip from her glass; the wine was very good. At least Max wasn't stingy with wine, ordering the cheapest bottle possible. This was a good vintage Chablis. It mollified her enough to make her give him a genuine smile. 'So, tell me about yourself, Max.'

'My name's Max Houghton. I'm a financier and I live in Norfolk.'

'Right.' Just what did a financier have in common with an English lecturer? An ex-lecturer, she reminded herself.

Max smiled. 'Rachel. I didn't ask Luke to bring you here so that I could play games with you. He's told me a little about you and your situation, and I think that I might know some people who could help.'

'Really?' Rachel's voice was frosty.

'But I can't say too much about it right now.'

'You don't say.'

Luke winced at the caustic tone. 'Rachel – '

'Luke, you tell me that you're taking me out for lunch. You bring me here, you inform me on the doorstep that we're also lunching with a friend of yours, you tell me absolutely nothing about him or why you want me to join you, and then you both start talking in riddles, saying that you can't tell me the whole story right now.' Rachel glared at him. 'How do you expect me to react?'

'We've handled it badly, I admit,' Max said, giving her an appealing look. 'But let me make it up to you over lunch. Luke's told me about you, and I wanted to meet you, get to know you a little better.'

'Why?'

'Because I might know someone who can help you with your job situation. If you're suitable,' Max said.

'So this is an interview, of sorts?'

'Of sorts,' Max admitted. 'But I'm not going to start giving you a grilling about the finer points of nineteenth-century literature. For a start, I'd have no idea whether or not you were bluffing; and secondly, I'm more interested in you as a person.'

'I see.' Rachel took another sip of wine, trying to give herself time for it all to sink in.

'Do you like fish, Rachel?'

Rachel smiled. 'That sounds like a question out of a magazine questionnaire.'

Max grinned. 'It's more to do with the menu. The salmon and avocado mousse is very good, here – and the Dover sole is to die for.'

'And goes well with Chablis.'

'Exactly.' He tipped his head on one side. 'So may tempt you?'

Rachel had the distinct impression that he mean tempting her to more than just the fish, but nodded. 'Al right.'

'Luke?'

'Better make that three,' Luke said.

Max smiled. 'Good. Nice and easy.' Again, a waite appeared at Max's discreet signal; he gave the order then they chatted lightly and inconsequentially, Max and Rachel sipping their wine until the first course arrived Max ordered a second bottle of Chablis, then turned expectantly to Rachel. 'Well?'

Rachel tasted the mousse. 'Mm, Max, you're right. It' very good.'

'I'm so glad that you agree.'

Rachel suddenly noticed that Luke was eating with his right hand – and that a hand had settled on her righ knee and was bunching her skirt up as a prelude t sliding under the hem. She frowned at him but h ignored her, continuing to stroke her thigh.

Then she became aware that another hand had settle on her left knee and was also sliding under the hem o her skirt. She gave Max a sharp look: he was eating with his left hand. Which meant that it was *his* hand on he other knee. Just what the hell was going on?

She didn't want to make a scene; on the other hand she was annoyed at the way they seemed to be perform ing some kind of double act. Max and Luke obviousl knew each other extremely well, either well enoug virtually to read each other's mind, or to be able to rea a set of unobtrusive signals. Rachel suddenly wondered just how many other women had been in the same situation as she was, sandwiched between these two very attractive men, maybe even in this same restaurant. How had they reacted? Had they been shocked, outraged, left the table? Or had they settled back, enjoying the way that two attractive men were pleasuring them?

All the time, their hands were working on her, stroking the soft skin of her thighs above the lacy welts of her stockings, teasing and tantalising. Whether it was the amount of wine she'd consumed or something more primeval, she wasn't sure, but she was suddenly aware that her sex was softening, growing wet. What they were doing to her was turning her on in a big way.

Part of her was shocked. They were, after all, in a public place. True, their table was secluded and the tablecloth was long enough to hide what Max and Luke were doing – but it was still a restaurant. The waiter or another guest could walk past and see from the look on her face exactly what was going on. Another part of her, a more defiant part, liked the way that Luke and Max were touching her and didn't care what other people thought.

Almost in perfect synchronisation, she felt their palms pressing against her inner thighs, encouraging her to part her legs more widely and give them the access they wanted; then she felt a finger slide under each leg of her knickers. One slid down her quim, tracing her intimate folds and crevices, discovering just how wet she was, while the other settled on her clitoris. One pushed into her sex and began to move, very slowly, back and forth; the other began to rub her clitoris in a figure-of-eight motion, arousing her even more.

Rachel swallowed hard. It would be, oh, so easy to drop her fork, close her eyes and tip her head back, giving herself up to the increasingly pleasurable sensations and not caring if anyone overheard her ecstatic moans. And yet she couldn't do that, not in such a public place. It was too much. The only thing that she could do was to behave outwardly as if nothing was happening, as if the men either side of her weren't teasing and coaxing her body into spasms of pleasure.

She risked a glance at Luke; his eyes had grown luminous, his pupils large and dark. She knew then that he was the one who'd just added a second finger to the first, filling her and bringing her closer to the edge. He smiled at her, licking his lower lip, hinting that he'd like to do more than just touch her so intimately. Rachel, remembering the feel of his mouth on her sex, had to stifle a moan and stared back down at her plate.

'Delicious,' Max said quietly. 'Utterly delicious.' On the surface, he was talking about the mousse; but all three of them knew what he was really referring to. Rachel flushed. 'Such a perfect texture,' he continued. 'Soft to the touch and taste. Creamy and spicy. Delicious.'

Rachel's colour heightened as she had a sudden sharp vision of herself sitting in a chair, her legs splayed widely and Max kneeling between her legs, her skirt bunched up and the gusset of her knickers pushed to one side, his palms flat against her inner thighs. She could so easily imagine him drawing his tongue down her glistening quim, and then working on her in earnest – while Luke stood behind him, unbuttoning her shirt and playing with her breasts. Her nipples hardened immediately; from Max's soft chuckle, she knew that it was obvious through the thin stuff of her shirt.

He renewed his assault on her clitoris with renewed vigour, pressing hard on the erect nub of flesh in a way that made her quim flex; at the same time, Luke added another finger, so that it was almost like being fucked by a short thick cock. Rachel nearly dropped her fork, but managed to continue eating. Her hand was shaking slightly, but it was the only outward sign she gave.

Max bent towards her; the warmth of his breath fanned against her ear. 'Rachel.' His voice was slightly

108

husky; Rachel knew then that he was enjoying what he was doing as much, if not more, than she was. 'What I'd really like to do,' he said, 'is to sweep all this stuff from the table, take off your clothes and lay you across the white tablecloth – in full view of everyone. And then I'd dip my fingers in this mousse, spreading it across your breasts and your belly. I'd lick it off, tasting the sweetness of your skin under the savoury mousse.'

Rachel shivered; the way he was talking, she could imagine the scene only too clearly.

'I'd take your nipples between my lips, pulling gently at them. Maybe using my teeth, keeping just the right side of the pain-pleasure barrier. And then I'd work my way very slowly downwards, past your navel, over your belly. You'd spread your thighs for me, because you'd be aroused by then, wanting something to fill you and pleasure you. I'd spread a little more mousse over you, wanting to taste the coolness of salmon and avocado against the heat of your beautiful cunt: and I'd lap at you, licking you long and hard until all the traces of the mousse had gone, and you were writhing beneath me, moaning and clenching your fists.'

Rachel swallowed hard; she could feel the familiar warmth of her orgasm starting at the soles of her feet, a delicious fizzing sensation which grew sharper and harder as it rose up through her calves, moving inexorably forward.

'And then,' Max whispered, 'I'd fit the tip of my cock against the entrance of your sex. You'd feel so hot, so wet; sinking into you would be like pushing my cock into warm damp crushed velvet. You'd wrap your legs round my waist and I'd push into you hard, my hand between our bodies and rubbing your clitoris, until you were coming again and again and again. You'd be wailing and sobbing my name, not caring about the other people looking on: the only thing that mattered would be the way I made you feel. Only then would I allow myself to come, to fill you.'

As he finished speaking, her orgasm coiled in her gut and exploded; she stifled a cry, biting her lip, and covered her confusion by pretending to wipe her mouth with her napkin. She took a gulp of Chablis and heard Max laugh very softly; then his hand cupped her mons veneris in a cherishing gesture, almost a 'well done'. He slid his hand from her knickers and raised it to his lips, under the guise of wiping his mouth on his napkin; Rachel couldn't help looking at him and noticing that he breathed in the scent of her arousal, licking her juices from his fingers. Then he winked at her and resumed eating his mousse.

When the aftershocks of her climax had died away, Luke removed his fingers too, although he didn't make such as a display as Max. He merely smiled encouragingly at her and let the hem of her skirt fall back into place.

Rachel was unable to speak as their empty plates were removed and the second course appeared. Max and Luke didn't seem to notice; they chatted happily to each other, concentrating on their food. Rachel forced herself to eat, hardly able to believe what had just happened. She'd only just met Max and she'd allowed him to fondle her so intimately, to make her come under the table. It was the second time in a week that she'd allowed another man, one she wasn't involved with emotionally, to touch her like that. Christ. It wasn't even as if she could use the excuse of being shocked at losing her job, because the incident with Hollis had taken place before Gilson had told her. So what the hell was happening to her?

'Rachel.' Luke nudged her gently.

'Huh?' She rested her fork on her plate, aware that although the food was delicious, she'd been toying with it. 'Sorry, I was miles away.'

'I know.' He smiled at her. 'Max has just invited us away for the weekend.'

'Us?' She turned to Max. 'Where?'

'To my house, in Norfolk.'

'You mean, your palace,' Luke teased.

'Hilbury Manor isn't *that* big,' was the immediate retort. 'Ignore him, Rachel. I'm having a small house party and I'd like you and Luke to be guests – if you're not busy?'

'When?'

'This weekend.'

Something in his face made Rachel sure that there was a little more to it than met the eye. This meal, too, had been more than just three people meeting for lunch. She'd been set some kind of test; and this invitation meant that she'd passed. Max had said something about knowing someone who could help her with her job situation: maybe this person would be at Max's house, that weekend.

Luke took Rachel's hand, squeezing it. 'You'd like Hilbury. It's the kind of place where you can just relax, be yourself.'

Rachel was thoughtful. On the other hand, was there something else behind Max's invitation? A repeat of what had just happened between them, or even living out the fantasy he'd just outlined to her, in front of his other guests? 'I don't know,' she said finally.

'Rachel. It'll do you good to get out of London.'

'My friend Jennifer – you know, Jude Devereaux – is meant to be staying for a few days.'

'Then ask her if she'd mind moving her visit back a week,' Max said. 'Please. I'd like you to be there, Rachel.'

Luke's fingers tightened round hers. 'You'd enjoy it. Trust me.'

Her eyes met his. 'Luke, I . . .'

'You've nothing to lose, Rachel,' he said softly. 'And everything to gain.'

So it *was* something to do with a job. She nodded. 'All right. I'll ring Jen tonight and ask her to change the date.'

'Thank you. You won't regret it,' Max said. 'I promise.'

The rest of the meal was uneventful. Max and Luke both behaved with perfect decorum and Rachel relaxed enough to agree to Max's suggestion of crème brûlée for pudding. It turned out to be as good as Max had said; Rachel ate it with gusto, suddenly realising that she was hungry after all.

Eventually, after coffee, Max glanced at his watch and looked regretful. 'I'm afraid I have an appointment in half an hour,' he said. 'But thank you for coming today, Rachel. I look forward to seeing you in Norfolk tomorrow evening.'

'Yes.'

He took her hand, kissing the back of it; the look in his eyes made her shiver. There was definitely something more than met the eye about Max's invitation: she had a feeling that he'd make some excuse to be on his own with her at some point over the weekend. And the way things were going . . . she wouldn't resist him.

'Luke Holloway.'

'Can you talk?'

Luke chuckled as he recognised Max's voice. 'Yes.'

'Rachel's back at her place, then?'

'No. She's in the bath actually,' Luke said.

'Right.' Max coughed. 'You're sure that you can talk?'

'Absolutely.' Luke paused. 'What did you think?'

'You're right. She's delicious. Utterly delicious. And so responsive.' He coughed. 'Though I was half-expecting her to walk out at first.'

'You're the one who said not to say anything,' Luke reminded him. 'So I didn't.'

'True.' There was a tapping noise, as though Max were drumming his fingers on the table. 'I liked her, though. I think that she'll be perfect for the job.'

Luke smiled. 'I told you so.'

'And how many years have you been waiting to say that?' Max asked archly.

'Too long,' Luke said.

'Can she be trusted?'

'Yes. Absolutely.' Luke paused. 'She's not one of *them*.'

'I didn't think for a moment that she was.' Max coughed. '*À bientôt.*'

'Tomorrow night,' Luke said softly, replacing the receiver.

Friday afternoon was bright and sunny. Luke met Rachel after lunch – they both had a clear afternoon, or at least could do their work outside of the university – and they headed for Norfolk. The roads were almost empty and, within two hours, they were at the outskirts of Norwich.

'Tell me about Max,' Rachel said as they turned off the bypass on to a narrow road.

'What do you want to know about him?'

'Everything. How you met him, what he does for a living; that kind of thing.'

'He's about forty-five and he's in finance. He made quite a lot of money on the stock market in the boom years of the 1980s, and he bought this fabulous pile in the country – Hilbury Manor. It's quite unusual, for Norfolk: instead of being built of brick-and-flint, it's pure red brick. Very Gothic, all spiky arches and turrets and ivy and mullioned windows. I think it's seventeenth century, although Max could obviously tell you more than I could about the history of the place. The grounds are gorgeous too: acres and acres of grass and trees.'

'It sounds lovely,' Rachel said carefully, 'but what about Max himself?'

Luke sighed. 'There isn't that much to know.'

'Then tell me what you do know,' she persisted.

'Well, he likes art, music and good living. He's the original *bon viveur*, in fact. He's made enough to be able to indulge himself with any fancy he chooses. Oh, and he can down more red wine than anyone I know, so don't ever, ever, get caught up in a late-night conversation with him and agree to share a bottle or two of wine. He'll keep your glass topped up, so you'll have no idea how much you've drunk. You'll feel great at the

113

time, but your hangover the next morning will be incredible.'

'Thanks for the warning.' She paused. 'So Max is in finance and you're a history lecturer. How did you meet him? Through work?'

Luke shook his head.

'How then?' Rachel persisted.

'Ah.' Luke scratched his chin. 'He's my cousin.'

'Your cousin?' She was surprised. 'You didn't say so, the other day.'

'No. Well. I think of him more of a friend than as a relative. We get on very well.'

'So I gathered,' she said drily.

He chuckled. 'You're not still cross about the restaurant, are you?'

'Meaning the fact that it was lunch for three, or the hors d'oeuvres?'

It was the first time she'd mentioned what had happened between the three of them; Luke decided to tread carefully. 'That's just Max,' he said lightly. 'He took to you. Otherwise he'd have been very polite and left us early, with the excuse of an urgent business meeting.'

Rachel frowned. 'But that's what he said – that he had an appointment.'

'A genuine one,' Luke told her. 'He stayed until after coffee. Rachel, just relax, will you?'

'I want to know what's going on, Luke.'

'Max will tell you in good time.'

'Why can't you?'

'I – just can't.'

'Can't or won't?'

'Both,' Luke said. 'So can we change the conversation, please?'

Her eyes narrowed. 'This house party – '

'Is also genuine,' Luke said. 'Max entertains most weekends. He likes good company. There are usually at least four people staying at Hilbury.'

'Right.' She paused. 'So why did he ask us?'

'Because he'd like our company. And maybe because there's someone he wants you to meet, I don't know.'

'Someone who's going to offer me a job?'

'Maybe.' Luke shrugged. 'Anyway, I need to concentrate on the road for a bit. There's a turn-off and I don't want to miss it – otherwise we'll have to go miles out of our way.'

'All right.' Rachel lapsed into silence, wondering just what had been planned for their weekend. And why had Luke been so secretive about his relationship to Max? Why hadn't he told her at the restaurant that Max was his cousin? Or even when she'd first asked him about Max, in the car? Again, her questions were unanswerable. For the moment, anyway; maybe Max would enlighten her during the weekend.

# Chapter Nine

$E$ventually, Luke turned off down an even narrower, slightly bumpy road; as they neared the crest of a hill, Rachel's eyes widened. Hilbury Manor was just as Luke had described it: built of soft dark red brick, three storeys high, with three pointed arches at the front. There was a small turret on each side of the house and ivy grew around the mullioned windows. The front door was Gothic, too, a large wooden affair with ancient studs.

The road to the house was lined with beech trees, which met overhead in a canopy; Rachel thought with a shiver that it would be very spooky at night. In daylight, it was incredibly pretty, with light dappling through the leaves on to the ground. There was a large gravel area to the front of the house, where several cars were parked – newish and expensive cars, Rachel noted. A shiny MGF in British racing green, a navy top-of-the-range Audi, a convertible white BMW and a smart blue Range Rover. Either Max enjoyed cars or his guests were equally well-off and able to afford to drive whatever they wanted.

Wisteria grew among the ivy and there were a couple of rosemary trees at the front of the house – ancient trees, judging by the spread. No doubt at the back of the house there would be a formal garden with immaculate flower beds, and maybe a fountain. Perhaps a walled garden, too, and an orchard; Rachel smiled to herself. Here she was, falling in love with the place before she'd even got there!

She could imagine what the house was like inside. The hall would have a scrubbed flagstone floor, with rush matting on top. There would be large wrought-iron candle-holders and pot-pourri and heavy oak benches everywhere and lots of portraits on the walls, a big sweeping staircase and room after large well-proportioned room opening off the hall.

Luke parked next to the MGF. 'Max's latest baby,' he said, nodding at the numberplate. MDH 5.

'Flash. Are they all his?'

Luke shook his head as he took their cases from the back of his car. 'He's got another in the garage, the one he uses on a day-to-day basis. The MGF's just for fun.' His lips twitched. 'And, considering what Max says about Bess . . .'

'He's just as bad, right?'

'Right. In fact, he was the one who found Bess for me.' He smiled at her. 'So, what do you think of the place?'

'It's amazing,' Rachel said.

'Isn't it? It's right in the middle of nowhere – well, there are a couple of market towns within a twelve-mile radius and the village of Hilbury is about two miles down the road. But that's "road" in inverted commas,' Luke said. 'They're more like country lanes than roads around here, and it's a fair bet that you'll end up stuck behind a tractor.'

'We didn't, on the way here.'

'For once. Believe me, I've been here enough times to know,' Luke said drily. 'Anyway, let's go in.'

'Shouldn't we – well, ring the bell or something?'

Luke shook his head. 'Max leaves the door open. He has a slightly different alarm system.'

Rachel was about to ask him what kind of system,

117

when Luke opened the door and ushered her inside. Approximately five seconds later, two black and white springer spaniels raced into the hall, barking madly.

'Hey, hey, you two, it's me!' Luke dropped their cases and knelt down; the spaniels, recognising him, flung themselves upon him, licking every bit of skin in sight, their feathery tails waving madly. 'And this is Rachel.' He looked up. 'Um – Rachel, you're not scared of dogs, are you?'

She shook her head. 'My parents have a labrador. I grew up with dogs.'

'Come and meet Bill and Ben, then.'

'Bill and Ben?' She was amused.

'Yeah. Max reliving his childhood,' Luke explained.

Rachel followed his lead, kneeling down to greet the dogs; a couple of minutes later, Max walked into the hall. 'I see that you've met the terrible twosome.'

'Yes.' Rachel fondled the ears of one spaniel. 'They're lovely.'

'Once they know you, yes. But their bark's enough to frighten off anyone who shouldn't be here. And I certainly wouldn't trust Ben with a stranger. He's very protective.' He held out his hand; Rachel stood up to shake it.

'Did you have a good journey?' he asked.

'Yes, thanks. This place is lovely.' She looked round. It was nothing like she'd imagined. It wasn't furnished in a gothic and slightly uncomfortable style; if anything, it was more like a very expensive country hotel. The floor in the hall was chequered black and white, with Turkish rugs scattered over it: silk rugs, Rachel realised, which changed colour in the rippling light. The carpet on the sweeping staircase was thick pile, and the walls were all pale, rather than the Gothic dun colour she'd imagined.

There were indeed paintings in the house – but they weren't the dark and dingy portraits she'd expected. There were clean sepia-toned line-drawings and small oils in glowing jewel colours: all original art, Rachel realised with a shock. Luke had said that Max was rich enough to indulge his whims: that obviously included art. She didn't recognise any of the paintings; they were an eclectic mix of modern and what looked to her like Victorian art. The modern art was all remarkably similar in style. Perhaps, she thought, Max had become an old-fashioned patron to a local artist.

'Come and have a tour,' Max said, linking his arm through Rachel's. 'Luke will sort your cases out. You're in your usual room, Luke, and Rachel's next door.'

'I'll come and find you,' Luke promised.

Rachel raised an eyebrow as Max led her down the hall, the spaniels padding behind them. 'Separate rooms?'

Max grinned. 'For comfort's sake. There's a connecting door, if you want to use it – or you might even enjoy creeping round the corridors. I should warn you that the floorboards creak outside every door.'

She chuckled. 'Thanks for the warning.'

'Oh, and you've a bathroom each. There's an ensuite to all the bedrooms.'

Rachel was stunned into silence, and let Max show her round. As she'd expected, the rooms were all large and well-proportioned; there were heavy drapes at all the windows, but there was still more than enough light to give the place an airy feel. Each room had a thick carpet, and she literally sank into the pile as she walked. More of the silk Turkish rugs were scattered around, toning in with the decor of each room: blues, golds and dusky rose.

There was a sitting room, with large overstuffed sofas and mahogany furniture which looked antique rather than reproduction, leading to a large conservatory filled with palms and orchids; a large dining room, with a table to seat twelve and an old-fashioned sideboard; another sitting room, this time with a baby grand piano and a grandfather clock. All contained more of the art she'd noticed in the hall.

Then there was Max's study, a minimalist room with pale walls, a large oak desk, and state-of-the-art office equipment: PC, fax, copier and a rack of files. Rachel's eyes widened as she noticed one of the line drawings: a naked and very beautiful woman, touching her breasts with one hand and the other working between her legs, her head tipped back and the beginnings of a mottled flush spreading over her skin.

Max followed her eyes. 'Like the picture?'

'Um – it's unusual.'

'Coward,' he teased.

'Don't tell me – all your own work?'

He grinned. 'Touché. No. Though I saw it in progress.'

'You mean – you . . .'

'Yes, I watched the artist at work. And the model. She's a good friend of mine.' He spread one hand nonchalantly, then led her through to the next room.

Rachel gave a sharp intake of breath as she took in where she was. The library. It was fantastic: a whole room lined with floor-to-ceiling shelves, all filled with leather-bound books. 'Max – this is . . .'

'I know.' He gave her a lopsided smile. 'I have to admit, I haven't read *all* of them.'

She loosened her arm from his and went over to scan one of the bookcases. She noticed that some of the books were Victorian, and idly picked one from the shelves, wondering whether Max had had them rebound. Her eyes widened as she realised that it was actually a first edition. 'Max – this is amazing.'

'I thought you'd like this,' he said. 'But you can have a proper look later. I want to finish showing you round.'

The kitchen was huge, with red pamment flooring, beech Shaker cabinets and an Aga with a large wicker basket beside it, which obviously belonged to Bill and Ben. There was a scrubbed pine table in the middle of the room and a rack for saucepans above the large stone sink. A door led to a large walk-in pantry which was well stocked with food. There were herbs growing on the windowsill in little terracotta troughs, and there was a large painted dresser displaying an assortment of plates. There were also some bells above the door; Max grinned. 'A relic of times past. I wouldn't dare ring them. Maggie Stewart would put salt in my coffee, to teach me a lesson!'

'Maggie Stewart?'

'My housekeeper. There are a couple of girls from the village who come in and help her, and her husband does the garden.' He shrugged. 'Well, I need staff here – I can't look after the place on my own. Besides, it's nice to have company.'

'Luke said that you entertained most weekends.'

Max nodded. 'I enjoy it. I think you'll get on well with my other guests this weekend.'

'Other guests?'

'You'll meet them later this evening. They've gone for a ramble round the grounds.' He rolled his eyes. 'They'll be all afternoon.'

'I see.' Rachel suddenly remembered what Luke had said about Hilbury having acres and acres of grass and trees. It was the sort of place where you could ramble for hours.

'There's a scullery over there, but it isn't very interesting,' he said. 'It's stuffed with wellington boots, discarded brollies and the like. It's where Bill and Ben dry off when it's wet. Anyway, come and see upstairs.'

There turned out to be ten bedrooms – five on each of the upper floors, all furnished with double beds, roomy wardrobes and chests; and all contained more of the erotic line-drawings Rachel had seen in Max's study, with the same model.

'Is the artist a friend of yours, as well as the model?' she asked.

He grinned. 'You could say that. Yes.'

And Max had no doubt been at the sittings for every single one of the drawings, Rachel thought.

Luke found them as they walked back into the upstairs hall. 'Incredible place, isn't it?' he said to Rachel.

'Yes. It's lovely,' Rachel said, meaning it.

'Well – do you mind if I leave you with Max? I have one or two things to sort out,' Luke said.

'All right.'

'See you later.' He kissed her lightly and walked down the stairs.

Max squeezed Rachel's hand. 'Unfortunately I, too, have a few things to sort out. You're welcome to have the run of my library – or I could send Stella up to you.'

'One of your maids?'

'Sort of.' Max pulled a face. 'She's a beautician, actually. She's setting up her own business. When I have guests for the weekend, I ask her to come along on the Friday afternoon – so if you'd like a facial, or a manicure, or anything like that, all you have to do is say.'

'Thank you, Max.'

'From what Luke tells me, you need to relax.' Again, there was that light pressure on her fingers. 'You'll have the chance to do whatever you wish here. If you'd like to go for a walk, feel free; if you want to spend your time in the library, that's fine. As long as you don't actually do any work.'

Rachel smiled ruefully. 'Luke and I both bunked off, this afternoon. We were supposed to be preparing tutorials or lectures. And then there's my thesis.' Her thesis, which she intended to finish, regardless of Colin Gilson.

'I'm sure you put in more than enough hours,' Max said. 'Tell you what – you go and unpack, and I'll send Stella up to you. Her neck massages are excellent.'

Rachel suddenly remembered the way that Luke had massaged her the other evening. Had he learned from Stella, she wondered. But it wasn't important. 'All right, Max.'

'Good girl.' He led her back to her bedroom. 'If you need anything else, ask Stella. She knows this place like the back of her hand.'

'I will. Thanks.'

As Max called the dogs after him and closed the door, Rachel surveyed her room. It was light and airy, with sunny yellow walls and curtains sprigged with yellow and blue flowers, a pattern matched in the border round the room and by the king-sized duvet. There was a white sculpted vase in the middle of the chest, filled with irises and gypsophilia.

The floral theme didn't extend to the paintings, though. The one by the bed held Rachel's attention the longest. It was a watercolour, and the model had glossy dark hair with red lights, and very green eyes. She was naked, lying on her left side on what looked to Rachel to be a sheepskin rug, her left elbow at an angle and her hand supporting her head. Her left leg was stretched out straight, the toes pointed and the leg tensed, the muscles of her calf clearly outlined.

Her right foot was placed flat against the rug, with her knee pointed towards the ceiling. Her head was tipped back slightly and her mouth was open; she had a teasing look on her face, as though she were performing for her lover, warming herself up. Her right hand was placed on her delta, the heel of her palm resting against the curve of her belly, and her middle finger extended and parting her labia.

Rachel flushed. Max obviously liked to watch women masturbating. And she knew from experience, he enjoyed touching them, too. She had half-expected Luke to excuse himself at some point during the weekend, leaving her alone with Max – and for Max to have started making love to her. Or maybe he judged that right now wasn't the moment: there were still two days to go.

She shivered, turning away from the painting. Luke had placed her case on the bed; swiftly she undid it and unpacked, hanging her clothes in the wardrobe and putting the rest of her things away in the spacious chest. She was glad that she'd thought to pack a little black dress: it was quite old, but she hadn't worn it much. It would at least pass muster for dinner. She had a feeling that dinner, that evening, would be a black tie affair.

She wandered over to the window. Her room overlooked the back of the house. Just as she'd thought, there was a formal garden, with clipped yew bushes and a fountain in the middle. The flower beds were well stocked and immaculate, and the lawn looked very tempting. She could imagine running barefoot over it, how it would feel soft and springy beneath her toes.

A knock on the door startled her; she turned round from the window. 'Come in.'

The door opened and a woman of about her own age walked in, carrying a small valise. Rachel's eyes widened. She was the woman from the painting.

If she noticed the shock on Rachel's face, the woman said nothing. She merely smiled, closed the door behind her and walked over to Rachel, extending her free hand. 'Hi. I'm Stella. Max sent me up – he said he thought that you could do with some pampering.'

'I'm Rachel.'

'I know. Max told me.'

Yes, and what else has he told you? Rachel thought, but said nothing.

'There's about four hours until dinner, so we've more than enough time for a facial and a massage, if you like?'

'Thanks.'

'Pleasure.' Stella smiled. 'I expect Max told you about me – that I decided to retrain and change my career, after failing my accountancy exams for the third and critical time.'

'Accountancy?' Rachel's eyes widened. 'You don't look like an accountant.'

'Nah, well. It didn't really suit me. I like working with people rather than figures. Max has been good to me; he's supported my business by giving me weekend contracts here. And the nice thing is, his friends are more interested in talking about things other than holidays

124

and the colour of nail polish. So I get the best of both worlds.'

'Right.' Rachel smiled at her. 'I know how you feel. I'm at the stage where I might have to change my career, too.'

'Oh?' Stella's tone was light and interested; she sat on the bed and patted the duvet.

It was natural for Rachel to sit beside her and tell her about Gilson and how she had to find herself another job – though she didn't hold out much hope of getting the sort of job she wanted.

'Ouch,' Stella said. 'Tell you what, let's close the curtains and I'll do your facial. It won't get you another job, but it'll make you feel a lot better. By the time I've finished with you, you'll feel on top of the world.'

The more Stella talked, the more Rachel liked her; she grinned. 'I'll hold you to that!'

'I'll do the curtains; take your jeans, shirt and bra off and lie down on the bed,' Stella said. 'Width-ways; then I can kneel on a pillow beside you, and it'll be more like having a couch.' She smiled. 'The amount of work I do for Max, I ought to persuade him to turn one of the bedrooms into a beauty parlour. But he says he thinks his guests like it this way.'

'Right.' Rachel stripped down to her knickers and lay down on the bed, as Stella had directed. She didn't feel the slightest bit embarrassed or self-conscious; it was like being with a close friend, chatting and not paying attention to each other's bodies.

Stella took a pillow from the bed and knelt behind Rachel. 'Lift your head up, a moment – I don't think you want all this gunk going over your hair.' She removed Rachel's Alice band, replacing it with a wide stretchy band which pulled Rachel's hair away from her face. 'Now, just close your eyes and relax. It looks like your skin's sensitive. All the stuff I use is hypo-allergenic, but if you feel even the slightest sensation of burning or discomfort, tell me, and I'll whip off whatever I'm using, pretty smartish.'

'Thanks.' Rachel smiled and closed her eyes, giving herself up to Stella's clever and professional hands. The cleanse, tone and moisturise routine was familiar to her: Jennifer always gave her a voucher for a facial for birthdays and Christmas, saying that it was always good to be pampered; Rachel had gradually drifted into the habit of having a facial every couple of months when Gilson was upsetting her too much or her thesis was going particularly badly. And Stella was right: it didn't change things, but it made her feel much better, more able to cope with things.

'Better?' Stella asked, when she'd finished.

'Mm. And I love the smell of the stuff you use.' Rachel opened her eyes. 'At the risk of sounding like all the rest of your clients, I'd like a price-list, please.'

'No need,' Stella said. 'If you look in the bathroom, you'll find that Max has provided a little coffret with about two months' supply of cleanser, toner and mois-turiser, plus the de-stress aromatherapy bubble bath. He expects you to take it with you when you leave.'

'Max is so thoughtful, isn't he?' Rachel said. 'Have you known him long?'

'For about five years. He's become a close friend.' Stella smiled at her. 'Roll over. I'm going to do your back – but it's probably easier if you lie properly on the bed this time. I find it easier to back massage when I'm astride my clients.'

'Right.' Rachel coughed.

Stella grinned. 'Yes, it does sound bad, doesn't it? Relax. I'm not going to leap on you.' She stroked the curve of Rachel's throat. 'Though you'd tempt a saint.'

Rachel flushed deeply. 'I . . .'

'You're completely straight and you arrived with Luke,' Stella finished. 'On your front, there's a good girl.'

'All right.' Rachel rolled over, stretching her arms in front of her and resting her forehead on her hands.

'Now, I'm going to use a relaxing oil on you – a mixture of lavender, lemon and neroli. Do you know if you're sensitive to any of them?'

'I don't think so.'

'Good. Now, just lie there and enjoy it, as the saying goes. If I'm working you too hard, yell.'

'All right.' Rachel closed her eyes. The next thing she felt was the bed giving way slightly as Stella joined her, then the soft cotton of Stella's trousers against her thighs as the beautician straddled her. This was the way Stella preferred to work, she told herself sharply. There was nothing more to it than that.

Then she felt the beautician's oiled hands smoothing up and down her back, and then firm, knowing fingers working on the knots of tension in her neck. Rachel made a small murmur of pleasure and wriggled slightly under Stella's fingers. It reminded her of the way that Luke had massaged her that evening, only better. She could almost imagine what it would be like if Stella's hands drifted a little further, stroking her buttocks and parting them, then sliding lower to caress her open sex . . .

She swallowed hard. This was crazy. She didn't think about other women in this way. It was just the fact that Stella had half-suggested it, and the way Stella was touching her made her think of Luke, the pleasure she felt at his touch.

'Relax,' Stella directed, leaning forward and virtually breathing the command into Rachel's ear. But Rachel couldn't. She kept seeing the images of Stella masturbating, and wondering if the other woman's fingers were just as skilful with a lover's body.

'Rachel . . .' Stella stopped the firm caressing movements on her back.

'I'm sorry. I'm just a bit on edge.'

'You're telling me.' Stella climbed off her and Rachel rolled over on to her back.

'I'm sorry,' she said again.

'Hey, it's all right.' Stella stroked her face. 'Want to talk about it?'

'Yes – no – I . . .' Rachel squeezed her eyes shut. How could she possibly tell Stella what she'd just been thinking? How could she voice the words that made her feel so uneasy, the sheer longing she felt?

'It's the pictures, isn't it?'

Rachel opened her eyes in surprise. 'The pictures?'

'Mm. Max met me when I was modelling for a friend of his.' Stella gestured to the watercolour by the bed. 'Hence these. Max commissioned the lot.' She paused. 'They make you uncomfortable, don't they?'

Rachel's colour deepened. 'I'm not a prude.'

'That's not why they make you feel uncomfortable,' Stella asked softly, 'is it?'

'I . . . No,' Rachel admitted.

'You're a woman with one hell of an imagination – whether you've used it yet or not. Max can tell these things; and he only invites people he likes down to Hilbury.'

Rachel was almost tempted to tell Stella what had happened in the Mayfair restaurant and her suspicions that Max had several ulterior motives in inviting her here; at the last moment, she chickened out. 'Oh.'

'Oh,' Stella teased softly.

'Stella, I . . .'

'Would it help if I did this?' The other woman leant over, touching her lips very lightly to Rachel's.

To Rachel's shock and surprise, she found herself responding, sliding her hands into Stella's hair and opening her mouth. Stella's tongue slipped into her mouth and one oiled hand slid downwards to caress Rachel's breasts.

Rachel's nipples were already hard; Stella broke the kiss, making a small murmur of satisfaction as she rolled one hard peak of flesh between her thumb and forefinger. 'Mm, Rachel. I think that you need this,' she said softly. 'Your body's aching for fulfilment.'

'I – I've never –'

'Sh.' Stella placed her finger gently against Rachel's lips. 'You don't have to say anything. I know.' She smiled. 'The first time it happened to me, I was pretty shocked, too. Especially when I found out how good it was. Is,' she amended. 'And it will be just as good for you,' she promised huskily.

Rachel swallowed. This was so far out of her experience. She'd never been sexually attracted to another woman before, and she wasn't sure how to handle it.

'Just leave it to me,' Stella said softly, and Rachel flushed as she realised that she'd spoken aloud. 'We'll take it slow and easy. If I do anything that makes you uncomfortable, just stop me. And if you want me to do anything in particular, touch you in a certain way – well, all you have to do is say. OK?'

Rachel nodded, unable to speak. Stella smiled in satisfaction and climbed off the bed, swiftly removing her trousers and her loose shirt. Her figure was as voluptuous as in the watercolour, and Rachel found herself appraising the other woman warmly. Stella noticed her intense stare and smiled at Rachel, reaching behind her back to undo the clasp of her bra and let the garment fall to the floor. Then, very slowly, she peeled her knickers downwards and rejoined Rachel on the bed.

Rachel swallowed, feeling suddenly shy. She'd been naked in the presence of other women before, but it had been in a completely different context – the changing room of a gym. This ... this was something else. A prelude to love-making. 'Stella – '

'Sh. It's all right.' Again, Stella put the tip of her finger against Rachel's lips; unable to help herself, Rachel drew Stella's forefinger into her mouth, sucking gently on it. Stella smiled and let her free hand drift down Rachel's body, moulding her curves. 'I think,' she said quietly, 'you'd feel better if we were really equal.'

Frowning, Rachel stopped sucking her finger. 'How do you mean?'

Stella gently removed her hand. 'Like this.' She hooked her fingers in the waistband of Rachel's knickers. 'Lift your bottom up,' she directed; Rachel did as she was asked, raising her buttocks. Stella gently removed the offending knickers, drawing the scrap of material down over Rachel's thighs; then she leant over to kiss Rachel again, her lips soft and warm and coaxing.

Rachel couldn't help opening her mouth, letting the other woman kiss her more deeply; she ran her hands down Stella's sides, then up again to curve round the other woman's breasts, stroking their soft undersides. Stella gave a small murmur of pleasure, and then her mouth began to track down Rachel's body. Rachel closed her eyes and tipped her head back against the soft feather pillows as Stella took one hard nipple into her mouth and began to suck. She could feel the soft curtain of Stella's hair against her skin, and she was shocked to find how much she liked the feeling.

Luke had made love to her in a similar way and she'd loved it: but this, feeling the softness of another woman's skin and hair, was just as arousing, although in a different way. Her sex pooled. Would it be the same when Stella went down on her? Or would it be better, because Stella, as a woman, knew exactly what gave a woman the most pleasure?

Slowly, Stella moved down the bed, nuzzling Rachel's skin and murmuring soft endearments; Rachel slid her hands into Stella's hair, massaging her scalp and urging her on. Stella moved lower, lower, until at last she was crouching between Rachel's thighs; she placed the flat of her palms against Rachel's inner thighs, exerting a very light pressure, and Rachel spread her legs.

'That's better,' Stella said quietly, and then she bent her head, kissing Rachel's inner thighs. Rachel moaned, tipping her pelvis up; she was so aroused now that she was past caring that it was Stella rather than Luke crouched between her thighs. She needed to come. She

130

needed to feel a mouth working against her sex, sucking and licking and probing.

Stella's finger drifted along Rachel's quim, exploring her folds and crevices; Rachel bucked her hips, wanting more. Stella laughed softly and then pushed one finger against the entrance of Rachel's sex. Rachel moaned and pushed upwards; Stella's finger slid deep inside her.

'Oh, yes,' Rachel breathed. 'Yes.'

Stella began to move her hand back and forth; at the same time she dipped her head, making her tongue into a hard point and flicking it across Rachel's clitoris, teasing the little bud of flesh from its hood. Rachel groaned, pushing up again, and Stella pumped her hand more rapidly, taking Rachel's clitoris between her lips and sucking hard.

Rachel's climax took her by surprise; her internal muscles contracted sharply around Stella's finger and she cried out. Stella kissed her thighs and straightened up again, leaning over to kiss Rachel so that she could taste her arousal against the other woman's mouth.

'That's just for starters,' Stella said, climbing off the bed and opening a drawer of the bedside cabinet.

Rachel lifted herself up on to one elbow. 'What are you doing?'

'You obviously haven't had a chance to explore yet,' Stella said, with a grin. 'Max likes to make sure that his guests have – let's say, all the amenities they need.'

# Chapter Ten

'*A*menities?' Rachel frowned, not understanding.

Stella withdrew a thick vibrator from the drawer. 'Like this,' she said. 'As you and I both know, a finger helps to ease the ache – but it's not as good as being filled properly.'

Rachel's eyes widened. Max provided this sort of thing for his guests? And Stella was intending to use that on her? 'I . . .'

'Sh, sweetheart. Go with the flow.' Stella came back to lie beside her on the bed. 'Close your eyes.' She stroked Rachel's face. 'Just relax.'

Rachel closed her eyes and Stella slowly stroked down her body, playing with her breasts and caressing her abdomen until Rachel was aroused again, lifting her body up to be touched. Then Rachel felt Stella straddle her body again; she opened her eyes, realising that the beautician was facing away from her. She couldn't resist stroking the other woman's buttocks, the pads of her fingertips smoothing her soft skin; Stella's wriggle indicated her pleasure and Rachel grew bolder, letting one hand drift down to the crease of Stella's bottom.

'Oh, yes,' Stella murmured, shifting slightly so that her quim was presented to Rachel. 'Do it. Do it now.'

It was more of a request than a command; gi̶
not sure if she was doing it right, Rachel rea̶
forward, stretching out her tongue, and slowly drew̶
along the length of Stella's musky slit. Stella's gasp ot
pleasure encouraged her and Rachel began to explore
her lover properly, parting her labia and lapping at her
clitoris. All the while, she stroked and fondled her lover's
buttocks, pulling them apart slightly to give her easier
access to Stella's quim.

At the same time, Rachel felt the tip of the vibrator
pushing against her sex. She widened the gap between
her legs and Stella slowly eased the thick plastic tube
into her. There was a soft click as Stella turned the
machine on and Rachel's quim flexed as the tube began
to vibrate. Stella began to wield the vibrator deftly,
sliding it in and out of Rachel's quim, then teasing her
lover, pushing just the bulbous head rapidly in and out.

Rachel, in turn, began to lap harder at her lover,
pushing her tongue deep into Stella's sex, her tongue
gathering up the sweet nectar and spreading it along the
length of Stella's quim. Stella moaned with pleasure and
worked the vibrator harder, settling a finger on Rachel's
clitoris and circling the hard nub of flesh.

Rachel bucked her hips and Stella turned the vibrator
up to full speed; Rachel felt her quim begin to ripple
again and her orgasm snaked through her, making her
internal muscles contract sharply round the vibrator. At
the same time, Rachel felt Stella's quim flexing against
her mouth, and suddenly her mouth was filled with
sweet-salt juice.

Stella groaned and switched the vibrator off; she left it
buried deep in Rachel and shifted position, curling into
Rachel's arms. 'God. I think we both needed that.'

'Mm.' Rachel stroked her lover's hair. 'You're right.'

Stella felt Rachel's slight withdrawal and kissed her
lover lightly on the lips. 'Hey. Don't start analysing it
and worrying.'

'I'm not.'

Stella smiled wryly. 'Oh yes, you are. Rachel, we've just given each other pleasure. A lot of pleasure. It's as simple as that.' She stroked Rachel's abdomen. 'Just enjoy it. Let yourself fill your potential.'

'Potential?' It was almost like the encouraging comment of a tutor whose pupil had just passed another test. Rachel's brain snapped into gear. 'Stella – do you know what's going on around here?'

'Just Max, indulging himself.'

Rachel frowned. 'How do you mean?'

'He likes company. He chose you because he likes you. That's all there is to it.'

'Are you sure?'

'Yes.'

Rachel wasn't, but it was obvious that Stella wasn't going to give her the answers she needed, so she kept her doubts to herself.

Max lay watching the screen on the ceiling of his four-poster bed. Rachel and Stella were the perfect foils for each other, the one so dark and the other so fair. He smiled, freeing his hard cock from his trousers and slowly began to stroke the shaft. As he'd hoped, Rachel was a quick learner. Her boundaries would stretch – and stretch well. Luke had been right. Rachel was perfect.

He tightened his grip on his penis, rubbing more quickly. It was a sight he loved even more than the vision of a woman masturbating: two women exploring each other's bodies, bringing each other to the peak of pleasure. Especially two bright, intelligent women like Rachel and Stella. He'd known that the two of them would get on well.

'Ah yes,' he breathed, as he watched Stella slowly slide the vibrator into Rachel's quim. He continued to rub himself, pressing slightly on his groin with his other hand. He was looking forward to the moment when he, too, would enjoy Rachel's body – when it would be her hand wrapped around his cock, rather than his own: or

134

maybe her delectable mouth. Or her even more delectable quim, dripping with the sweet honey he loved so much.

He smiled as he remembered her reaction in the restaurant, when he and Luke had tested her. She'd known that she was being tested and she'd passed with more than flying colours. She could have walked out on them both, then and there, but she'd stayed – and she hadn't drawn attention to their actions. Rachel would be very good at control, he thought. All she had to do was learn how.

He moaned as he felt his orgasm bubble through him; he pushed his shirt up out of the way and tightened his grip on his cock as it throbbed in his hand. A warm streak of semen spattered over his abdomen. 'Oh, Rachel,' he said softly. 'I'm looking forward to this, so much . . .'

Rachel and Stella made love again, this time with Rachel sliding the vibrator into Stella and Stella using her mouth to bring Rachel to another climax. Afterwards, Stella glanced at her watch and exclaimed with horror. 'I'd better be going!'

'Stay. Max won't mind,' Rachel said lazily.

'No, but I'm supposed to be somewhere.' Stella's lips twitched. 'With someone else.'

'Right.'

'Mm, and he's a bit of a stickler for time,' Stella informed her, uncurling and standing up. She stretched and dressed swiftly. 'Anyway, you've got to get ready for dinner. Max is a stickler for punctuality, too – although Luke's probably already told you that.'

'Not really.' Max was still an enigma to her. All she knew about him was that he was Luke's cousin, that he worked in finance, and that he was rich enough to indulge his whims. He was also a superb host and she had a feeling that he'd be good company: but she still didn't know what made him tick.

'Well, I'm sure that you'll get to know him better over the weekend.' Stella leant over to kiss her lightly on the lips. 'Have a long bath and take your time getting dressed for dinner.'

'Stella – do you know who else is here this weekend?'

'Some of the regulars,' Stella said. 'They're a nice crowd. You'll like them. Anyway, I have to go.'

'Take care,' Rachel said.

'You too.' Stella grinned. 'Though I think that our paths will cross again some time.'

'Yes.' Rachel smiled back.

When Stella had left, Rachel padded into the bathroom. Exactly as Stella had said, Max had provided everything Rachel could possibly need, even down to cotton wool balls and cotton buds. She smiled. Max really was a thoughtful man. But, still, she itched to know what made him tick and what he was really planning. She was still sure that there was more to the weekend than met the eye. And she was beginning to suspect that Max had known what would happen between herself and Stella.

She ran the bath, pouring in liberal quantities of the aromatherapy bath foam. She tested the water, adding a little cold water to lower the temperature slightly, then climbed in and let the taps run until the bath was almost full. The scent in the air was delightful, a mixture of citrus and something else that she didn't recognise; she lay back and relaxed, almost falling asleep. This was pure decadence, she thought, being pampered, making love all afternoon, and then spending as long as she liked in the bath. She stretched and washed her hair; as Stella had predicted, by the time that she climbed out of the bath again, she felt on top of the world.

The oversized bath towels were thick and fluffy; and there was even a towelling robe hanging on the brass hook at the back of the door. She dried herself, wrapped a towel round her hair, then wrapped herself in the robe and padded back into the bedroom. She sat in front of

he dressing table; as she'd half-expected, the top drawer
ontained a hairdryer. She went over to her bag, taking
ut her hairbrush, and smiled wryly. Only a few days
efore, she'd used the handle of that same brush to ease
he mad surge of lust caused by meeting Luke. And
ow . . .

No doubt Max had provided a similar vibrator for the
ther female guests – assuming that there were some,
he thought. She wondered idly what he'd provided for
he men. Magazines, videos perhaps. A nasty thought
truck her, but she dismissed it as ridiculous. It was
nuch too fanciful. Of course there wouldn't be closed
ircuit TV concentrated in the women's rooms for the
nen to view whatever the women did when they were
lone and restless, relieving the ache deep within their
odies.

Pulling a face at herself, she dried her hair and did her
nake-up. Just as she was dressing, there was a knock at
he door. 'Rachel?'

She recognised Luke's voice immediately. 'Come in.'

He walked into the room, closing the door behind
im. 'Hi. Sorry I've been so long.'

'That's all right.'

'I trust that Max looked after you?'

'He had to do something – but he sent Stella to give
ne a facial and a back massage.' Rachel flushed. No way
ould she tell him what else Stella had given her. 'And
've been lazing around in the bath.'

Luke sniffed. 'Mm, I can tell. You've used Max's
pecial too. I love the smell of that bath foam.' He
tooped to kiss her lightly. 'I'll just shower and change,
hen I'll meet you in about fifteen minutes to go down to
linner, if that's all right with you?'

'Fine. See you in fifteen minutes.'

'Precisely.' He winked at her, and went to the door.

'Oh – Luke?'

'Yes?' He turned round, the door half-open.

'Do you know who else is here?'

He shook his head. 'Maggie Stewart tells me that ther
are seven of us, including you, Max and me.'

'Oh.' She felt slightly foolish. As if it mattered wh
else was there, that weekend.

'See you in a bit, then.'


Luke was absolutely on time and he smiled appreci
atively at Rachel. 'You look lovely,' he said.

'Thanks. So do you.' Luke was wearing a black dinne
jacket, teamed with a brightly patterned silk waistcoat,
toning bow tie and a white shirt; the formal clothe
suited him. Rachel was suddenly glad that she'd packe
her black dress.

The other guests were already waiting in the dinin
room: two men and two women.

'Rachel, Luke.' Max beamed expansively at them. 'Le
me introduce you.'

Rachel and Luke took their places at the dining table
Max was at the head of the table; Luke was opposit
Rachel. On her left was Michael Berisford, an exporter
he was about five years older than she was, she thought
His dark curly hair was streaked with grey at the temple
and he had a good-humoured face and startling blu
eyes. On her right was Euan Patterson, a broker. He wa
about the same age as Max, with floppy blond hair an
kind brown eyes.

On the opposite side of the table, either side of Luke
there were two glamorous-looking women. Rachel fe
slightly ill-at-ease, until Max introduced them. Th
titian-haired Rebecca Stone was a lawyer; Rachel coul
have guessed that from her power bob and large ear
rings. But her green eyes were kind and there wer
laughter lines around them. Luke already seemed t
know her; the fact that he was at ease with her mad
Rachel feel better. Madeleine Jones turned out to be
dealer in antiquarian books; as Max said, she and Rache
had a lot in common. Rachel liked the dark-haire

Madeleine on instinct; she was small and lively, with a vibrant sense of humour.

Dinner turned out to be a sumptuous affair, starting with Brie and redcurrant filo parcels, a rich Beef Wellington, and ending with a choice of three puddings. There were half a dozen cheeses on the cheeseboard, and by the time that coffee arrived, Rachel felt thoroughly stuffed – as well as more than a little tipsy. Michael and Euan had managed to keep her glass topped up, so she had no idea how much she'd drunk. It didn't seem to matter. Everyone else was just as relaxed and contented.

Even so, something nagged in the back of her mind. These people were connected, somehow. Experts in their fields: antiquarian books, law, export, finance. Luke was a lecturer who'd worked in the States; and she was a nineteenth-century literature specialist. There was a reason why Max had gathered them together, something going on behind the scenes – but she couldn't work it out.

In the end, she gave up and took them all at face value. They were just Max's friends: four people who were good company, entering into lively debates and teasing each other.

Later that evening, when Luke escorted her to her room, the questions returned to haunt her. 'Luke?'

'Mm?'

'These other people in the house party . . .'

'What about them?'

'They're linked in some way.'

He grinned, pulling her into his arms and rubbing his nose against hers. 'Yes. They're all friends of Max.'

'That's not what I mean, Luke.' She fought to keep control as he dipped his head, kissing the curve of her neck. 'There's something going on, isn't there?'

'Yes. One of Max's weekends. Lots of good food, good company and very good wine.'

'Luke, I – '

He stopped further questions by the simple method of

jamming his mouth over hers. Rachel couldn't help responding, opening her mouth under his and kissing him back. He made a small noise of pleasure in the back of his throat and began to unzip her dress; Rachel made no move to stop him and stood still as he removed her dress.

He held her at arm's length, just looking at her. 'God, Rachel, you're so lovely.' He licked his lips. 'I've been thinking about this all evening. I was watching you talk to Euan and Michael – and I think they fancied you, too.'

'Rubbish.'

'Seriously,' Luke protested. 'Either one of them would have liked to be in my place, tonight. Or even both together.'

Rachel thought about it. Two men pleasuring her; two men stroking and kissing and caressing her body. One man's cock filling her, the other in her mouth ... She said nothing but her eyes glittered, and Luke was watching her intently enough to notice.

He smiled and continued removing her clothes; he left her stockings on, but that was all. Then he stripped swiftly and drew her over to the bed. 'Rachel. I want to make love with you. Right now.'

In answer, she reached up to cup his face, drawing his mouth down to hers. Luke kissed her deeply, his tongue exploring her mouth, and pulled her down on to the bed. She closed her eyes, turning on to her back and putting her hands behind her head. Luke smiled as she placed her feet flat on the mattress, widening the gap between her thighs. 'Is that a hint?' he teased.

'What do you think?'

He smiled again and kissed his way down her body; Rachel sighed with pleasure as he settled between her thighs, his cheeks rubbing against her soft skin. He'd shaved earlier and his face felt as smooth as Stella's had.

Stella. A hot wave of shame raced over her. She'd come here with Luke, and yet the moment the beautician had touched her, she'd ended up making love with her.

She squeezed her eyes tightly shut. She felt such a slut. She didn't usually behave like that and she couldn't work out what was happening to her; at the same time, she couldn't help herself. Part of her felt that she ought to tell Luke what had happened; part of her wasn't sure how he'd react. Would he be shocked? Disgusted? Aroused?

Luke didn't seem to notice her distraction; he continued licking her, his mouth exploring her intimate topography. Rachel felt herself sliding into a warm sea of pleasure and stopped thinking, giving herself up to Luke's consummate skill. She slid one hand down her body, squeezing her breasts and then easing lower so that she could tangle her fingers in Luke's hair, urging him on. He took the hint, his tongue whipping across her clitoris in a way which made her buck and writhe beneath him.

At last she came, her internal muscles contracting sharply; Luke shifted up the bed to lie next to her and stroked her face. 'Better?'

'Better,' she agreed huskily.

'Good.' He smiled at her. 'Though I haven't finished yet.'

She curled her fingers round his erect cock. 'So I see.'

Gently, he removed her hand. 'Not yet,' he said softly. He leant across to the bedside cabinet, opening the drawer and removing the vibrator.

Rachel's eyes widened. 'How did you know about that?'

'I know Max,' Luke said simply. He stretched out beside Rachel, the thick plastic tube in his hand. 'He believes in giving his guests whatever they want. What they need.'

'I . . .' Rachel fell silent. Was he going to ask her if she'd already used it – and if she'd been alone?

He smiled at her. 'Relax, Rachel. I want you to enjoy this.'

'Mm.'

He leant over to kiss her. 'Rachel. Don't be shy. I'm not going to ask you to perform for me.'

Her colour heightened. 'Perform?'

'Masturbate for me.' He grinned. 'I think every man I know must love the thought of that – the sight of a beautiful woman giving herself pleasure. And you did say that that was what you were going to do, in that email you sent.' His lips twitched. 'Not that I ever got the chance to read it.'

'No.' She couldn't meet his eyes, remembering what she'd written – and the unexpected consequences.

He nipped gently at her lower lip. 'But tonight, I want to use this on you, Rachel. I want to make you come so hard that you're screaming.'

Her eyes dilated as she remembered Max's other house-guests. 'But – '

'The walls of this place are several feet thick. No one's going to hear you,' Luke soothed. 'Besides, your bathroom's on one side of this room and my room's on the other. So we're a long way away from anyone else. We won't be disturbed.' So saying, he stroked her thighs apart again and Rachel felt the tip of the vibrator pressing against her still warm and puffy sex.

She closed her eyes as Luke pushed the vibrator into her. He pushed it back and forth, very slowly, twisting it slightly as he moved it. Rachel felt her climax begin to build again; Luke seemed to sense it and quickened his pace, moving the vibrator rapidly back and forth. She tipped her head back against the pillows, baring her teeth; Luke smiled. 'Rachel.'

'Yes.' Her voice was cracked with desire.

'Touch yourself. Touch your breasts.'

She did so, bringing her hands up to cup the soft globes and massaging them gently, her thumbs rubbing her nipples. Luke made a small sound of satisfaction and continued to work the vibrator. Rachel cried out as her orgasm snapped through her, bringing wave after wave of pleasure.

When her pulse had slowed, Luke gently removed the vibrator and turned her over on to her front, guiding her on to her hands and knees. Rachel buried her face in the pillow, pushing her buttocks up in the air; she'd completely forgotten about the other people in the house. All she could concentrate on was Luke and the way he made her feel.

She felt the tip of his cock press against her sex and he eased inside her; she flexed her internal muscles round the hard length of his cock and he smiled, caressing her buttocks. He leant forward, kissing his way down her spine, and then began to thrust.

'Does it feel good, Rachel?' he asked.

'Mm. Yes.'

'Good.' His voice was slightly throaty. 'Rachel. Remember Euan and Michael? They were watching you, all through dinner. I bet they're lying there in bed, imagining you like this right now.' He paused. 'Imagining themselves both here with you. So you'd be straddling one of them, his cock deep inside you – exactly as mine's inside you now.' He thrusted hard, each thrust emphasising his words. 'And the other ... he'd be kneeling behind you, like I am now. He'd be touching you, Rachel. He'd be stroking your back and your buttocks and your breasts. Your skin's so soft, he'd want to touch you all over.' Luke imitated the action, stroking her back and squeezing her buttocks. 'And then ... he'd do this.' He slid his finger down the crease of her buttocks and pressed lightly against her anus. Rachel cried out as his finger pushed into her and he began to move it back and forth.

It brought back all the memories of how she'd been in Hollis's office, naked and spread over his desk while his cock had pushed deep inside her and his finger had massaged her anus lewdly. She shivered, remembering how she'd felt: how angry and ashamed and turned on, all at the same time. And here was Luke, doing the same thing to her, albeit his feelings towards her were com-

143

pletely different. And it made her reaction different, too: because, this time, she didn't feel angry. She wanted him. Though, at the same time, she felt faintly uneasy, as if she were yearning for something forbidden and dark.

'Can you imagine it, Rachel?' Luke whispered. 'They'd find you irresistible. They wouldn't be able to stop themselves – and you wouldn't want them to. Because you'd be enjoying it, too, wouldn't you? Two men making love to you. Two men filling you and fucking you until you were sated. Taking it in turns ... and then doing it together, in synchronisation.'

Rachel swallowed; a hot pulse was beating between her legs. If Luke was suggesting what she thought he was suggesting ... She couldn't. She'd never done that. He was too big; it would hurt. And yet something deep and dark inside her welcomed the idea. The thought of two men filling her, one with his cock buried deep inside her quim and the other with his cock pushing into her forbidden passage ... She shivered and Luke laughed softly.

'Oh, yes, Rachel. You'd be scared at first, maybe, not sure if you could accommodate them both – but they'd keep touching you and caressing you until you were relaxed and your whole body was loose and fluid. They'd kiss you and lick you until you were shaking, you wanted them both so much. They wouldn't be cruel, though, and force you against your will. They'd make you beg for it. They'd make you tell them what you wanted. And then, when you told them that you wanted them both to fill you, they'd start touching you again. They'd make you ready for them.' He removed his finger and reached over to the drawer again. Rachel felt something cold and greasy against her buttocks, and stiffened with shock as she realised what Luke was doing. Lubricating her, making her ready for penetration – just as he was describing how Euan and Michael would do it.

'You'd tense again,' Luke continued, 'as the idea

144

started becoming reality. You'd want it, but you'd be scared. Scared that it would hurt. But they'd be experienced. They'd know how to do it to give you the most pleasure, just the right side of pain. They'd kiss you and touch you and soothe you.' He kissed the nape of her neck, stroking her spine. 'And eventually, you'd relax.' He withdrew from her for a moment; Rachel frowned, and then felt him push back into her again. Then she realised that it wasn't Luke's cock filling her. It was the vibrator.

'And then, they'd ease into you. One, like this, where you were used to it: and the other, right here. So very, very gently.' Luke ran the tip of his cock over her perineum; despite her sudden fear, Rachel felt a kick of desire. Yes, she was scared – but she also knew that she wanted this. She wanted him to take her, the way no one had ever taken her before. She wanted him to do it. 'Just like this,' Luke continued softly, pushing the tip of his cock against her forbidden portal.

Rachel couldn't help tensing; he caressed her, kissing the nape of her neck. 'Relax, Rachel. This is going to be good. So very good. You like it when I touch you there, don't you? And this is going to be even better, even stronger.' She cried out as the tip of his cock eased into her bottom. 'Easy, easy,' Luke soothed; even so, he continued pushing into her, until he was in her up to the hilt. Then he stayed perfectly still, letting her get used to the feeling of being penetrated.

Part of Rachel thought that she was going to disgrace herself; her bowels roiled, protesting. And then the pain and the panic eased, and she was aware of a white-hot flame of lust ripping through her. Luke was penetrating her in the most primal way; and he'd filled her vagina at the same time, with the vibrator.

'This is how it would feel, Rachel, if you had a cock up your glorious cunt and another up your pretty little arse. They'd wait until you were ready, until you were used to it – and then they'd take you properly. They'd work in time.' Luke reached under her belly and took hold of the end of the vibrator. He began to move it slowly back and forth; at the same time, he began to thrust into her, using long, slow and very deep thrusts.

Rachel cried out; the sensations were indescribable. Her mind was whirling. What she was doing – it was way, way outside anything she'd ever done before. Part of her was shocked, almost ashamed at how easily she'd let Luke manipulate her in this way; yet part of her gloried in it. She buried her face in the pillow to hide her moans as Luke continued to push into her.

Her climax was quick, almost immediate, and it was stronger than anything she'd ever felt before. Her whole body seemed to pulse hotly, her sex and her sphincter both contracting sharply. And then she felt Luke tense, heard him cry out, and felt his cock throbbing deep inside her, lengthening her orgasm. As her body flexed round his, she felt everything fade around her, and she blacked out.

# Chapter Eleven

*T*he next morning, Rachel woke to find herself alone in bed. She lay there for a moment, thinking. Had last night really happened – or had she dreamt it? She turned over and the sudden ache in her body made her aware of the truth. It had all happened.

She shifted again, plumping the pillows behind her and sinking back into them, closing her eyes. She still couldn't quite believe that she'd been so abandoned with Luke – letting him use a vibrator on her and bugger her at the same time. There was nothing illegal about it nowadays, she knew: but it was still way, way beyond anything she'd ever done before. Way beyond the realms of her friends' experiences, too – except maybe for Jennifer, and even then, Rachel wasn't sure.

Heat rose in her cheeks. She'd passed out, in the end, her orgasm had been so strong. Her whole body had thrilled and shivered, flexing sharply with her climax. She'd come to, to find herself lying in Luke's arms, cherished and close; he'd said nothing, merely stroked her hair and kissed the top of her head, keeping her exactly where she was in his arms. The combination of the wine she'd drunk, the country air and the sheer exhaustion of her body had made her sleepy; she'd ended up falling asleep in his arms.

Where was he now? She opened her eyes again, sitting up. There was a note on the pillow next to her, written in Luke's small neat script, in black fountain-pen ink.

*Rachel, I've had to do something this morning. I'll see you later this afternoon. Don't worry about breakfast: Maggie Stewart will get you what you want when you're ready. Max says he thinks he knows where you'll be – and so do I!*

Rachel's colour deepened. If Max had any idea about why she'd slept so late ... But of course he didn't. How could he? He just meant that she'd be in the library, discovering just what treasures lay behind the cool leather bindings.

She glanced at her watch. It was half past ten. No doubt everyone else had already had their breakfast; still, she didn't fancy a cooked breakfast. A cup of coffee and some toast would do just nicely. She was surprised to find that she was hungry; she climbed out of bed and was relieved to discover that she didn't have the trace of a hangover. She had a quick shower, dressed in casual trousers and a shirt, and padded downstairs.

As she'd expected, there was no one in the dining room. She headed for the kitchen; Bill and Ben were there, sitting under the table and being fed scraps by a thick-set woman in her fifties.

'Hello,' Rachel said, feeling slightly shy.

The woman turned and smiled at her. 'Hello – you must be Rachel. I'm Maggie Stewart.' She wiped her hands on her apron. 'You must be dying for some breakfast. Would you like some scrambled eggs?'

Rachel shook her head. 'Just coffee and toast would be lovely, please.'

'Sit yourself down then. And ignore those two if they start scrounging. They love toast. They love anything, really.'

Rachel felt immediately at ease. Thank God that Max didn't have a Mrs Danvers-type housekeeper. But then again, she didn't think that he was the sort to put up with someone like that.

'Help yourself to milk and sugar. This is your first time at Hilbury, isn't it?' Maggie asked as she placed a mug of steaming coffee in front of Rachel.

'Yes. Max met me, with Luke, and invited me here for the weekend.'

'Mm, he told me.'

Rachel took a swig of coffee to cover her embarrassment. It was ridiculous, she knew. Of course Max wouldn't have told Maggie Stewart everything. He wouldn't have told her about the way that he and Luke had made her come in a public place.

'Are you looking forward to the party tonight?'

'Party?' Rachel frowned. 'Max didn't say anything about a party. He just said that a few people were staying for the weekend.'

'That's Max for you.' Maggie rolled her eyes. 'Well, he's expecting a few more people to arrive tonight – though they won't be staying. Max always has a party, this time of year.'

'Don't tell me that it's his birthday,' Rachel said, a horrible thought striking her.

'No, it's the anniversary of when he moved into the house.' Maggie smiled. 'He said that this place probably held loads of masked balls in its heyday – and that's precisely what he's done, organised an annual masked ball. But don't worry about a mask. Max always supplies those.'

'Right.' Rachel took another swig of her coffee and Maggie placed a plate of toast in front of her. 'There's honey, raspberry jam or marmalade, if you'd like any.'

Rachel shook her head. 'Just butter's fine, thanks.' She ate ravenously and wasn't surprised to find a head on each knee and two pairs of very soulful brown eyes looking at her. In the end, she slipped a piece of crust surreptitiously under the table to both dogs; and then looked up to meet Maggie's wry grin.

'What?' she asked.

'I knew that they'd soft-soap you.'

'They look so appealing,' Rachel said, trying to justify herself and feeling embarrassed at being caught.

'I know. Hard to resist them, isn't it?'

'Very.' Rachel finished her toast and coffee and went to the sink.

'Leave that,' Maggie said. 'I'll do it later.'

'I can't expect you to wait on me,' Rachel said.

Maggie shrugged and gave Rachel another wry grin. 'That's what Max pays me for. If I can wash up after everyone else's breakfast, I can wash up after yours.'

'Well – thank you.' Rachel paused. 'Where is everyone?'

Maggie shook her head. 'No idea. I think a couple of them went into the city this morning; the rest of them could be anywhere. Walking in the grounds, taking a swim – anything.'

'A swim?'

'Didn't Luke tell you that there's a pool here?'

Rachel frowned. 'No. I wish he had; I would have brought my swimming costume. It would have been nice to do a few lengths, too – to work off some of the calories I consumed last night!'

'Maybe next time,' Maggie said comfortingly.

'Is there anything I can do to help you?'

'No. Everything's under control. Go and relax – that's why you're here,' Maggie told her. 'I'll see you later.'

Rachel wandered out of the kitchen and found herself heading towards the library. Max had said the previous day that she could have the run of the place and she wanted to take a closer look at the Victorian first editions. She spent a happy half-hour combing through the shelves; then she came across two small leather-bound books with no titles. She picked one of them up and opened it at random. Her eyes widened as she realised that it was a diary. A woman's diary, judging by the small and very neat handwriting. An educated woman, at that.

Unable to resist the lure, Rachel took the two books over to one of the large leather armchairs and curled up. She began to read; as she turned the pages, her excitement grew. The diaries were really special. If the contents were true, then George Randolph Burton – one of the leading poets and novelists in Victorian times – had had a blazing affair with the woman who had written the diary.

Rachel's eyes glittered. There had been a lot of speculation about Burton's work, and some of his poems had been written to an unknown woman. Scholars had been trying to find out her identity for years; and it looked as though Rachel had just found out the answer to the mystery.

The diary was obviously a private one, not meant for public view; Rachel was almost shocked at how explicit it was, detailing every bit of the affair. The first time they'd met and the woman's feelings about him; the first time they'd touched, kissed; even the first time they'd made love.

Rachel's hands were shaking as she continued to turn the pages, reading avidly. Something like this . . . It was the stuff of dreams. Just about every academic she knew harboured secret longings of finding some lost letters or manuscripts of their pet author – work never seen before, or maybe some kind of correspondence which gave a new insight into the true character of the author.

She'd almost done her thesis on Burton. As it was, his novels featured prominently in the work she'd done so far. 'God, if only I could use this,' she said softly. It would be perfect source material, showing the difference between the representation of women in his novels, and the part they played in his real life.

The sound of a door clicking shut startled her. She looked up to see Max watching her, a smile on his face.

'Oh – Max. Hello.' She uncurled from the chair. 'I hope

you don't mind me being here. You did say that I could have a look through the shelves.'

'Yes.' He continued watching her closely, his blue eyes glittering with a light she couldn't interpret. 'Have you found anything interesting?'

'Oh, yes.' The words were out before she could stop herself.

'May I?' Max walked over to her, holding out one hand. Reluctantly, she handed him the diary. He looked at it and grinned. 'I thought that you might come across this.'

Rachel's eyes widened as she suddenly realised that Max had meant her to find the diaries. He'd planted them there deliberately. 'You wanted me to see these, didn't you?' she accused.

'Yes.' He looked levelly at her. 'Rachel, I know all about your job situation. Luke told me, and it's bloody unfair. If only Gilson didn't hold all the cards.'

'Tell me about it,' she said drily.

'This job I was talking about, the one I couldn't say anything about before – well, I just wanted to get to know you a bit better, find out what you were really like, before I offered it to you. Luke was fairly sure that you were right for the job.'

'So Luke knows all about this?'

Max nodded. 'When I first found them and realised what they were, I asked him if he knew anyone – a colleague who was interested in Burton, or at least a Victorian specialist. At the time, he didn't.' He paused. 'Rachel, I want these diaries edited for publication. I need someone who can do it sensitively, who understands the period – and who understands Burton, of course.' A wry smile spread across his face. 'And someone who won't be fazed by the nature of these diaries.'

Rachel stared at him. He was offering her something that most people in her line of business only dreamt about. 'Max, you do know that it's the standard academic dream, don't you – to find some new material, something that's been lost for years? And that working on this would be a privilege?'

Max grinned. 'I hoped that you'd see it that way. So you'll do it, then?'

'Yes, of course I will!' Rachel was half-tempted to hug him. 'Max, I'd really love to do it. The only thing is, I have to work out my notice first.' She grimaced. 'Not that I have any loyalty to Gilson. He can go to hell, as far as I'm concerned; but it wouldn't be fair to my students just to dump them.'

'I don't have a problem with that. It's taken me long enough to find the right person to work on the diaries; a couple more months won't make much difference.' He paused. 'And I'll be flexible about the time you spend on them. If you want to finish your doctorate at the local university, that's fine.'

'I can hardly finish it in London, can I?' Rachel asked ruefully.

'Well, good. I'm glad that that's settled.' Max held out his hand; Rachel shook it warmly.

'Thanks, Max. This is going to be a lifeline for me.'

'It's not entirely altruistic, you know,' Max said. 'You're going to be working for me, doing what I want.'

'I know.' Rachel paused. 'Um – would you prefer me to work here or to take the stuff back to London and work there?'

'It's entirely up to you,' Max said. 'You can even do a mixture of the two. Whichever's more convenient. I assume you'll need access to some material in London.'

'Yes.' Rachel smiled. 'I think that I'm going to enjoy having you as my boss, Max.'

His eyes held hers for a moment. 'I think that we're both going to enjoy it.'

Rachel had the feeling that he meant more than just working on the diaries and flushed as she remembered the first time that she'd met Max. She could understand now why he'd tested her to see just how shockable she was. She'd obviously passed the test with flying colours or he wouldn't have offered her the job now.

So what else could she look forward to, working for him? The possibilities swam enticingly in her mind. Making love with Max, in his swimming pool. Or with Max and Stella, the three of them caressing each other's bodies ... She shivered. God, what was she doing, having fantasies like this? The very fact that Max was going to be her boss meant that he was off limits; let alone the fact that he was Luke's cousin.

'I think,' Max continued, 'that we should celebrate with champagne. This evening.'

Rachel nodded. 'Luke didn't tell me before that you were having a masked ball tonight. No one mentioned it last night, either.'

'It's an annual event. I think people are just used to it.' Max was quite blasé.

'I – um – I don't know how dressy you're expecting me to be, Max, but last night was about as dressy as I get. Ever.'

He chuckled. 'If you want to come to the party in trousers, that's fine. Luke did say that you almost never wore skirts.'

'And that's why you insisted that I wore a skirt when I first met you, hm?'

'How do you know that it was at my insistence?' he parried.

She grinned. 'Because, Max, I think that I'm beginning to learn to read your mind.'

'I wonder.' He smiled at her. 'Well, I'll leave you to it, then. Is there anything that you need?'

'Actually, yes. Could I borrow your photocopier, please?'

'My photocopier?' He was surprised.

'Yes. I'd like to copy the diaries; I could start working on them this afternoon. If I work on a facsimile, I can make notes all over them without damaging the originals.'

'Sure, help yourself. You know where my study is.'

'Thanks.'

'Would you like some lunch first?'

She shook her head. 'I've only just had my breakfast.' She flushed. 'I don't usually get up this late.'

'It's the Norfolk air,' he informed her. 'It makes people eat a lot and sleep a lot – particularly people who are used to London.'

Rachel chuckled. 'Come off it.'

'I'm serious. Ask Maggie – she'll tell you.'

'Right. It has nothing to do with the amount of wine your friends plied me with last night, then?'

He laughed back. 'Partly, I suppose. Well, don't forget that you're here as my guest this weekend. I don't expect you to start working on those diaries straight away.'

'Maybe, but I've read enough not to be able to help it,' Rachel said quietly. 'I want to know what happened between Burton and the diarist.'

'Yes. I was the same and I hadn't really read any of his books at that point. Only the one they always make you do for O-level and I didn't really appreciate it, at the time. I was more interested in maths and economics.'

Rachel nodded. 'I didn't tell Luke but I very nearly did my thesis on Burton. I've got the complete works – in rather elderly and battered paperback editions; nothing like this – ' she waved her hand at the leather-bound volumes on the shelves. 'But if you want to borrow any of them, you're very welcome.'

Max smiled. 'Oh, Rachel. I think that this is going to work out perfectly – for both of us.'

Rachel spent the rest of the day carefully photocopying the diaries, then poring over them in her room, sprawled face-down on her bed in her favourite working position, with her legs kicked up behind her and her chin propped up by her left hand. She read until there was a knock at the door. She looked up. 'Come in. It's open.'

155

Luke walked in and closed the door behind him. 'Hi. You look deep in something.'

'Yes.' She shifted position abruptly, to sit up with her legs crossed. 'Luke, you knew about this, didn't you?'

He frowned. 'Knew about what?'

'The diaries.'

'The diaries?' Luke's expression was blank.

'Luke, you don't have to cover up any more. I found them in the library today. You knew about them and that Max wanted to have them edited. That he was looking for a Victorian specialist, someone who wasn't afraid of erotic material, to work on them.'

Luke winced. 'Yes, I did know; but I couldn't tell you. I promised him that I wouldn't say anything. I mean, they were his diaries and it was up to him to choose who he wanted.'

'He told me that he'd asked you to look out for someone.'

'Yes.'

'And you recommended me.'

Luke nodded.

'And that's why he wanted to meet me in the restaurant and why he asked me down here for the weekend.'

'Yes. Look, I'm sorry, Rachel. I didn't lie to you.'

'Unless you're counting lies of omission.'

'Rachel, I just couldn't tell you.'

'I know.'

'So – have you accepted?'

She nodded. 'It's a godsend. I have a job lined up now, something to look forward to.' She smiled wryly. 'It's the stuff that academic dreams are made of.'

'Mm. I almost wish that I was a Victorian specialist,' Luke said. He came to sit next to her on the bed. 'Rachel. What are you planning to wear at the party tonight?'

'Ah, yes. The party. You didn't tell me anything about that, either.'

'I forgot.'

'You forgot?' Disbelief made her voice sharp. 'Maggie told me this morning that it's an annual event – and you forgot?'

'It slipped my mind,' Luke said. 'Honestly.' His grey-green eyes were sincere. 'There's nothing ulterior in it, I promise.'

'What do people usually wear to Max's party?'

'The same sort of stuff as last night. Max provides all the masks.'

'That's what Maggie said.' Her lips twitched. 'And Max also said that I could wear trousers if I wanted to.'

Luke chuckled. 'You really must have made an impression on him then. He has very definite ideas about how he likes women to look, and trousers are not included.'

'Yes, well. I think that my black dress will just have to do for another night,' Rachel said.

Luke glanced at his watch. 'We haven't really got time to drive into Norwich and find you something, even if you were a super-fast shopper.' He kissed her linger-ingly. 'So I wondered if you'd like me to wash your back instead?'

Her lips twitched. 'And this is something else without an ulterior motive, is it?'

He grinned. 'No.'

'I thought not.'

He stood up, drawing her to her feet. 'Come on.' He led her into the bathroom and pulled her back into his arms, kissing her hard. Rachel found herself responding, sliding her arms round his neck and kissing him back.

He broke the kiss and lifted her hands, kissing her fingers one by one in a gesture which thrilled her and left her aching for more. Then he bent over, putting the plug into the bath, and ran the water. He added liberal quantities of the aromatherapy bath-foam she'd dis-covered the night before, then turned back to her, his eyes glittering with desire.

He kissed her lightly on the lips, and Rachel's legs

turned to jelly as he took tiny nibbles from her lower lip, soothing the sting by running his tongue over it. As she opened her mouth, he slid his tongue into her mouth, kissing her more deeply; she felt her sex begin to pool. She wanted him, so very badly.

She arched against him and he tugged at her shirt, freeing it from her jeans. Then he unbuttoned it very slowly, moving from the lowest button upwards; by the time that he'd finished undoing her shirt, Rachel was shaking. He continued kissing her, sliding the garment from her shoulders and dropping it on the floor; then he deftly unclasped her bra, letting that, too, drop to the floor.

Rachel made a small noise of pleasure as he cupped her breasts, his thumbs rubbing against the hardening nipples. She wanted to feel his mouth there, as well as his hands: she wanted him to lick and suck her, taking the hard peaks of flesh between his teeth and biting them gently, arousing her still further.

Still kissing her, he slid his hands down her sides, moulding her curves in a way that made her shiver; then he undid the button of her jeans and the zip, easing the soft denim over her hips and stroking her buttocks as he did so. He left her jeans at half-mast, nuzzling her throat, and slowly tracked his mouth down her body, licking and nuzzling her skin, until he reached her breasts. He buried his face in them for a moment, inhaling her scent, then turned his attention to one of the hard rosy peaks, sucking gently.

Rachel groaned, and he switched to her other breast, making his tongue into a hard point and teasing her nipple, then taking it into his mouth properly, sucking it and using his teeth just hard enough to make her gasp with pleasure. He dropped to his knees, nuzzling her midriff and pulling her jeans down further, removing her knickers at the same time. She leant on him for balance, lifting first one foot and then the other, so that he could remove her clothes.

158

He smiled, and traced the outline of her navel with the tip of his nose, finally blowing a raspberry against her skin; she chuckled. 'Luke.'

'Mm.' He got to his feet again, faintly disappointing her; she'd half-expected him to touch his mouth to her sex, bring her to a delirious climax with his tongue. Instead, he tested the water, then lifted her up and placed her in the bath.

He rolled up the sleeves of his sweater. 'Lean forward,' he said, kneeling down beside her, then picking up the soap so that he could lather his hands.

Rachel did as he asked and closed her eyes, revelling in the way that he soaped her back and then sluiced the suds from her skin. His hands were very gentle, very sure; by the time that he'd finished her back, she was feeling incredibly relaxed and sensuous.

'How do you feel?' he asked.

She looked up at him and smiled. 'Relaxed, happy – and bloody randy.'

'Good,' he said. He soaped his hands again, this time paying attention to her breasts. 'Mm. You're beautiful and lush and ripe, Rachel. I can barely keep my hands off you.'

The huskiness in his tone thrilled her. 'I'm not complaining.'

'I know.' He continued to soap her, washing her feet carefully and gradually working his way up her legs, massaging her calves and the sensitive spot at the back of her knees.

Rachel closed her eyes and relaxed. She had no idea who'd taught him this – Stella, maybe? – but whoever it was, Rachel sent her a silent thank-you. Luke had a sure touch, gentle and yet firm. She ached to feel him touch her sex, his fingers sliding over her labia and then finally pushing deep inside her, relieving the nagging ache.

Almost as if he could read her mind, he parted her thighs; she shivered as he washed her sex, his fingers playing lightly over her intimate flesh. She waited for him to touch her more deeply, to slide his fingers into her; instead, he leant over to kiss her lightly on the mouth. 'Right, then, let's be having you.'

He finished washing the soap from her skin and pulled the plug. As she stood up, he wrapped a towel round her and lifted her out of the bath. He dried her carefully, paying attention to every inch of skin; by the time he'd finished, Rachel was tingling all over and longing for him to finish what he'd started in the bath. 'Luke. Don't tease.'

He grinned. 'I'm not. I just wanted to make sure that you were properly relaxed, first.'

'And?'

'And I think that you're just about ready now.' He stripped swiftly, yet with finesse; Rachel watched him, smiling. His sex was rigid, betraying the fact that he was just as aroused as she was.

'I want you, Rachel,' he said softly. 'Turn round.'

She did so; he came to stand behind her, sliding his hands round her waist and pulling her back against him. His cock pressed hard and hot against the cleft of her buttocks; she shivered, remembering the previous night. Was he intending to take her like that again – or did he have something else in mind?

He rested his chin on her shoulder, so that his lips were by her ear. 'Rachel. One of the nice things about Max's bathrooms is that he has mirrors everywhere. You can see exactly what I'm doing to you.'

Rachel swallowed hard as she looked at the mirrored wall. It was steamy from her bath, but she could still make out their reflections. She could see Luke's hand slide down over her abdomen, as well as feel it; she could see the way he squeezed her breast with his other hand. The sight turned her on almost as much as what he was doing.

'Lean over,' he directed gently. 'Put your hands on the side of the bath.'

She did so; Luke, too, leant over, once he'd picked up

the towel he'd dropped on the floor and wiped the steam from the mirror. Then he gently repositioned her, widening her stance and pressing down lightly on her back so that she stuck her bottom up in the air. 'Look up,' he told her, his voice husky.

She did so, and her eyes widened. She looked incredibly lewd, like that.

'No. You look beautiful,' he corrected.

She was mortified to realise that she'd spoken aloud. 'I . . .'

'Hey, it's all right.' He stroked her buttocks. 'A perfect heart-shape. Oh, Rachel, if you had the view that I do . . . Your quim's beautiful. All shades of red, from a rich deep crimson through to a dusky pink. You're glistening, as if someone's painted you with runny honey; and you're irresistible. All I want to do is to sink my cock into you.' He curled his fingers round his shaft, fitting the tip of his cock to the entrance of her sex. Rachel couldn't help pushing backwards slightly, and he sank into her with a groan.

'Christ, you feel so good,' he told her. 'I love the way you feel. Warm and wet and tight. You're delectable, Rachel. Utterly, utterly delectable.' Then he began to move, pumping into her; Rachel couldn't take her eyes from the mirror. When he pulled back so that his cock was almost out of her, she could see his shaft, glistening with her juices; and when he pushed back in, her whole body moved forward, her breasts swinging.

'Ah, Rachel.' He spread his hands over her buttocks. 'And here, you're beautiful. Your skin's so soft, and yet you're firm at the same time. I love the way you feel.' He squeezed her buttocks. 'And here . . .' He rested his thumb lightly against the puckered rosy hole of her anus and she tensed. He leant forward, kissing her shoulder. 'I'm not going to do that,' he said. 'Not right now. Your body needs time to get used to the feeling, and I don't want to spoil the memories of last night.'

She flushed deeply. 'I . . .'

'It was good for me, too,' he said softly. 'But right now, all I want to do is touch you there.' He licked the pad of his thumb and continued to massage her, very gently; although he didn't penetrate her, Rachel's memories were so strong that it felt almost as if he had. She closed her eyes as his rhythm speeded up; and then her internal muscles contracted sharply round him. It was enough to tip him into his own orgasm; he cried out her name and then she felt his cock throbbing deep inside her.

He waited until the aftershocks of her orgasm had died down, then withdrew. He lifted her into the bath, washing her clean, and then dried her tenderly again, wrapping her in a towel. 'I think I'd better go next door while you get dressed,' he said, rubbing his nose against hers, 'or I don't think either of us will make the party.'

She smiled at him. 'I know.'

'I'll see you later, then.' He kissed her lightly, and left the bathroom.

# Chapter Twelve

*R*achel dressed slowly. She felt languid and warm and content; she really wasn't in the mood for a party. What she felt like doing was padding down to the kitchen, sneaking a large plateful of canapés, and going back to bed with Luke, alternately sating her hunger for his body and for food. But she knew that it would be selfish and rude to do that. Max had invited them for the weekend; and he'd already said that he wanted to drink champagne with her, to celebrate their new working partnership. She couldn't let him down.

Just as she finished doing her make-up, Luke knocked on their connecting door. In response to her call, he walked in. 'Max asked me to give you this.' He handed her a mask.

'Oh.' She examined it in silence. It was an old-fashioned Venetian mask which was designed to cover only the top half of her face, though it was enough to disguise her completely. She put it on and looked at herself in the mirror. Staring back at her was a woman in a black dress, with full red lips. The top half of her face was adorned with peacock feathers; the porcelain mask almost matched her own skin tone, and there was a domino painted around her eyes: a mask within a mask. There was a tiny diamond which glittered in the place of a beauty spot, just above her mouth.

'You look incredible. If it wasn't for the fact that I don't want to ruin your lipstick,' Luke told her, standing behind her and sliding his hands round her waist, 'I'd kiss you, right now.' His lips lightly touched the curve of her neck, and she shivered.

'Luke . . .'

'Later,' he promised, disentangling himself from her with obvious reluctance.

'What's your mask?' she asked.

He smiled and put it on. His mask was full-faced, in the design of a Green Man made of oak leaves; she grinned. 'It matches your waistcoat.' Luke's sober black dinner jacket, white shirt and black silk bow tie was in sharp contrast to the richly patterned green silk waistcoat he wore.

He removed the mask again and held her at arm's length, looking at her. 'Rachel.'

'Mm?'

'Can I ask you something?'

'Of course. What?'

He looked thoughtful. 'I'm not sure how to ask you this.'

She frowned. 'Try asking me straight.'

'Well . . . would you do something for me, tonight?'

'That depends what it is.'

He drew her closer, putting his lips by her ear. He licked her earlobe. 'What I'd like you to do is to take your knickers off.'

'Now?'

'Mm-hm. It'd really turn me on, dancing with you tonight and knowing that you're not wearing any knickers. And then maybe I can show you Max's rose-garden.'

She digested what he'd just said. 'You want me to go out without any knickers on.'

'Yes.' He stroked her buttocks, then began to bunch

up the material of her dress; the lining was slippery, and he found it easy to push the skirt of the dress upwards.

'Luke, I . . .'

'Too outrageous for you, is it?'

There was a slightly taunting note in his voice which annoyed her. She lifted her chin. 'No.'

'Then why not do it?' His eyes glittered. 'No one else at the party will know. Just you and me. Of course, if you'd rather not . . .' What he'd left unsaid was obvious. If she'd rather not, he'd know how much of a coward she was.

She didn't want to lose face with him. 'All right.'

'Good.' He hooked his thumbs into the sides of her knickers, dropping to his knees as he peeled the lacy garment downwards. Rachel leant against him, lifting one foot and then the other so that he could remove her knickers properly. He placed the flat of his palms against her thighs, the gentle pressure forcing her to widen her stance slightly. 'Beautiful,' he said huskily. 'I can't resist you, Rachel.' He bent his head, kissing her inner thighs, and Rachel closed her eyes as she felt his breath against her sex-flesh, cool and inviting.

She felt the long slow stroke of his tongue along the length of her quim; and then he slid his hands upwards, holding her labia apart. She gave a small moan of pleasure as he began to work on her clitoris, his tongue teasing the hard bud of flesh from its hood and then rapidly flicking across it.

Her sex grew wet and puffy; he pushed one finger into her, moving his hand back and forth with slow, teasing movements which made her wriggle and squat slightly, pushing her sex against his hand. Just as she was about to slide her hands into his hair and push his face against her sex, forcing him to please her properly, he stopped abruptly and stood up. Rachel opened her eyes in shock and disappointment as she felt him slide the skirt of her dress down to its normal position. 'Luke?'

'Later.' He gave her a wolfish grin. 'I just thought I'd give you a taste of what I have in mind.'

She flushed. 'That's unfair. You've turned me on, and you know it.'

'Mm, I know it all right.' He brushed his knuckles against her breasts, tracing the outline of her hardened nipples.

'You did that on purpose,' she accused.

'Yep. I think I've worked your clitoris to just the right point.'

Her eyes narrowed. 'Meaning?'

'Meaning that your sex is going to tingle as you walk. You're going to think of what we'll do later tonight ... and by the time we finally make it out to the rose garden, your sex is going to be so hot and wet. And every man who dances with you will smell just the faintest scent of musk, and they'll know how aroused you are, how hot and ready for a man you are.'

Her colour flared. 'Luke!'

'Of course,' he continued, 'you could always put your knickers on again and pretend it hasn't happened.'

She lifted her chin. 'Why do I get the feeling that you're trying to push me for a reason?'

'Oh, I am,' he agreed. 'Personal reasons. The best kind.' He licked his lips, removing all traces of the glistening musky juices from his mouth. 'So, are you ready?'

'I'm ready.'

'Good.' He replaced his mask and escorted her from the room.

Exactly as Luke had predicted, Rachel's sex tingled as she walked. He'd taken her just far enough for her to need to come: and too far for her to put it out of her mind. She could imagine her juices seeping slowly down her leg, the musky aroma of her arousal obvious to anyone who came near enough; it shocked her but, at the same time, she was conscious of a growing feeling of excitement.

Max met them at the bottom of the stairs, his full-faced Harlequin mask pushed up to the top of his head. Like Luke, he was wearing a formal dinner jacket and bow tie. 'Rachel.' He smiled and gave her a formal bow. 'You look beautiful,' he said, taking her hand and kissing the back of her fingers.

'Thank you.'

He tucked her arm through his. 'Come on. I promised you some champagne, earlier.'

He looked at Luke. 'You don't mind if I spirit Rachel off, do you?'

'Of course not.' Luke smiled back at him. 'I'll see you later, Rachel.' His eyes glittered behind the mask; Rachel licked her lips, knowing that she was being obvious, but unable to help herself.

Max led her through into the dining room. Chairs had been scattered round the room and the table pushed against the wall. Maggie had excelled herself with the buffet: there were tiny delicate smoked salmon canapés, little parcels of Brie in filo pastry and a large selection of dips, saté and small savoury nibbles, as well as the more usual party food of cocktail sausages, nuts and crisps.

'Help yourself, whenever you fancy,' Max said. He handed her a glass of champagne. 'Well – cheers. And here's to a good working relationship.'

Rachel echoed the toast and clinked her glass against his before taking a sip. She quickly realised that although it was a party, Max hadn't bought cheap champagne. The wine had a sharp lemony tang, mixed with the delightful creaminess of top-class fizz. Perfect. She savoured the taste and took another sip. 'This is lovely, Max.'

She could hear the sound of soft bluesy jazz from one of the other rooms and realised that Max hadn't used piped music. He'd hired a proper band.

The room was already filling with men dressed in dinner jackets and women in little black cocktail dresses or brightly coloured taffeta ballgowns; all wore masks.

'When did you decide to start holding a masked ball?' she asked.

'A long time ago.' He smiled. 'It's more fun. People are more likely to mix and stop being shy, if they're wearing a mask and nobody knows who they really are.'

'Except you.'

He grinned. 'That's the host's privilege. You can be who you like, behind your mask.' He glanced over her shoulder and frowned slightly, before putting his mask into place. 'If you'll excuse me, Rachel, there's someone I need to talk to. You'll be all right on your own, won't you?'

'Sure. I'll find Luke; or maybe I'll just mingle with the other guests and pretend to be a high-born Venetian lady.'

He nodded in approval. 'Yes, I don't think that you'll be on your own for very long.'

As he left, Rachel wandered over to the table, taking a plate and helping herself to a selection of nibbles. She ate slowly, savouring the rich tastes and textures of the food; then helped herself to a second glass of champagne and went in search of Luke. Max's words kept echoing in her head: *you can be who you like, behind your mask*. Given the amount of champagne that everyone was likely to consume, she imagined that this was going to be one hell of a party.

She wandered into the sitting room where the band was playing, and stayed to watch them for a while. Even they wore masks: the singer, the pianist and the bass player. Obviously this wasn't the first time that they'd entertained at one of Max's parties, she thought, sipping her wine.

A hand descended on her shoulder and she whirled round, startled. Even without his mask, she wouldn't have recognised the man who stood beside her. He was slightly too broad-shouldered to be Euan or Michael, Max's guests of the previous evening, and he wasn't Luke – he wasn't wearing the Green Man mask or the bright waistcoat.

'Would you like to dance?' he asked.

His voice was quiet, cultured, rather than the braying City type Rachel had dreaded; it was enough to tip the balance. She nodded. 'Why not?'

She placed her empty glass on one of the small occasional tables and allowed herself to be led round the room by the stranger. He was a good dancer and Rachel found herself relaxing, enjoying herself. He moved well, and although Rachel had never learned any formal dances, she didn't need to: he guided her effortlessly.

When the song finished, he bowed slightly and kissed the back of her hand. 'Thank you.'

'My turn, I think,' a voice said behind her.

Again, Rachel didn't know who he was; she didn't recognise his voice. But what the hell. It was a party; and, as Max had said, she was free to be whoever she chose, behind her mask. She smiled at him. 'Fine.' She danced with him to the next two songs, then changed partners twice more; finally, she protested laughingly that she needed a break.

She wandered back into the dining room, collected another glass of champagne and went in search of Luke. The fact that she'd been dancing with all those men and not one of them had known that she was wearing no underwear ... she wasn't sure whether it excited her, frightened her or shocked her. All the same, she was aware of how warm and puffy her sex felt.

She flexed the muscles of her quim, feeling her clitoris throb dully. God, if only Luke were there with her. Maybe he'd take her into the garden, as he'd promised, and give her the satisfaction she needed. She drained her champagne. Or maybe he'd dance with her, teasing her and rubbing his body against hers, knowing that he was driving her slowly mad with longing and desire, before taking pity on her and taking her back to one of their rooms.

At that precise moment, she felt a hand touch her shoulder, and spun round. 'Luke!' She recognised him

169

instantly. He was still wearing his mask; but he was the right height, the right build, and wore that beautiful green silk waistcoat. So even if someone had had the same mask, she knew that this was definitely Luke.

He didn't respond to her greeting; he merely took the empty glass from her hand and began dancing with her. He moved fluidly; obviously he'd been formally taught. She wondered how: whether he'd taken classes when he'd been younger, or whether a woman had taught him. An older woman, perhaps; a lover, who had taught him all kinds of other things as well.

She shrugged the thought away; the next thing she knew, Luke had waltzed her out through the French doors to the patio. Although it was a warm and pleasant night, no one else was outside; she smiled. 'Don't tell me – you're going to show me Max's rose garden?'

He inclined his head; she smiled to herself. Obviously he was playing a part behind his mask: the silent green man. Fertility. If this was the way he wanted to play it . . . She remembered again how he'd persuaded her to go without her knickers, and a thrill shot through her at the memory.

She let him slide his arm round her shoulders and guide her over towards the wall at the side of the garden. She hadn't explored the outside of the house, having been captivated by Max's library, but there was a formal garden at the back, with low lavender bushes, clipped box, fragrant herbs and large marble statues on pedestals.

There was a small green door in the wall. 'Don't tell me – this leads to the walled garden?'

He nodded and opened the door, ushering her though. To her delight, she discovered that the walled garden was actually a rose garden. She could imagine how beautiful the place would be on Midsummer Eve, filled with fragrant old English roses spilling their scent into the night, moonlight glistening on the flowers. Because it was late spring, the roses were merely in bud, but she could still appreciate the beauty of the place.

She was about to turn to him, tell him what she'd been thinking, but he took the initiative, pulling her back against his body and moulding her to him so that she could feel the heat and hardness of his cock against the cleft of her buttocks. His hands spanned her waist; he let one hand drift up to curve over her breast, squeezing the soft globe gently. Her nipple hardened almost immediately in reaction, and he made a small soft sound of pleasure in the back of his throat. He let his other hand drift down over her abdomen, stroking her; she arched against him, willing him to go further. They were alone. No one knew where they were and no one could see them. She wanted to make love, oh, so badly.

She felt him bunch the material of her dress between his fingers, hoisting her skirt up. She closed her eyes and tipped her head back against him, luxuriating in the feeling. He was going to do it. He was going to bare her to the night and take her.

When her quim and her buttocks were bare, he slid one hand along the inside of her thighs, finally letting his hand come to rest on her delta; the heel of his palm pressed against her mons veneris and his fingers lay against her warm, wet quim. She willed him to touch her more intimately; he waited for a moment, tantalising her, and then at last she felt his finger part her labia.

She moaned softly as his finger slid up and down her satiny cleft, dabbling in her musky juices. He drew his hand up to her mouth, smearing the glistening juices against her lower lip; still with her eyes closed, she opened her mouth and sucked gently on his finger. She could feel his cock starting to pulse, and she knew that he was as excited as she was. She turned to face him. 'Luke. Finish what you started earlier.' Her tone was a mixture of pleading and command; he remained silent and she knew what he was waiting for. 'I want you to fuck me,' she said. 'I want you to fuck me, right here and right now. I want to feel your cock deep inside me, filling me and stretching me. I want you.'

She undid the button of his dark formal trousers, sliding the zip down. He was wearing silk boxer shorts and the rigid outline of his cock was clearly visible through them. She curled her fingers round his shaft, squeezing gently, and then pushed his trousers down, pulling his boxer shorts down at the same time.

He groaned and lifted her up, balancing her against the wall. She didn't care that ivy was ruffling her hair into wild disarray, that the wall was slightly crumbling; all she wanted was to feel him inside her. She slid her arms round his neck, resting against him for balance, and crossed her legs round his waist. He tilted his hips forward and she could feel his cock butting against the entrance of her sex. She moaned as he slid into her. God, it felt so good, the way he filled her and stretched her.

He began to thrust, all the time balancing her weight against his and keeping her still so that the bricks at her back wouldn't scratch her or ruin her dress. She threw her head back, ignoring the ivy as he thrust into her. If only he'd remove that damned mask, so that she could kiss him properly. But then, what the hell? The rhythm between their bodies was more important than anything else, right at that moment.

She felt her orgasm building, flowing through her body. It was though she were at one with the night, and it made her want to howl, almost, wail her desires at the moon. She couldn't help crying out his name as her climax suddenly ripped through her. Her internal muscles contracted sharply, tipping him over the edge into his own orgasm. She felt his seed fill her; then, gently, he withdrew, letting her slide down his body until she was on her feet again. He steadied her, putting her dress to rights, and then straightened his own dress. She noticed that he still hadn't kissed her, that he still kept his mask in place; it irritated her mildly, but she decided not to push it. Besides, she was still wearing her own mask.

Without another word, he traced the curve of her

lower lip; then he led her back out of the rose garden. As he closed the green door behind them, she suddenly noticed another couple standing in the formal garden, behind one of the statues, hidden from the rest of the party. She flushed deeply. Christ. They must have heard her cry out in orgasm, known exactly what she was doing. But then again, she thought, maybe they were too engrossed in what they were doing to have noticed.

The man was leaning back against the statue, his hands gripping the top of the fluted marble column; the woman was on her knees in front of him. The top of her black dress was pushed down, to expose her breasts. Her skin was creamy in the moonlight and her nipples were large and dark, erect and elongated where he'd obviously been touching and kissing them earlier. His trousers were halfway down his thighs, as were his underpants; the woman was fellating him, her head bobbing back and forth rapidly.

Rachel's eyes widened. This was something that she hadn't been expecting. To her shock and surprise, Luke didn't lead her straight back to the house. Instead, he guided her towards the couple. She opened her mouth to protest, but he anticipated her move, putting a finger to her lips to warn her to stay silent.

As they neared the lovers, Rachel realised that the man wasn't wearing a mask. There was a harlequin mask lying in the middle of the lawn: obviously the one that he'd discarded. She looked at his face and realised with shock that the man groaning in pure bliss as his cock was being sucked was none other than Luke himself. Rachel didn't know the woman who worked him; she was about to turn to her companion and demand to know who the hell he was, who the woman was and what they were playing at, but he was too quick for her. He slipped his hand over her mouth. 'Sh,' he breathed in her ear. 'All in good time.'

He held her close to him; Rachel watched, fascinated and appalled, as the woman continued to work Luke to orgasm, taking him deep into her mouth. She heard Luke's cries and moans as though through some kind of fog: sounds which were so familiar to her from their own love-making, and yet he was like a stranger to her at that moment. She had no part in his pleasure.

Shaken, Rachel allowed the stranger – the man she'd just made love with – to lead her back to the party. She still couldn't quite take it in. Luke was the one being fellated by the woman in the garden – and he knew that the woman wasn't her. She was wearing a different mask, a different dress – she even had different coloured hair. How could he do that to her?

Another part of her remembered the way that she and Stella had made love, the first afternoon at Hilbury. And she'd just made love with a complete stranger – not only a man whose name she didn't know, but a man whose face she'd never seen. As they reached the patio, she stopped. 'I want to see your face.'

He nodded and removed the mask. Rachel stared at him, surprised. She didn't recognise him; she'd never met him. Part of her had begun thinking that her incognito lover had been Max, that the harlequin mask on the lawn had belonged to their host; now she realised that he wasn't. 'Who are you?' she asked.

'My name's Edmund.'

'And you're a friend of Max?'

'And Luke.'

'I thought that you were Luke.'

He raised a disbelieving eyebrow. 'Luke was, shall we say, otherwise engaged. As you've just seen.'

'But you're wearing his mask, his waistcoat.'

Edmund nodded.

'So Luke knew that I'd think you were him?'

Edmund's eyes glittered. 'Yes.'

Rachel frowned. 'But – why?'

'Why not?' was the annoying answer. 'Rachel, it's a party.'

'So you know my name. How?'

'Max pointed you out to me.'

She sighed. 'Christ. I'm beginning to think that I'm out of my depth here.'

He smiled, stroking her face. 'Rachel. Don't be angry. Max believes in pleasure – he believes in giving people what they want. And you wanted to come, didn't you?'

She flushed dully. Of course she had. He'd known that, the minute he'd touched her sex and found how aroused she was. 'Did you know that I was . . . dressed like that?'

He nodded. 'Luke told me.'

'Luke planned this?'

'No. I think he'd genuinely intended to do it himself. But . . . circumstances changed.'

'I see.'

Edmund replaced his mask. 'Look, if you want to have a fight with him, do it later. Right now, I feel like drinking champagne and dancing. It's a party. Either you can sulk on your own – or you can join me. The choice is yours.'

A choice, a decision: it was almost as though Max enjoyed playing games with people, enjoyed putting them in circumstances where they had to choose. Choose something unfamiliar, something unsettling – but something that they really wanted, at the same time. She nodded. 'All right.'

He slid his arm round her shoulders, squeezing her to show his approval. 'Come on. I think we both need a drink.' He stooped slightly so that his lips were next to her ear. 'Because the more I think of what you're not wearing beneath that demure dress of yours, the harder it's going to be not to take you into some dark secluded corner and make love with you again. At least champagne will help to take my mind off it.'

His words were so outrageous, so deliberately chosen, that it made her smile. 'Mm. Let's go inside.'

# Chapter Thirteen

$S$he didn't see Luke until later that night – when she'd already gone to bed and he tapped softly on the connecting door. 'Rachel?'

'Mm?' She was still half-asleep.

'Can I come in?'

'Mm.' To her relief, he didn't switch the light on; she shifted drowsily in the bed as the mattress gave beneath his weight.

'Rachel.' He pulled her into his arms, kissing her lightly on the mouth. 'Forgive me, for tonight?'

'Forgive you for what?'

'Kate, in the garden.'

'That.' She cuddled into him. 'Yes. You set me up, though, didn't you?'

'Yes.'

'Why?'

'Why not?'

'Don't you start. That's what Edmund said.'

He chuckled. 'Rachel, it's just how it is at Hilbury. Either you're comfortable with it or you're not.'

'It's like some kind of test,' Rachel said. 'This whole weekend – it's all been a kind of test.'

'Believe me, you've passed,' Luke told her softly. His

hand stroked down the curve of her body, lingering in the dip of her waist and then smoothing over the soft plains of her flanks. 'Rachel.'

'Mm?'

'I want to make love to you. Would you mind?'

She smiled wryly. 'Do I get any choice in the matter?'

'Of course. If you'd rather go to sleep . . .'

'Mm. Luke, I've been drinking champagne all night, I was almost asleep when you knocked on my door, and I'm not feeling that with it.'

He rubbed his nose against hers. 'I don't need your brain for what I have in mind. Just your body.'

'Indeed.'

'So, may I?'

'May you what?'

It was Luke's turn to groan. 'You haven't listened to a word I've said, have you?'

'I told you, I'm not feeling very with it.'

'Hm. Well, I can do something about that.' He moved her gently so that she was lying on her side. He parted her thighs, pulling her back towards him slightly so that she was resting her weight on him. She could feel his cock pressing against the cleft of her buttocks; then he eased his hand between their bodies, positioning the tip of his cock at the entrance of her sex.

She gave a small murmur of pleasure as he pushed, his cock sliding into her.

'Comfortable?' he asked softly.

'Mm. Very,' she murmured drowsily.

'Good.' He kissed the nape of her neck and tilted his pelvis, penetrating her as deeply as he could. His thrusts were slow and measured; it was gentler and less urgent than their love-making of the previous night, but Rachel found herself enjoying it just as much. Whatever was going on at Hilbury, whatever the test that Luke had admitted to really meant, she didn't care.

Her climax was rapid, but gentle: a slow soft rippling which seemed to fill her whole body with a delicious warmth. Luke held her close, cherishing her, his face buried in the soft skin of her neck; and Rachel drifted into sleep, sated, with Luke still inside her.

When Rachel and Luke finally woke, late the next morning, there were no signs of the party. Everything in the house was as pristine and elegant as the day before. No crumbs, no empty glasses, no spills on the carpets: it was hard to believe that only a few hours before, the house had been filled with people.

Maggie was in the kitchen; she looked up in surprise as they walked in. 'Hello. I wasn't expecting anyone to surface yet.'

'Max isn't up, then?' Luke asked.

'Not yet.' She smiled at them. 'Would you like some coffee?'

Rachel, who had the suspicions of a hangover, nodded gratefully. 'Please.'

Maggie gave her a knowing look. 'What you need is vitamin C and plenty of water.'

'I'm never going to drink champagne again,' Rachel said.

Luke grinned. 'I'll remind you of that.'

'Hm.' Rachel pulled out a chair and sat down. 'Do you mind if we have our coffee in here, Maggie?'

'Of course not.' Maggie, who'd been busy in the fridge, handed her a glass of freshly squeezed orange juice. 'Can you face a cooked breakfast?'

Rachel grimaced. 'I don't even know if I could face toast!'

'You need to eat something,' Maggie chided, cutting slices from a granary loaf. 'Toast will help.'

Rachel submitted, but fed half the toast to the spaniels, who had settled hopefully at her feet.

'Rachel, do you want to stay for lunch?' Luke asked, munching his own toast.

'Why? Do you need to get back?'

He nodded. 'There's something I have to do in London.'

'Right.' It was probably something connected with his disappearances over the past couple of days, Rachel thought. 'Well, if that's convenient for you, Maggie?'

'Whatever you like. Max won't mind.'

'Great.' Luke smiled happily and demolished another pile of toast. 'Well – I'd better pack my stuff. We'll set off in half an hour, Rachel.'

'Hadn't we – well, shouldn't we at least wait until Max is up?' Rachel asked, feeling that it was rude to disappear without even thanking their host for his hospitality.

'I'll ring him from London,' Luke said.

Rachel still felt slightly uncomfortable about it, but gave in. Maggie refused to let her help wash up, so Rachel went back to her room to pack. Just as she finished, Luke rapped on their connecting door and came into the room. 'All set?'

'Yes. Though I still think that we ought to wait at least until Max gets up.'

'Max won't mind. He's my cousin, remember? And I've left him a note anyway,' Luke said. 'Come on.'

After saying goodbye to Maggie, they left for London. The roads were fairly clear and they were back in Walthamstow within a couple of hours. Luke took Rachel's luggage from the boot of the MG and kissed her lightly on the cheek. 'Well, I'll see you later, then.'

'Don't you want to come in for a coffee or something to eat?'

He shook his head. 'I'd love to, but I have things to do. I'll see you later, OK?'

'All right.' Rachel felt vaguely disappointed: but then remembered the work that she hadn't done on Friday afternoon. And then there was her thesis and the photo-copy of the diaries – she'd left the originals with Max at Hilbury. She had more than enough to occupy her. 'See you, then.'

Luke smiled at her and climbed back into the car. Rachel watched him drive away, then let herself into the house. There was a pile of post waiting for her, including a formal letter from the university expressing their regret at letting her go – 'As if,' she snarled – and a small A5 jiffy bag which contained an advance copy of the latest Jude Devereaux novel.

She put them to one side, then went into the kitchen to switch on the kettle. She took her bags upstairs, emptying most of the contents into the laundry basket; then finally settled down at her dining-room table with the photocopied diaries and a cup of coffee. She felt a slight pang of guilt at not doing her university work first – but then again, in the circumstances, it really didn't matter. She wouldn't be there for that much longer, thanks to Gilson.

She worked until it was dark, making notes about things she wanted to trace further; then, finally, she stretched in her chair, feeling her muscles creaking in protest. She stood up, pushing the chair back, and walked over to the phone. Maybe Luke had finished doing whatever had been so urgent and fancied having dinner with her. She dialled his number; the phone rang four times, and then the answerphone cut in. 'You've reached Luke Holloway's answering machine. Please leave a message after the beep and I'll call you when I can.'

Rachel hung up without leaving a message. Obviously he wasn't back. She wasn't that hungry anyway. She went into the kitchen and made herself a sandwich, then put some Vivaldi on her CD player and curled up on the sofa with Jennifer's book. There was more than one way to spend a pleasant evening; and she didn't need Luke that much.

The next morning brought a summons to Gilson's office. Rachel stood in front of his desk, her hands on her hips and a defiant look on her face. If he was intending to give her a bollocking for taking the Friday afternoon off – well, she was more than a match for him at the moment. She didn't have to bite her tongue and remember how much damage he could do to her career; in fact, she thought, she could have the satisfaction of telling him exactly what she thought about him. 'So what can I do for you?' she asked, her expression making it clear that the question was merely for politeness' sake.

'More like, it's what I can do for you,' Gilson said.

There was a hint of menace in his tone; Rachel's eyes narrowed. Who the hell did he think he was? 'Indeed,' she said, her voice crisp.

'Let me put this another way. If you cooperate now, things might not be so bad.'

'Cooperate?' She frowned. 'What are you talking about?'

'I think you know.'

'Know what?'

'Don't play games. We know everything. If you cooperate now and tell us the truth, I'll see what I can do to make things easier for you. And if you don't . . . you'll have to face the consequences.'

Rachel shook her head. 'I'm sorry, I don't have the faintest idea what you're talking about.'

'The papers,' Gilson said. His small piggy eyes glittered behind his glasses.

'What papers?'

'Don't play dumb. It doesn't suit you. You know exactly which papers I mean. Original papers. Papers to do with your thesis. Victorian documents. Does that ring a bell?'

His sarcasm annoyed Rachel. 'Of course I've been using original papers. If you remember, we discussed it and you said that the best thing I could do was to go back to the original sources. I finished using them months ago and I returned them then. They're all signed for.'

'I don't think so.'

'Well, call the library. They'll tell you.'

'The library called me, actually. Some of the papers have gone missing.'

'They've *what*?'

'Some of the papers have gone missing,' he repeated, enjoying the shock on her face. 'Now, we know that a certain university in America's shown a lot of interest in those papers. So I suggest that you sit down, Rachel, and tell me what you know.'

Rachel remained standing. 'I don't know anything. I . . . I . . .' She shook her head. 'I don't know what you're talking about. I haven't taken any papers. All I did was work on my thesis, using source materials, and I handed those papers back in when I finished with them.'

'There's no documentation.'

'There must be! I signed for them.'

'The last thing in the records is that you had the papers. Now, where are they, Rachel?'

'They're in the library. I told you.'

'They're not.' He looked at her, his face grim. 'We have proof, Rachel, so you might as well admit it now.'

'Proof of what?'

'Your connection – with Luke Holloway.'

Rachel stared at him in disbelief. 'And since when has it been a crime to have a relationship with another lecturer?'

'When they've been working for a university in America, take up a position here and then suddenly the papers that a private buyer in that same part of America's been interested in go missing; what else are we to think?'

Rachel's lip curled. 'You're insane. I wouldn't do anything like that and you know it.'

'We have proof.'

'We?' Her eyes narrowed. 'What do you mean, we?'

'That's not for you to know.'

She scoffed. 'You don't know a bloody thing, Gilson – because there's nothing to know.'

'I think there is, Rachel. You know it too.' He folded

182

his arms. 'I was hoping that you'd be reasonable about this and that you'd cooperate. Obviously, since you're not, then I have no choice in the matter. You're dismissed.'

'Dismissed?'

'As from now. Sacked, for stealing university property.'

'But I haven't stolen anything.' Rachel shook her head, shocked and angry and confused. 'This is England. What happened to being innocent until proven guilty?'

'You were. We gave you the benefit of the doubt. Now we know that you're guilty.'

'But I haven't done anything!'

'Just clear your personal belongings from your office and leave. The police will be in touch.'

Rachel stared at him in horror. She hadn't expected this at all. She'd merely expected him to make some snide remarks about her commitment to the university, torment her a little about her thesis, and then leave her to get on with her job. 'But – I've got a lecture this morning.'

'I'll take care of that. You're dismissed.' Gilson stood up and walked to the door of his office. Opening it, he said, 'Now. Leave.'

Stunned, Rachel looked at him. 'You mean it, don't you? You want me to clear my things from my office.'

'Actually, on second thoughts, perhaps you'd better just go. We don't want you taking any other university property.'

Rachel's temper snapped. 'You bastard! You know I wouldn't take anything. There isn't a dishonest bone in my body and you know it. If there's anyone around here who'd lie and cheat, it's you!'

'You'd better leave now, before you make things worse,' Gilson told her. 'Of course, I could call security and ask them to escort you from the premises if you persist in being difficult.'

'I'm going – but you haven't heard the last of this,

believe me,' Rachel stormed. 'I'll be talking to my solicitor within the next hour.'

'You do that.' He looked faintly amused. 'But you don't have a leg to stand on. It's an empty threat, Rachel, so don't waste my time. Goodbye.'

If Rachel had had some hot coffee in her hand, she would have thrown it in his face, then smashed the mug and dashed that in his face, too. As she left Gilson's office, the absurdity of her thoughts struck her. It reminded her of the scene in *Wuthering Heights*, where Heathcliff had dashed the apple sauce into Edgar's face. It had been a pointless, empty gesture – and throwing coffee over Gilson would have been just as useless. It wouldn't even have made her feel that much better.

Slowly, she walked into her own office. She opened the bottom drawer of her desk, taking several carrier bags from it, and began to pile her books into them. There was no way that she could carry this lot home on the tube. She'd need help. Luke. Of course.

She picked up the phone and dialled his extension. It rang interminably; at last, the line switched through to the departmental secretary. 'Faculty of Arts, History Department.'

'Can I speak to Luke Holloway, please?' Rachel asked.

'Luke Holloway?' There was a pause. 'I'm sorry, I'm afraid he's called in sick today.'

Rachel frowned. She'd been with him only the day before and he'd been fine. 'He's called in sick?' she repeated, hoping that she'd misheard.

'Yes, that's right. Can I take a message and ask him to call you when he comes in?'

'No – but thank you anyway.' Rachel cleared the line and dialled Luke's home number. The phone rang twice and then clicked in to the answerphone. 'You've reached Luke Holloway's answering machine. Please leave a message after the beep and I'll call you when I can.'

Rachel cleared the line. Bloody hell. He was probably just call-screening. If he'd gone down with one of those twenty-four-hour bugs, he wouldn't be in the mood for talking to anyone. She sighed. It looked like this was something she'd have to face on her own, for the moment.

She finished packing her belongings, then switched through to an outside line and dialled her local taxi firm's number. They arranged to meet her in twenty minutes; time to kill, she thought. Enough time to take down her postcards – and enough time to send Luke an email. She knew that he had an internet connection at his flat. Maybe he'd log on later that morning, see her message and get in touch.

Quickly, she switched into the email program. This time, she was more careful when she typed in the destination ID, being sure that she'd typed in Luke's ID and not Hollis's. 'Luke,' she typed, 'I'm in trouble. Gilson's sacked me. He says I'm involved in stealing some original documents and giving them to some private buyer in America. It's not true. Please ring me, Luke. I need you. I'll be at home.'

She sent the email; then, dejectedly, she carried her bags out of her office, closing the door and locking it behind her. No doubt Gilson expected her to hand in her keys but she had no intention of doing that. Not just yet. She left the building, trying not to cry. By now, she should have been taking her lecture. It was one of her favourite ones, on the role of women in Hardy: and Gilson was taking it in her stead, giving completely the opposite viewpoint. Maybe he'd even turned it into a Dickens lecture.

And God only knew what he was telling her students about her, the reason why she wasn't giving the lecture herself. Would they believe him? She gritted her teeth, trying not to think about that. Of course her students wouldn't believe him. They knew her. Gilson wasn't that plausible a liar. He couldn't turn everyone against her.

The taxi was waiting for her outside. She climbed into the back and gave her address. The driver recognised that she wasn't in the mood for talking, and didn't try to strike up a conversation, the way that London cabbies usually did. She brooded in silence all the way home, paid him and let herself back into the house. She left the bags of books in the hall, not really having the stomach to rearrange her shelves; then made herself an extremely strong cup of coffee.

Even the caffeine kick didn't revive her. She could still hardly credit that Gilson actually believed that she could do something like that. Or maybe it had been an excuse, another of his fake reasons for getting rid of her. He only had to wait until the end of term: but he hadn't even been able to do that. He'd hated her that much. Rachel still wasn't sure why; but was there ever a reason for personality clashes?

She glanced at her watch. Everyone she knew would be at work by now. Everyone, except Luke, who was ill and not answering his phone; and Jennifer. Jennifer. Thank God for sensible Jennifer, who'd clear this mist and fog from her brain and make her start thinking straight again. She marched over to the phone and picked up the receiver so hastily that she nearly knocked the phone to the floor, then dialled the number.

She crossed her fingers, going over a kind of litany in her head. Please, God, don't let her be working. Please don't let her have the answerphone on. The phone rang three times, four; she squeezed her eyes closed, hoping that the answerphone wouldn't click in. But it did. 'Hello, this is Jennifer. I can't come to the phone right now, but if you leave your name and number after the tone, I'll call you back.'

Rachel swallowed. This time, she couldn't hang up. 'Jen, it's Rachel. There have been developments. Can you ring me – '

The phone was snatched up, cutting her off. 'Rachel?'

'You were call-screening! Thank God for that.'

Jennifer could hear the tears in her friend's voice. 'Rach, what's happened?' Rachel quickly told Jennifer the whole sordid story; Jennifer whistled. 'Jesus. You wouldn't do a thing like that. Everyone knows that.'

'Gilson doesn't.'

'What about Luke? What does he have to say about it?'

'I haven't been able to get hold of him. I rang him at the university, but they said that he'd called in sick. I rang him at home and got his answerphone.'

'Did you leave a message?'

'No. I couldn't. I didn't want to talk to him about it on the phone – not at the university, anyway.'

'Look, why don't you drive over to his place? OK, maybe he's off sick with a bug, but I'm sure he'd want to know about something like this.'

'Maybe.'

'Look, Rach, don't worry about it. We'll sort everything out. You can always come up here and stay with me for a few days, give yourself a breathing space until things have blown over.' She paused. 'Actually, why don't you do that? Speak to Luke, then drive up to my place. I'll have wine in the fridge and we can sit down and talk about it.'

'But, Jen, you're working.'

'I've always got time for my friends,' Jennifer said. 'Ring me from Luke's just before you set off, and then we'll work out what to do next. Have you spoken to a solicitor?'

'Well – no. The only one I know did the conveyancing on this house. That's a mile away from criminal law, isn't it?'

'I'll ask around,' Jennifer said. 'I'm sure I can find someone good. And then we'll fight that bastard Gilson all the way and clear your name.'

'Thanks, Jen.' Jennifer, as usual, exuded such a positive attitude that Rachel was momentarily heartened. 'I'll ring you later.'

'Great. Bye.'

Rachel cleared the line and tried Luke's number once

more. Again, the answerphone cut in. She sighed. Jennifer was right; the only thing she could do was to go round and see him. She went upstairs and packed a small suitcase, quickly throwing in the bare essentials. If necessary, she could always go shopping in Leeds or borrow something from Jennifer.

She left the house, making sure that she'd locked the door behind her. To her relief, her small Renault started first time and she drove to Holborn. Parking seemed to take an age; she was almost grinding her teeth in frustration by the time she found a space. She reversed into it, then walked down the street towards Luke's flat. She rang the bell and waited. There was no answer.

Frowning, she rang the bell again. Still there was no answer. She couldn't understand it. Luke couldn't be that ill. The way the departmental secretary had spoken, it had sounded like a minor bug, something that would disappear in a day or so. So why wasn't he answering? She rang the bell again; then she noticed the curtain of the ground-floor flat twitching. Maybe whoever lived there might know what was going on. It was worth a try. She knocked on the door and an elderly woman opened it. 'Yes?'

'Excuse me – I'm sorry to trouble you – but I'm looking for Luke Holloway. He lives in the flat above yours,' Rachel said.

The old lady nodded. 'I wouldn't waste your time ringing the bell, dear. He's not in.'

'He's not in?' Rachel was surprised.

'He left quite early this morning – not his usual time, I'm sure – and he hasn't been back since.'

'I see. Well, thank you very much.' Rachel forced a smile to her face.

'I'll tell him that you were looking for him. What did you say your name was?'

Rachel shook her head. 'Don't worry. He'll be in touch later.' Like never, she thought, as she returned to her car.

188

Luke had called in sick – but he'd left his flat earlier. What the hell was going on?

Maybe Hollis had had a point, she thought bitterly. Maybe he really had been on her side and had tried to warn her – albeit not very effectively. She'd been Luke's fall guy. He hadn't been a lecturer at all. It had been a pose. He'd purposely bumped into her in the first place – it hadn't been an accident at all. He'd planned it right from the start. He'd worked out who was interested in the documents that the private collector wanted, and who was the last person to use them at the library. He'd struck up a friendship with her, make her think that there was some future in their relationship.

Then, once he was sure that she trusted him, he'd acted. He'd taken the documents – and left her to take the blame. Her lips twisted. Yes, he'd fooled her, hook, line and sinker. Max was probably involved too. And his house guests. Why else had Luke kept trying to avoid the subject, making love to her to avoid her questions? An antiquarian book expert, an exporter, a lawyer and a broker . . . They'd all been in it together. Even the diaries had probably been stolen.

What a mess, she thought. What a complete and utter bloody mess. And she'd walked straight into it. She squeezed her eyes shut for a moment; then lifted her chin. No, she wasn't going to burst into tears. She was going to stay with Jennifer, talk to a solicitor and clear her name. She started the engine, then drove off, heading for the M1.

# Chapter Fourteen

$R$achel drove straight up to Yorkshire, only stopping to fill up with petrol. Four hours later, she arrived at Jennifer's moorland cottage, a chocolate-box place built of pale yellow stone with roses round the door. Before Rachel had even taken her cases from the boot, Jennifer had already opened the front door and walked across the gravel.

Jennifer hugged her friend. 'Rachel, it's good to see you.' She smiled wryly, her blue eyes filled with sympathy. 'It's just a shame that the circumstances are like this. Come on, I'll fix us a drink.' She looked at Rachel. 'You haven't stopped for anything to eat either, have you?'

'No.'

'Bad girl.' Jennifer ushered her into the cottage and closed the door behind them. Her black-and-white cat walked sedately down the hall to greet them, and twined lovingly round Rachel's legs; Rachel smiled, picking the cat up and making a fuss of her.

'Leave your case there. We'll deal with that later. In the meantime, food,' Jennifer said decisively.

Rachel followed her into the kitchen and Jennifer opened a bottle of wine, handing it to Rachel with two glasses. Rachel took them over to the scrubbed pine kitchen table and poured out the wine, while Jennifer busied herself in the fridge.

A few minutes later, the table was filled with a plate of savoury biscuits, a large tub of taramasalata, a box of grissini and a plate of cheese, with a big bowl of black grapes. 'Eat first, talk later,' Jennifer said.

Rachel was surprised to discover that she was actually hungry. She ate with relish; Jennifer shared her love of cheese, and the selection included a large hunk of soft extra-creamy Brie, rich dolcelatte and a sharp lemony goat's-milk cheese. Finally, Rachel pushed her plate away. 'I'm stuffed.'

'Good.' Jennifer looked at her. 'So, tell me the whole story.'

'Well, I've been thinking about it all the way up here. I've been set up,' Rachel said. Her face darkened. 'By Luke.'

'But, Rach, normally your instinct about people is so good. I can't believe that he'd do something like that to you. Not when you'd become so close.'

'There's always a first time.' Rachel bit her lip. 'Oh, Jen. I really thought that it was working between us. I can't believe that he's done this to me – but there's no other explanation. I've thought about it and thought about it, and he has to be the one behind it all.'

'How come?'

'I went to his flat. There was no one in. In the end, I noticed these curtains twitching in the window of the flat below his. I knocked on the door and this woman told me that he'd gone out that morning, earlier than usual. He also phoned in sick, so it looks like he's probably halfway across the Atlantic at the moment.' She sighed. 'This weekend, at Max's house – all the time, I was sure that something was going on. Luke kept distracting me whenever I asked him a question. Hollis warned me to stay away from Luke, saying that he was trouble; I thought it was because Hollis didn't like him, not because he was concerned about me.'

'Hollis being the sexy librarian?'

Rachel grimaced. 'I don't know about sexy. He's not my type. He's too old, too prissy.'

'But he made you come,' Jennifer reminded her.

Rachel took a gulp of wine. 'I don't want to think about that at the moment. Or about the weekend.'

'What happened at the weekend?'

'It was a house party,' Rachel said. 'On Friday night, there was just a normal dinner party but I thought at the time that there was something funny about it. The people who were there were all very nice, but their jobs seemed to link in. There was a broker, a lawyer, an antiquarian book specialist and an exporter. All experts in their fields.' She coughed. 'Then there was Luke and there was me. I was the one who had access to the documents that Luke wanted, and, through me, he managed to get hold of them. In my name.'

'How do you know?'

'Gilson told me.'

'And you believe him?'

'He's a bastard, but he doesn't have any reason to lie to me. Not about something like that. He was gloating when he told me, Jen. He started pretending that he wanted to help me, but I knew that that wasn't true. He wanted me out of the way and he was enjoying every second. He knew damn well that I'm not the type to steal books.' She closed her eyes. 'Oh, Jen, I can't believe that my life is disintegrating like this. Everything was going OK until a couple of weeks ago. So I could have cheerfully swung for Gilson on a few occasions, but I could put up with him. There was a light at the end of the tunnel. Only a few more months and I'd have my PhD and I could go somewhere else. Then suddenly, he came out with all this crap about having to let me go, because the university needed to make cuts – and now, this.' She swallowed. 'Max offered me a job, editing these diaries he'd come across. Very intimate diaries, written by a woman. They were about Burton.'

'Burton? As in George Randolph Burton?'

'Yes.'

Jennifer whistled. 'So now you know who those gorgeous poems were written to?'

'Exactly. What academic would resist a chance like that?'

'None,' Jennifer agreed.

'I should have known that it was a trap. They were probably stolen; and I bet they're not even in the country now.' She took another swig of wine. 'I took photocopies, but that's not the same thing – and besides, it makes me look guilty. Why would I have photocopies of stolen books?'

'Because you were tricked.'

'I'm finished, Jen. I'll never ever get another academic job. And because I've been sacked, no one's going to employ me in industry either.'

'Don't be so defeatist. You're innocent and we're going to clear your name. I spoke to a solicitor and we've got an appointment for tomorrow afternoon. You can tell him the whole story and we can get it sorted out.'

'I can't afford an expensive legal battle,' Rachel protested.

'Ever heard of legal aid?' Jennifer said.

'I suppose you're right.'

'Of course I'm right.' Jennifer topped up their glasses.

'I'm so angry with myself, ' Rachel said. 'Falling for a stunt like that. I always thought that I was bright.'

'You are,' Jennifer assured her.

'I don't feel it at the moment.'

'Everyone makes mistakes.' Jennifer squeezed her hand. 'I'm really sorry that it ended up this way. From what you told me, he sounded absolutely gorgeous.'

'He is. That's just the point.' Rachel shook her head. 'He was everything I wanted in a man. I liked his personality, he was intelligent, I enjoyed talking to him.'

193

'Not to mention the fact that he was extremely good in bed, hm?'

'Yeah. He wasn't one of these "I'm good-looking and I know it" types. He was so laid-back about it all. When we made love, he was always insistent that I should enjoy it as much as he did.'

'Which is how he managed to distract you at Max's place, then?'

'Exactly.' Rachel flushed at the memory of the Friday night.

'Want to talk about it?'

'I . . . Yes, I do. Though if the scene *ever* turns up in one of your books,' Rachel warned, 'I think I'll murder you.'

Jennifer laughed. 'Of course I wouldn't. I magpie the odd thing – like a mannerism or an occupation or a favourite piece of music – but I'd never embarrass a friend like that.'

'Well, that night of the dinner party, I said to Luke that it was a bit odd, that I thought the other people were all connected in some way. He just said that they were friends of Max, and when I tried pushing it, he started talking to me, fantasising about the other two male guests and how they were thinking about making love with me.' Rachel's colour deepened. She couldn't tell Jennifer everything. 'Let's just say that Luke stretched my boundaries a bit that night. I wasn't in a fit state to ask any questions by the time he'd finished. In fact,' she said ruefully, 'I actually passed out.'

Jennifer whistled. 'It's a rare man who can bring a woman to that kind of pleasure.'

'Mm. It's just a shame that he's turned out to be such a callous, unprincipled bastard – the more so, because he tricked me into thinking that he was different.' Rachel decided not to tell Jennifer about the party and the way she'd ended up making love with Edmund in the walled garden, thinking that he was Luke. 'All during the weekend, he kept disappearing, saying that he had to do

194

something or be somewhere. He was quite mysterious about it, now that I think about it; at the time, I just assumed that it was something to do with work. Then, when I was looking through Max's library and found the diaries and Max offered me the job, I thought that Luke had known about it and had just tried to be tactful about things.'

'Oh, Rach, I'm so sorry.'

'Yeah, well. At least I'll know better in future.'

'Though it looks to me like you're sitting there, eating your heart out over him.'

Rachel nodded wryly. 'But I'll get over it.'

The phone rang in the hall; Jennifer looked at Rachel. 'Do you mind if I answer that?' she asked. 'It's just that I'm expecting my agent to ring about something, and I really want to get it sorted out today.'

'No problem.'

'The paper's over there and I'll even let you do the crossword,' Jennifer said. 'Make yourself a coffee if you want one. I might be a while.'

Rachel grinned. 'Just go and answer your phone, woman, before your agent leaves a message on your answerphone and makes another call!'

'All right, all right.'

While Jennifer was away, Rachel amused herself by fussing the cat and flicking idly through the paper. A few minutes later, Jennifer returned.

'Everything OK?' Rachel asked.

'Fine.'

Jennifer looked slightly ill-at-ease, but Rachel decided not to press it. She knew how much her friend hated discussing business. 'I meant to say, thanks for sending me the latest Jude best-seller. I really enjoyed the first six chapters.'

'Only the first six? Losing my touch, am I?' Jennifer asked.

'Not at all. That's as far as I got.' Rachel winced. 'I meant to pack it and bring it with me.'

Jennifer grinned. 'I think there are enough copies kicking around. I'm sure you can find one and finish it here.'

'Thanks. I was really getting into it.'

'Flattery,' Jennifer told her, 'will get you just about anywhere. Including out of doing the washing-up.'

'Jen, that's not fair. I can't expect you to wait on me hand and foot.'

'I'm not going to,' Jennifer said. 'Look.' She pointed to the corner. 'It's the latest Clark purchase.'

'A dishwasher. Jen, you're becoming a yuppie.'

'Yes.' Jennifer stretched. 'But I deserve it. I have better things to do with my time than washing up.'

'Mm, and you really ought to be doing it now,' Rachel said. 'If you want to carry on working, don't feel you have to stop because of me. I can amuse myself with the cat, your bookshelves and your CD player – and I promise I'll keep the volume down.'

'I'll hold you to that. Cheers.'

'In fact,' Rachel said, 'I could even cook dinner for us tonight if you like.'

'No need. Good old Tesco ready meals – fresh pasta, salad and garlic bread.'

'Right.'

On her way out of the room, Jennifer stopped, adding, 'Oh, by the way, Rachel, I meant to tell you. A friend of mine was planning to come over this evening. You don't mind, do you?'

'Not at all,' Rachel said. 'I'm just grateful that you've given me a bolthole.'

'Any time.'

Rachel spent the rest of the afternoon curled up on the sofa, fussing the cat and reading the rest of Jennifer's latest novel, listening to some of the baroque music which Jennifer claimed helped her to work.

When Jennifer had finished working for the day, she came back into the sitting room, brandishing another bottle of Chardonnay and two glasses. 'We deserve this,' she said. 'We've both had a hard day.'

Rachel smiled wryly. 'You're giving me some bad habits, Jennifer Clark.'

'Actually,' Jennifer said, 'you're the bad influence on me.'

They grinned, toasted each other, then sat back, sipping wine and chatting. The doorbell buzzed; Jennifer stood up. 'I'll be back in a minute.' She closed the door behind her. Rachel continued taking occasional sips of wine, listening to the background music Jennifer had put on earlier and trying not to think about Luke.

Two minutes later, the sitting-room door opened again. Rachel looked up, expecting to meet one of Jennifer's friends, and her colour vanished as she saw Luke. 'What the hell are you doing here?' she demanded. 'And Jennifer – how could you let him in?'

Jennifer winced. 'Rach, let me explain.'

'Explain? You mean you're in on it too?'

'That phone call – it wasn't my agent, though I really was expecting a business call. Luke told me a few things, and I think that you two have a hell of a lot of things to talk about. If you'll excuse me, I have a couple of things to do; I'll leave you to it.'

'But, Jen – ' It was too late. Jennifer had already gone. Rachel looked at Luke, her eyes blazing. 'You bastard. I don't know how you have the nerve to show up here.'

'Jennifer told you, we have things to discuss.'

'I've got nothing to say to you – not after what you did to me.'

'Rachel, I – '

'Rachel, nothing,' she cut in. 'You're not going to soft-soap me this time. I've lost my job because of you. Gilson's sacked me and there's no way I'll ever get another academic job. In fact, I'll be bloody lucky to get any kind of job at all.'

'Rachel, just give me a chance to explain.'

'Give you a chance? Why the hell should I?' Seeing

him was enough to make all her emotions boil to the surface. She stood up; in a temper, she struck out at him. He caught her wrist before her hand made contact with his face.

'Rachel, this isn't going to help. Violence doesn't solve things.'

'I don't give a fuck. Just get away from me.'

'Rachel – '

'Let me go!'

'No way.' Luke caught her other wrist, holding it up so that she was powerless to hit out at him.

'Why the hell should I listen to you?'

'There's only one way to shut you up,' Luke growled, 'and I want you to listen to me, woman.' He walked her backwards until she was pinned against the wall, still holding both her hands above her head, and lowered his face towards her. Rachel, realising his intentions, twisted her head from side to side; but the moment that his lips touched hers, a surge of longing washed through her body.

She hated Luke. She hated him more than she'd ever hated anyone in her entire life, including Gilson. The way he'd betrayed her was unbearably callous. Yet, at the same time, she found him incredibly attractive. Her body couldn't resist him. She craved him, remembering the way he'd felt inside her.

His mouth came down over hers; she fought him, biting his lip, but he was stronger than she was and he didn't pull away. At last, she gave in, opening her mouth, and his tongue slid into her mouth, caressing her palate and her tongue, exploring her.

Rachel gave a muffled sob. This wasn't fair. He knew how she reacted to him. It wasn't fair. At the same time, her sex began to tingle and she found herself growing warm and wet. She could feel his body changing, too, his cock growing harder and larger as he pressed his body against hers. Her nipples hardened in response, her breasts swelling and aching.

Part of her wanted him to touch her; the more rational part of her knew that the moment he touched her, she'd be lost. She had to hold on to the truth, to the knowledge of what he was really like. The way he was touching her, the way that his body was arousing hers, was beginning to make her lose control. She forced herself to remember what had happened, that he'd stolen the documents and let her take the blame.

He pulled her wrists closer together, then pinned her with one hand, letting the other ease between their bodies. Rachel couldn't help arching against him as his kiss became less punishing, almost coaxing, persuading her to kiss him back. The next thing she knew, she was kissing him fiercely, sliding her tongue into his mouth and taking the lead. Luke slid one hand under her sweater, stroking her midriff and then pushing his fingers under the edge of her bra. She gasped as his fingers found her erect nipple and began to play with it, teasing it and tormenting it.

She wanted him to touch her more intimately. She wanted him now, right now. He freed her hands and she pushed him back slightly, so that she could reach the waistband of his jeans and undo the button and zip. She struggled slightly with the stiffness of the button; the fact that they were in Jennifer's house and that she could walk in on them at any minute was forgotten. The only thing that was important to her now was to feel him inside her.

She pushed his jeans down over his hips, pulling his underpants down at the same time. His cock rose, thick and hard. She curled her fingers round the shaft, luxuriating in the familiar feel of his flesh beneath her fingertips. As she began to caress him, she heard him moan in the back of his throat; and then his hands were at the waistband of her own jeans, undoing the zip and button and pushing them down.

The next thing she knew, he'd taken her jeans off, removing her knickers at the same time, then he'd picked her up, balancing her weight against the wall. It reminded her of the weekend, when she'd thought that she'd been making love with him in the garden, and yet it had turned out to be another man, a man with the same build and colouring. Edmund.

But this time there were no masks. She wound her legs round his waist; he fitted the tip of his cock to the entrance of her sex and pushed in. Then he began to thrust, pushing deeper and deeper. It was so good; it was more than just mechanical between them, she realised. It was chemical. Pheromonal. She'd never felt quite that way with anyone else.

He was still kissing her, his mouth moving warm and gentle over hers. She felt her orgasm build sharply, then suddenly she was flying, her body quivering and melting into his. Her cry of pleasure was muffled by his mouth; and then she felt his cock throb deep inside her as he, too, reached his climax.

When their pulses had slowed, Luke gently disentangled her legs from his waist, withdrawing and setting her down gently so that she was standing up. Then he dressed her, tender and solicitous, before pulling up his underpants and jeans and restoring order to his own clothes.

He stroked her face. 'Oh, Rachel. What the hell's been going on?'

'You tell me.' She was still angry with him, but it was no longer the violent fury she'd felt earlier. Their lovemaking had defused that.

'I got your email. I tried ringing you but I couldn't find you. In the end, I rang directory enquiries, found Jennifer's number and rang her. She told me some of what had happened, but – talk to me, Rachel.'

She stared at him. He knew what had happened. He'd been the cause of it, for God's sake. And yet his eyes were clear. He didn't look as though he was lying to her. 'You know what's been going on,' she said.

'All I know is that when I rang the university, they

told me that you were no longer there. They wouldn't tell me any more than that – even though they didn't know who I was.' He took her hand, leading her over to the sofa, and sat down, pulling her on to his lap and sliding his hands round her waist, holding her close. 'I tried your phone for about an hour, and when I realised that you weren't call-screening, I thought you must have gone somewhere. That's why I tried Jennifer.'

Rachel suddenly remembered something. 'You called in sick this morning.'

'I took a sickie. I had some business to attend to.'

'To do with missing papers, perhaps?'

He sighed. 'Rachel, I'm not a criminal. You'll have to trust my word for now; but tell me what happened to you.'

'Well, some papers have gone missing from the library – original documents that I'd been using for my thesis a few months ago. Gilson thinks that I've stolen them and that I'm trying to smuggle them into the States, in league with you.'

'That's ridiculous! You're not a smuggler and neither am I.'

'That's not what he says – and he reckons that he has proof.'

Luke shook his head. 'He's lying, Rachel. How can he have any proof? Neither of us has done anything wrong.'

'Haven't we? I've been thinking about that all the way up here. This weekend, you were so shifty. You kept disappearing – you said you had to do things and you wouldn't tell me what they were. When I made the connection between the people at Max's dinner party, you distracted me.'

He grinned. 'Mm, and we both enjoyed that, didn't we?'

She flushed, not wanting to admit it. 'So you admit that you distracted me?'

'Yes. Because, firstly, there wasn't any connection; and, secondly, I find you irresistible.' He stroked her face. 'You're more desirable than any other woman I've ever met, Rachel.'

'You're doing it again,' she accused. 'Changing the subject, avoiding questions. I want to know what's going on, Luke.' Her eyes held his. 'I want to know the truth. You're not really a lecturer, are you?'

He sighed. 'No, I'm not. I'm acting in the role of a lecturer.'

'So you are involved in this smuggling thing.'

'Not in the way you think,' he told her quietly. 'I'm not a criminal.'

'Then what's going on?'

'I'm working for the university. We agreed that I'd act as a lecturer and I borrowed some notes from a good friend of mine who happens to work in that subject.'

'I see.' Rachel's voice was cold.

'Rachel – look, I didn't want to tell you, because I didn't want you to be dragged into it.'

'It's a bit late for that now.'

'Yeah.' He sighed. 'I'm a policeman.'

'You're what?'

'A policeman. A detective. Some people at the university suspected that some documents were being systematically removed and sold to private buyers abroad. I've been assigned to find out who's behind it.'

'So the papers I was working on – they really are missing?'

He nodded. 'Probably. You've been set up, Rachel.'

'I'd already gathered that,' she said sharply.

'But not by me,' he added. 'Or by Max. Max really is my cousin; though I admit he knows about all this. He used to live next door to one of the bigwigs at the university and the subject just came up over dinner. He was the one who suggested that I could help. I've worked on these sort of cases in the past.'

'Successfully?'

'Yes.'

'So do you know who's behind it?'

'I think so.'

'Who is it?'

'Let's just say that they work in positions of power.'

'Luke, I think you owe me this much,' Rachel said. 'I want their names. I want to know who set me up.'

Luke sighed. 'I don't think this is a good idea. I don't want you involved.'

'I'm already involved. I've lost my job over this,' Rachel reminded him. 'Tell me what you know.'

'All right. I don't have the proof of it, yet, but I think...' He swallowed. 'Rachel, don't lose your temper, will you?'

'Just bloody tell me!'

'Gilson and Hollis.'

'Gilson and Hollis?' she repeated, almost in a shriek. 'You're joking.'

'I wish. But I don't have proof yet. I can't act, Rachel, until I have proof,' he warned. 'If I do anything without cast-iron evidence, they'll get away with it.'

'Gilson and Hollis. Well, whatever proof you need,' Rachel said, 'count me in, because I want them to pay for everything they've done to me.'

There was a discreet rap at the door. 'Come in,' Rachel called.

Jennifer put her head round the door. 'Is it safe to come in yet or are you still killing each other?' She noticed their position and smiled. 'Safe, methinks.' She walked into the room and sat down.

'When I first saw Luke,' Rachel said, 'and I realised that you'd had something to do with it – '

'Mm, I know.' Jennifer winced. 'He told me some of what had happened over the phone, and I liked the sound of his voice. You said before that you trusted him and you're usually a good judge of character. I found it hard to credit that it had gone pear-shaped like this.'

'Did he tell you who he thinks is behind the missing papers?'

'Yes. That's what made me decide to trust him –

because I know what's been happening between you and Gilson. I only met the guy once and I hated him on sight; so I thought that Luke was probably telling the truth.'

'Well, now you've both decided that I'm innocent, too . . .' Luke flexed his shoulders. 'Jennifer, can I ask a favour?'

'Sure.'

'Can I use your shower? I drove up pretty quickly and travelling always makes me feel grimy.'

'Upstairs, first room on the right at the top of the stairs. You get ten minutes and then dinner will be ready. We'll be in the kitchen when you've finished.'

'Thanks.'

'And you,' Jennifer told Rachel, 'can come and help me.'

Rachel stood up and followed Jennifer into the kitchen as Luke headed up the stairs.

'I like him,' Jennifer said, handing Rachel a block of cheese and a grater. 'I think he's telling the truth.'

'Maybe.'

'Look, you've got nothing to lose by trusting him.'

'True.'

'Anyway,' Jennifer added with a grin, 'he's one of the sexiest men I've met in ages. If you decide that you don't want him, then feel free to pass him on to me.'

Rachel chuckled as she grated the cheese. 'Jen, you're incorrigible.'

'Yep. And you,' she told Rachel, 'are just about to find your life changing for the better again.'

'I hope so,' Rachel said.

'More than that. I know so,' Jennifer said.

# Chapter Fifteen

'*I* hope you like Italian food,' Jennifer said. Rachel and Luke exchanged a grin. 'What's so funny?' Jennifer asked, catching their expressions.

'We're talking about a man,' Rachel told her, 'who sends out for takeaways to a certain Italian restaurant in Islington.'

'And?'

'He lives in Holborn.'

Jennifer chuckled. 'Well. And I thought that *I* was decadent! Help yourself, Luke.'

They all heaped their plates with pasta and salad; Jennifer topped up their glasses and raised hers in a toast. 'Well, here's to us – and to breaking the smuggling ring.'

Luke and Rachel echoed the toast. 'So you're in with us?' Rachel asked.

'You bet I am,' Jennifer said. 'Anyone who hurts my best friend gets me to deal with as well.'

'Thanks.'

'So what's the plan, Luke?'

Luke pulled a face. 'I can't do anything until I have formal proof that Gilson and Hollis are involved. They've been very clever, so far, and they've hidden their tracks well.'

'Not to mention setting me up,' Rachel added.

'Yeah.' He squeezed her hand. 'But it'll only add to their sentence.'

'How are we going to get this proof then, Luke?' Jennifer asked.

'What I really need to do is break into their offices and look around. I'm bound to find something incriminating if I get long enough to search the place without being disturbed.' He made a face. 'I can't really go in on the pretext of talking to one of them about something to do with the university. Apart from the fact that Gilson's in a different department, I don't think that Hollis would see me. And even if he did and I managed to get him to leave his office, it would only be for a couple of minutes.'

Jennifer was thoughtful. 'Do you need to break into both offices?'

'Probably not. One would do if I was lucky.'

'What are you thinking, Jen?' Rachel asked.

'Well, if you only need to get one of them out of the way . . . We could do it, Rachel.'

'How?'

Jennifer winced. 'On second thoughts, forget it. You won't like it.'

'Tell me anyway.'

'You seduce one of them. Get them out of their office, and Luke will have time to look around.'

Rachel stared at Jennifer, shocked. 'You're joking!'

'I knew you wouldn't like it.'

'Actually, she has a point,' Luke said. 'Remember that email you sent to Hollis by mistake? You told me the contents and I think it would turn any man on. He's probably still thinking about it, even now. He'd be a sitting duck.'

'I am not seducing the bastards who set me up,' Rachel said, her face set.

'Even if it's your best way of trapping them?'

'Look, just let me think about it,' Rachel said. 'I'm not happy about the idea.'

206

'Then we'll think of something else,' Luke said. 'Though I have to admit, I can't think of a better way right now. I need at least twenty minutes, if not half an hour.'

'Half an hour? You really need that long?'

'To make a proper search, yes.'

'Let's just drop the subject for now and eat, hm?' Rachel suggested.

They did so, the conversation turning to books, with Luke asking Jennifer where she got her ideas and displaying not only an interest but a lively knowledge of her books.

'I hope you don't ever go all Kathy Bates on me,' Jennifer teased. 'Being my number one fan and all that.'

Luke chuckled. 'Apart from the fact that I'm the wrong sex, I don't think I could imagine chaining you to a bed and smashing your ankle bones.'

'Being chained to a bed, without any violence, isn't a bad idea,' Jennifer mused.

Rachel giggled. 'Considering that one of your exes bought you a pair of fur-lined handcuffs for Christmas one year . . .'

'Handcuffs? Now, there's a thought,' Luke said.

'Don't get any ideas, you,' Rachel warned him.

He smiled. 'I'm glad we've sorted things out between us.'

'Mm, though you've still left a few questions unanswered.'

'Such as?'

'Such as, if Max is genuine, why did you keep disappearing during the weekend in Norfolk?'

'Because,' Luke explained patiently, 'I had phone calls to make, people to see. All to do with the smuggling ring – and I told you that Max knows all about that.'

'And that was the only reason why you kept disappearing?'

'No. I also knew about the diaries and I wanted to

207

give you a chance to chat to Max about them without me cramping your style.'

'And what about calling in sick to the university this morning?'

'I needed to see a colleague; it was the only excuse I could think of. Not very original, I know.'

'Hm. Maybe I should tell you that your neighbour downstairs virtually keeps a diary of your movements,' Rachel said.

'How do you mean?'

'I didn't believe that you were ill and I thought you were call-screening. So I drove over to your place; I rang the bell, but of course there wasn't an answer. She was twitching the curtains and she told me that you'd gone out much earlier than usual.'

'Maybe I should recruit her as my assistant,' Luke suggested, smiling.

'Maybe.'

When they'd finished the pasta, Jennifer brought out a large tub of the Italian fruits-of-the-forest ice-cream that Rachel adored and had introduced her to in London some months before.

'Bliss – utter bliss,' Rachel said, stretching like a cat.

'I don't know if a tub will stretch to three, but we'll have to try,' Jennifer said.

'Of course it will,' Luke said. 'That stuff's gorgeous, but it's very rich.'

'Well, I know someone who can eat a whole tub of it by herself, in one evening,' Jennifer told him.

Rachel flushed. 'Once. Just once, I did that. I'd had one hell of a bad day and I needed cheering up.'

'And who is it who always insists on going to the Haagen Dazs café when I come to stay with her?'

Rachel grinned. 'All right, so I'm an ice-cream junkie. There are worse things to be addicted to.'

Jennifer grinned back, and pushed the tub of ice-cream towards her. 'Help yourself.'

\* \* \*

After dinner, the conversation returned to Gilson and Hollis, and how Luke could get proof of their guilt. 'The more I think about it,' Luke said, 'the more I'm convinced that your seduction of Hollis is the best thing we can do, Rachel.'

Rachel shook her head. 'Not after what he's done.'

'But don't you see? This is the best way that you can get your revenge. Because while you're keeping him occupied, I can find the proof I need.'

'Supposing that you don't find it?'

'I think I will,' Luke said. 'I've worked on this kind of case before. I know the way these people work. No matter how clever Gilson and Hollis are, they'll slip up. They're so cautious at first, so clever; and then, as time passes, they become arrogant, start being careless. There'll be something in one of their offices, believe me.'

'And if it's not in Hollis's office?' Rachel coughed. 'I can't, Luke. Hollis, I can cope with, just; but I refuse flatly to do anything with Gilson. I'd rather die than let him put his disgusting grubby paws on me.'

'All right,' Luke soothed her. 'If we're unlucky with Hollis, we'll think of another way to distract Gilson. But I really think that we'll find what we need in Hollis's office.'

'He doesn't like you,' Rachel said. 'I've been thinking about that. He warned me to stay away from you. Does he know who you really are?'

Luke shook his head. 'He might have his suspicions, but he doesn't have any proof.'

'Yet,' Rachel said slowly. 'But supposing – '

'Rachel, we have to try,' Luke cut in. 'If we don't, they'll get away with what they've done. Would you prefer that to happen?'

'No, of course not – and you know it.'

'Will you do it then?'

'All right,' Rachel said finally.

They continued talking until late in the evening, agreeing that they would leave for London the next day.

Finally, Jennifer yawned. 'I'm going to bed,' she said. 'See you in the morning.'

'Night.'

Luke turned to Rachel. 'Do you want me to sleep on the sofa?'

Rachel looked at him. 'If you'd asked me that a few hours ago, I'd have said that I would have preferred you to sleep on a bed of nails.'

'But now you know the truth?'

'I'm sorry. I owe you an apology.'

'Hey, if anyone owes an apology, it's me,' Luke said. 'I should have told you before. I knew I could trust you.'

'So why didn't you tell me?'

'I couldn't afford to,' he said simply. 'It wasn't that I didn't trust you. Hollis and Gilson are very clever. If you knew about them and they so much as guessed that someone was on to them ... I couldn't risk it. You're a very open person, Rachel. What you see is exactly what you get, with you.'

'Mm. My mother once told me that I wore my heart on my sleeve,' Rachel said, her expression rueful.

'Let's go to bed,' Luke said. 'We have a long day ahead of us.'

Rachel coughed. 'You want me to see Hollis tomorrow?'

'Yes.'

She nodded. 'Luke – remember when we talked in the basement? You know, after Hollis hauled me over the coals about the email?'

'Yes.'

'Well, I didn't tell you the whole truth,' she said quietly.

'How do you mean?'

'Come to bed and I'll tell you.'

He followed her up the stairs. 'I'm glad that Jennifer's spare room has a double bed,' Luke said, as he opened the bedroom door.

'Me too.'

He started undressing her. 'So, what were you going to tell me about Hollis?'

'When he summoned me into his office about that email, he and I ended up having sex.' What had happened between them couldn't have been described as 'making love', Rachel thought. It had been physical, not emotional.

'I see.' He paused. 'Why didn't you tell me this at the time?'

'I suppose I felt ashamed.'

'For letting him take you?'

'He threatened to tell Gilson,' Rachel explained.

'And then you'd have played right into their hands.' Luke continued to undress her. 'So what happened then?'

'Well, he made me undress, in front of him.'

'In his office?'

Rachel nodded. 'And then he took a ruler from his desk. I thought that he was going to use it on me.'

Luke's face darkened. 'Did he hurt you?'

'No. It was just a threat. Then he made me stand with my hands on his desk, bending over. He switched out of his email, so I couldn't hack in and delete the message and leave; I knew that if I just dressed and left, he'd tell Gilson. I couldn't afford that. Then he came back and I discovered why he'd gone out.' She smiled wryly. 'He'd gone to buy some condoms.'

'So he's not that much of a bastard.'

'Then he took me.'

'I see.' Luke led her over to the chest of drawers. 'Show me.'

Rachel flushed. 'Luke . . .'

'No – show me.' He kissed her very lightly and turned her to face the chest of drawers. 'I want to see.' She leant over, her hands gripping the top of the chest of drawers. 'So he took you like this?' She heard the rasp of Luke's zip and then she felt the tip of his hard cock pressing against her sex.

'Yes,' she said softly. 'But that wasn't all. He touched me as well.'

'Oh?'

'He said that I had to stay perfectly still. I wasn't allowed to speak, either.'

'I see.' Luke paused. 'Where did he touch you, precisely?'

Rachel flushed. 'I . . .'

'I think I can guess.' He licked his finger and slid it down the cleft of her buttocks. 'Was it here, perhaps, Rachel?'

'Yes.' Her voice was little more than a whisper.

'And despite the fact that he'd virtually blackmailed you into this . . . you enjoyed it.'

Her flush deepened. 'Yes.'

'And then he did this, did he?' Luke massaged the rosy puckered hole of her anus, then pushed, very gently. Her muscles gave, letting him slide into her.

'Yes.' Rachel's voice grew huskier. 'And he rubbed my clitoris.'

Luke eased his other hand round the front of her body, stroking her midriff and then moving down to part her labia. He found her clitoris easily and began to rub the sensitive nub of flesh. 'Like this?'

'Yes.' It was more of a groan than a word.

'And all the time, you had to stay perfectly still and not make a sound? Hm. He's even more sophisticated than I gave him credit for,' Luke said, his tone half-admiring.

Rachel's protest was silenced by the orgasm ripping through her. The contractions of her internal muscles around his cock were enough to tip Luke into his own orgasm; he groaned, burying his head in her shoulder. 'Oh, Rachel. I adore you. You know that.' When their pulses had slowed down, he withdrew, turning her round and pulling her into his arms, holding her close. 'This thing with Hollis – if you'd really rather not, I understand.'

'No. I want him brought to justice, Luke. I'll do it.'

* * *

212

The next morning, after breakfast, they set off for London. Luke drove alone, and Jennifer travelled with Rachel. They stopped off at Rachel's house; Rachel changed her clothes, picking some underwear that she thought that Hollis would appreciate; then they caught the tube to the university.

Just before they reached the main door of the library, Rachel stopped. 'Luke, you don't think that they've revoked my security ID, do you?'

'I doubt it. Gilson just wanted you out of the way. They'll have to go through proper procedures before they can revoke you.'

'I hope that you're right.'

'As I don't have an ID,' Jennifer said, 'how about I wait in the café over the road?'

'Good idea,' Luke said. 'If there's any trouble, ring this number.' He took a card from his wallet and scribbled a number on the back. 'It's my cousin Max. He knows everything that's going on. If you can see anything suspicious happening, ring Max and he'll be in touch with people who can help.'

Jennifer nodded. 'OK. I've got a mobile phone and I'm pretty sure that the battery's charged up. We should have no problems. Well, take care, you two – and don't take any risks.'

'We won't,' they assured her. 'See you later.'

Luke and Rachel walked into the library. As Luke had predicted, Rachel's ID card was still valid and she was able to walk in unchallenged. 'Let's get our proof,' Luke said softly. He squeezed Rachel's hand as they walked up to Hollis's office. There was an empty office next door; Luke winked at her and went to the door. 'As soon as I hear his door close for the second time, I'll know that it's safe to go in,' he said.

'Fine.' She bit her lip. 'I just hope that he's on his own and not with Gilson.'

'The chances are, Gilson's taking one of your tutorials,' Luke reminded her.

'True.'

'Good luck.' He smiled at her again and she walked over to Hollis's office. She took a deep breath, nerving herself for what was going to happen, rapped on the door, and waited.

'Come in.'

She opened the door. 'Mr Hollis.'

His eyes widened as he saw her. 'Miss Kemp. What can I do for you?'

She smiled at him. 'It's more like, what I can do for you.'

He frowned. 'How do you mean?'

'Well,' she said. 'I've been thinking.'

'About what?'

'About what happened between us the other day.'

'Indeed.' He nodded. 'And I hope that you haven't been seeing Holloway.'

'Oh, you were right to warn me about him,' Rachel said. 'He's trouble. Mixing with him could cause all sorts of dangerous consequences.'

'I'm glad that you see sense, Miss Kemp.'

'Mr Hollis. Leonard.' She perched on the edge of his desk. 'Have you been thinking about it too?'

'About what happened?'

'Yes.' Her eyes held his. 'Remembering how it felt.'

His eyes glittered. 'And if I have?'

'Let's just say – you have sophisticated tastes, Leonard. And what I've been thinking about . . . I think that you're the one person who'd appreciate it.' Inwardly, Rachel was shaking. She'd never been into amateur dramatics and she was sure that she'd never be able to play this part convincingly – but she had to do it. For all their sakes.

'So what do you have in mind?' Hollis asked.

'Let's go down to the basement. We won't be disturbed there.'

'We won't be disturbed in my office.'

She shook her head. 'Supposing that your secretary

214

needs to talk to you, or a visitor arrives, or there's a problem and someone needs your help? The basement's much quieter. Hardly anyone goes down there – especially if we decided to go to the Old English section. Almost no one looks up that kind of literature now.'

Hollis looked at her. 'You've thought this all out, haven't you?'

She nodded. If only he knew. 'Yes. Very carefully. You see, if anyone sees us going there together, I can say that I'm asking you to help me find something rather obscure.' She licked her lower lip. 'Which is, in a way, true.'

'Then the basement, it is,' Hollis said, standing up.

Rachel's heart began to beat faster in a mixture of fear and elation. She'd done it. She'd managed to talk him into leaving the room. Now all she had to do was keep him interested for a good twenty minutes or so, giving Luke the time he needed.

Luke, who was waiting next door, heard the door close and smiled. He waited for a couple of minutes, giving Rachel and Hollis time to turn the corner of the corridor; then he pulled on a pair of leather gloves and left the room. He rapped on the door of Hollis's office, and waited: no answer. He tried the door: thank God, Hollis hadn't thought to lock it.

Luke closed the door behind him and began searching. He knew exactly what he was looking for: some correspondence between Hollis and Gilson, or with either one of them and their contacts abroad. He searched carefully, making sure that he put everything back in precisely the same place. The drawers of Hollis's desk yielded nothing and Luke cursed under his breath.

He turned to the filing cabinet. Something had to be there. It had to be.

Rachel and Hollis walked together in silence. When they reached the basement, Rachel paused. 'Just a moment,' she said. She opened her handbag, took out a dark red lipstick she'd borrowed from Jennifer, and quickly applied it.

Gilson raised an eyebrow. 'I think,' he said, 'that this is going to be very interesting.'

'I'm sure you'll find it so,' Rachel purred. They went to the back of the basement where the Old English books were kept, and Rachel smiled at him.

'So, what did you have in mind, Miss Kemp?'

'Rachel,' she told him. 'My name's Rachel.'

'Rachel.' His voice was slightly huskier and deeper than usual, betraying his excitement.

'Well,' Rachel said, 'I remembered your reaction to the email. I went shopping.' That much was true, but she hadn't been shopping for Hollis. She'd been shopping for herself. She'd found a teddy, made of the sheerest stretch black lace, which clung to her curves but was flexible enough to be worn any way she chose.

She unbuttoned her shirt, but didn't take it off; she left it open and slid one hand inside her teddy, pushing it down to reveal one breast. She did the same with the other side; the teddy was enough to keep her breasts supported.

Hollis's eyes widened as Rachel took the lipstick from her handbag again and proceeded to darken her areolae with it, teasing her nipples into hardness and colouring them fully. 'I thought that you might like this,' she said softly.

He licked his lips. 'Yes.'

Rachel's gaze travelled up and down his body, very deliberately and very slowly. As last time, he was wearing a dark grey suit, a white shirt and an understated silk tie; she could see the beginnings of his erection stirring in his trousers. She gave him her most coquettish smile and walked over to him, then slid her hands under his jacket and smoothed his crisp white shirt against his skin. Her hands drifted down to his belt; his breathing quickened as she proceeded to undo the

216

belt and the zip of his trousers, then pushed the dark grey material downwards.

To her surprise, he was wearing silk boxer shorts. But then again, she should have guessed that a sensualist like Hollis would like the feel of silk next to his skin. His cock had hardened fully and its outline was clearly visible through the thin soft stuff of his shorts. Despite her hatred of him, Rachel felt a small flicker of excitement in her quim. She could still remember how it had felt when he'd penetrated her – how good it had been, but how ashamed and angry and confused she'd felt at the same time.

She gave him another coquettish smile, and hooked her fingers into the sides of his shorts, pulling them down to reveal his cock. She dropped to her knees in front of him, and then looked up at him. 'I want you to hold the shelf behind you,' she directed. 'Right now.'

Hollis gave her a haughty look. 'I don't switch,' he said quietly. 'I give the orders. I don't take them.'

Rachel ran her finger along his frenum. 'Let's put it another way then. I'd like you to do it for me, Leonard. Indulge me. Let me play with you a little, enjoy your body the way I want to enjoy it. I've been thinking about this for such a long, long time.' She curled her fingers round his shaft and opened her mouth, sliding her lips over his glans. Hollis gave a small moan of pleasure and she felt his cock twitch.

She began to play with his cock, using the tip of her tongue. She made it into a hard point to tease the sensitive groove just below the head, then let her tongue grow soft again, swirling it over his glans. She could feel Hollis growing more excited, hear his breathing become irregular, and she began to massage his balls, using the same rhythm to stroke him as she used to fellate him.

Apart from slightly heavier and uneven breathing, he made no sound: Rachel gloated inside. He was struggling to keep control, she knew; and he was falling for this, every bit of the way. And she was about to shame him in the same way that he'd shamed her. She continued fondling him; then, with her free hand, she took the lipstick again. She'd buy Jennifer a new one to replace it, because it would be unusable by the time that she'd finished.

She uncapped the lipstick, swivelling the base so that the point of the dark red gloss showed, and slowly ran it along Hollis' perineum. He gasped and she pulled back, looking up at him in a mock-submissive pose. 'Indulge me, Leonard,' she said, trying to make it sound more like a plea than a command. 'I think you're going to enjoy this. Very much.'

He nodded and she smiled to herself. His grey eyes were almost black, and his mouth was slightly slack. Obviously he was too excited to trust himself to speak. Perfect. She resumed fellating him and again stroked the lipstick up and down his perineum, each time getting nearer and nearer to the puckered rosy hole of his anus.

Hollis gasped again, this time in pleasure rather than shock, as she rubbed the tip of the lipstick against the forbidden entrance to his body. She pushed slightly, feeling the tight ring of muscles give as she pressed the lipstick case against it. Then, when the case had penetrated him as far as possible, she swivelled the base so that the lipstick penetrated him even more deeply.

Using the swivel only, she moved the lipstick in and out of him. She could hear Hollis desperately trying to stifle his moans of pleasure, and she continued to work him, moving faster and faster, until at last, he gave a strangled cry, and her mouth filled with warm salty liquid.

She risked a quick glance at her watch. They'd hadn't been here for long enough. She couldn't risk it – she couldn't go back, not yet. Given Hollis's age, he wouldn't recover his erection quickly enough to have full sex with her, but there was something else that he could do. She removed the lipstick, leaving the case on one of the

218

shelves, and then stood up, sliding her hands round his neck and kissing him hard.

He was taken by surprise and opened his mouth. She kissed him deeply so that he could taste himself on her. She noticed with amusement that her lipstick had smudged over his face. His pupils were still dilated as he looked at her. 'Rachel, I . . .'

'I told you that you'd enjoy it,' she said. 'And now . . . perhaps you could repay the compliment.'

'How do you mean?'

'I want you to lick me. I want to feel your mouth on my sex. I want you to make me come. All the time when you fucked me over your desk, I wondered what it would be like if you used your mouth on me. I want to know, Leonard. Show me how good it is.'

For a moment, she thought that he was going to refuse; and then, slowly, he undid her jeans, sliding them downwards. She kicked off her high-heeled shoes and stepped out of the denims, then put her shoes back on again. He looked at her patent leather court shoes with obvious approval. She grinned. 'I thought that you might appreciate these.' She was also wearing lace-topped hold-up stockings, again thinking that they might appeal to him, keep his mind off kilter.

'Hm.' To her surprise, he sat down on the floor, uncaring that his suit would be marked. 'Come here,' he said softly. 'Stand over me.' Rachel did so, one leg either side of his body, and he smiled. 'Perfect.'

He pressed the flat of his palms against her inner thighs, and she widened her stance slightly; he continued pressing and Rachel's eyes widened. God. If he made her move much further, she'd fall over.

'No, you won't,' he said, reading her mind. 'But a little discomfort makes the pleasure even better.'

Despite herself, Rachel felt herself grow wet. This was something she loved. Luke had proved very skilled at it and she had a feeling that Hollis would be equally proficient. She closed her eyes, sliding her hands into

Hollis's hair; at least, she thought with relief, Hollis was clean, not faintly greasy like Gilson was.

He rubbed his face against her inner thigh; although he'd shaved, that morning, there was a faint rasp of stubble against her skin. She gasped and he turned his face, pressing his lips to her skin. She sighed and pushed her pubis impatiently against him; at last, she felt him push the gusset of her teddy to one side, his breath warm against her quim. She closed her eyes as she felt the first long, slow stroke of his tongue against her labia.

He teased her clitoris from its hood, making his tongue into a sharp point and flicking it rapidly over the sensitive nub of flesh. Rachel bit back a moan of pleasure and he began to lap at her in earnest, alternately pushing his tongue as deeply as he could into her vagina, pulling gently on her labia and sensitising her clitoris. His hands gripped her bottom; she felt him pull her cheeks apart, and then his finger pressed against her forbidden portal. As he entered her, she dug her fingertips into his scalp, urging him on.

And then her orgasm began, tiny ripples which swelled into a surge and then finally flooded her belly. Her internal muscles contracted sharply round his finger and his tongue; and then, when the aftershocks had died away, he withdrew from her, gently removing her hands from his hair and standing up.

'And now,' Rachel said softly, looking him in the eye, 'I think that we're even.'

Hollis smiled. 'Yes. I think that you're right.'

In more ways than you could imagine, Rachel thought, but she hugged her triumph to herself.

Luke started on the next drawer of the filing cabinet. Unless he'd misjudged Hollis very badly, there had to be something. A note, a tiny scrap of evidence. There had to be. He thought of his lover entertaining Hollis in the basement to give him time to search, and he gritted his teeth. Even the thought of a lying, cheating scum like

Hollis laying a finger on Rachel made him angry. If there had been another way, Luke would have taken it. But Jennifer had been right. It was their best chance of keeping Hollis distracted.

He looked through another file and a smile of mingled relief and triumph lit his face. Just as he was about to give up hope, it was there. A note from Gilson to Hollis: a note of the most incriminating kind. Stuck to the back of another piece of paper – or Hollis would certainly have destroyed it.

'This one's for you, Rachel,' he said, removing the A5 note and replacing the file exactly as he'd found it.

# *Chapter Sixteen*

*L*uke folded the piece of paper, intending to hide it in his wallet; then he noticed the fax machine sitting next to Hollis's desk. Maybe it would be safer to fax it to Max immediately, he thought. If he was caught leaving Hollis's office and was searched, they would find the piece of paper ... Making up his mind, he walked over to the fax machine, dialled Max's number and slotted the note in place.

All he had to do then was to print the fax journal and somehow destroy it – even if he had to eat the bloody thing, he would. 'Please, Max,' he muttered, 'please don't let your fax machine be engaged.' To his relief, the fax rang twice, and then the piece of paper started to go through. 'Yeehah,' Luke said under his breath.

At that precise moment, the door opened. He turned round in shock. He had been expecting another few minutes' grace. Surely Rachel wasn't back with Hollis yet? But it wasn't Rachel or Hollis standing in the doorway. It was a woman he didn't recognise. He judged her to be about thirty-five. She had mousy brown hair, pulled back from her face in an unflattering way. She wore no make-up or jewellery, apart from a slightly mannish watch; she had large horn-rimmed spectacles and was dressed in the kind of way that marked her out as the stereotype dragon secretary, all A-line tweed and buttoned-up collar and polished brogues. Miss Something-or-other, judging by the lack of a wedding ring. No engagement ring either.

'Who are you? What do you think you're doing in Mr Hollis's office?' she demanded, her voice sharp.

'I'm sorry,' Luke said. 'I'm a friend of Leonard's. He was expecting me. We were going to lunch together.'

'Mr Hollis is not going out to lunch today. He has a business meeting.'

Luke rolled his eyes. 'Dear oh dear. Len's becoming forgetful in his old age.'

'Len? Nobody calls Mr Hollis "Len".'

'I've known him for a long time,' Luke lied.

The fax machine beeped as the memo finished going through; her gaze darted to the machine and she saw the piece of paper. 'What's that? What are you doing?'

'I'm sending a fax to a friend of mine while I'm waiting for Leonard. I'm sure that he won't mind.' He smiled disarmingly at her. 'Actually, I was going to come and see you when I realised that he wasn't here, but I didn't want to disturb you because I know how busy you are.'

'Huh.' She gave him a look which clearly said that she wasn't going to let him soft-soap her.

He smiled again. 'Leonard's always talking about you, you know,' he said. 'He's always saying how good you are, how efficient, how capable. He feels that you could virtually do the job for him sometimes.'

'Oh.' A slight flush crept into her cheeks.

A sudden idea struck Luke. There was one sure-fire way to make sure that she didn't tell Hollis what was going on. If he made love with her and Hollis caught them, he'd throw her out on the spot without giving her the chance to tell him what was going on. If they weren't caught, then she wouldn't want to admit to Hollis what she'd been doing. She certainly wouldn't mention his visitor sending a fax – not until it was much too late.

'What Len didn't say,' Luke told her softly, 'was how attractive you are.'

'Attractive?' She was shocked.

'Yes. Your eyes, for starters. They're the most beautiful colour blue, like a carpet of bluebells in a wood at springtime.' Luke winced to himself. It sounded so corny. But he had to do it. 'And your hair – I bet when you're outside in the sun, in summer, it looks like sunlight dappling across a field of ripened corn.'

Her lips thinned. 'I don't take kindly to people mocking me.'

'I'm not mocking you or teasing you.' Luke walked over to her and took her hand, raising it to his lips and kissing the backs of her fingers, one by one. 'What's your first name?' he asked softly.

'Eunice.'

'Eunice. So unusual.' His eyes held hers. 'Has anyone told you that your mouth's a perfect rosebud?'

Her flush deepened. 'I don't wear lipstick or anything like that. I don't like painting my face.'

'Too true. A woman like you doesn't need paint to adorn her skin.' He traced her lower lip with his fingertip. 'A colour this perfect, this beautiful, shouldn't be hidden by paint.' He licked his lips. 'Eunice, I . . .' He bent his head, touching his lips to hers and kissing her very, very gently. He knew that he was taking a risk. Either she'd pull away, affronted, or she'd respond. Just at that moment, he wasn't sure which, but he hoped desperately that it would be the latter.

She stood still, immobile; and then her lips parted under his. Luke cupped her face and began to kiss her properly, his tongue probing her mouth. He took it slowly, making sure that she didn't feel rushed. At last, her hands came round his neck and he almost sagged against her in relief. He let his hands drop to her waist and pulled her in towards him, stroking her buttocks.

He broke the kiss and began a trail of kisses along her ear. 'Eunice.' He licked her earlobe. 'I don't know what

224

it is about you. I don't know whether it's your perfume or simply pheromones, but I find you utterly irresistible. I want you, Eunice. I want you, now.'

'But Mr Hollis – '

'Forget him.' Luke walked her backwards towards the door and turned the lock. 'We won't be disturbed. No one's going to see us. No one needs to know anything about this. It's just between you and me. Skin to skin, mouth to mouth.' He pulled the blind at the office window. 'I want you so badly, Eunice. I need you. Feel what you do to me.' He pushed his pelvis towards her so that she could feel his hardening cock; a thrill rippled through her. 'Eunice. Please. I need you.' He removed her glasses, putting them on top of Hollis's filing cabinet, and unpinned her hair, combing it through with his fingers. 'Eunice, if you wore your hair like this more often . . . I think a lot of the men in this building would have a hard time staying away from you.'

She flushed. 'You're teasing me again.'

'Not at all.' He rubbed his nose against hers. 'It suits you like this. It's softer, more flattering; it frames your face.'

'Oh.'

'I want you, Eunice. I want you, here and now.' Slowly, he removed her cardigan, folding it and placing it next to her glasses. Then he began to unbutton her prissy shirt, tugging it from the waistband of her skirt. She didn't stop him; he bent his head, licking the hollows of her collar-bones, and she shivered, arching against him. Luke finished unbuttoning her shirt and slipped it from her shoulders. She made no protest and he kissed her again, this time with more hunger.

Her bra was white and plain and functional, rather than pretty, with ugly wide shoulder straps; Luke unfastened it deftly, dropping it to the floor, and cupped her generous breasts in his hands. He gave a sharp intake of breath as he looked down. Naked, she was beautiful; this wasn't going to be a pretence, with him having to call up a picture of Rachel in his mind in order to make love to her.

'Eunice, you're lovely,' he told her, his voice cracking slightly. 'Your breasts are beautiful, even more than I'd imagined. Your skin's all creamy and soft, and your nipples, they're such a perfect colour. It makes me want to touch you and kiss you, Eunice. I want to kiss your breasts. I want to lick them, suck them, taste your skin.'

Eunice was flushed and quivering. Luke dropped to his knees in front of her, still massaging her breasts, and took one rosy nipple into his mouth. It hardened instantly and he began to suck, rolling its twin between his thumb and forefinger. She gasped and Luke pulled back slightly, blowing against her wet skin. She arched against him, giving a small cry of pleasure, and Luke nuzzled her midriff.

His hands slid behind her back; he undid the waistband of her skirt and slid the zip down. The skirt had a slippery lining and it was no effort for him to draw her skirt down over her hips. As Luke had half-suspected, she was wearing frumpy brown tights and big knickers. This was a woman who dressed to be practical, rather than sensual, and it saddened him that she was burying her sexuality in this way. Eunice was a woman who'd flower under the right touch, he was sure.

He drew his finger down the seam of her tights. 'I'd like to rip these from you,' he said. 'I'd like to hear the nylon hiss apart as I tear them from you. But it would be unfair to ruin your clothes, just for a whim of mine.' Slowly, he rolled down her tights, stroking her legs as he did so. Eunice lifted one foot and then the other, letting him remove her shoes and then take off her tights properly.

'Eunice. You're all woman.' He leant against her, kissing the soft skin of her inner thighs. She trembled slightly. Luke wondered for a moment whether she was a virgin, and then decided not. She had the look of a woman who'd expected more from her first lover, and had given up sex from disappointment rather than disinclination.

Slowly, he hooked his thumbs into the waistband of her knickers and drew them down. 'You're so beautiful. I want to touch you and taste you.'

'I . . .'

He pounced on her hesitation. She was scared: but interested, too. 'Let me, Eunice,' he said softly. 'Let me show you pleasure. Let me show you how good it can be.' Suddenly, Luke desperately wanted to give her pleasure. He wanted to make up for whoever had broken her heart in the first place. Maybe even it had been Hollis himself: though, from what Rachel had told him, Hollis was very sophisticated, and Luke assumed that Hollis had the skill to match.

He parted her legs and cupped her quim, the heel of his palm resting against her mons veneris. He could feel a pulse beating heavily in her quim; slowly, he pushed one finger between her labia, testing her wetness. She gasped as his finger slid into her moist channel. Luke settled his thumb on her clitoris and began to rub it, using a gentle figure-of-eight motion. He continued pushing his finger in and out of her; she slid her fingers into his hair, urging him on, and he added a second finger, working her harder and harder until he felt her internal muscles clenching round his finger.

'Beautiful Eunice,' he said softly. 'And this – this is the best wine known to mankind.' He bent his head and began to lap the musky nectar from her quim. Eunice groaned and he probed her more deeply with his tongue, licking and sucking until she was shuddering with pleasure. He brought her to another climax, and then, swiftly, he stood up. 'Undress me, Eunice,' he urged. 'I want to be as one with you. I want you to take me to the edge with you, this time.'

With trembling fingers, she undressed him. He allowed her to explore his body, her fingertips brushing his skin. Her hands were shaking as she struggled to

227

undo the button of his jeans. Gently, he helped her, his fingers twining with hers as she pulled the zip down.

Then, when he was naked, he lay down on the carpet. 'Make love with me, Eunice,' he urged. 'Let's show each other how good it can be.'

Looking slightly hesitant and unsure, Eunice sank to the floor beside him. He pulled her into his arms, kissing her and caressing her, building her to fever pitch. He took her hand, curling it round his cock. 'Feel what you do to me, Eunice.'

She trembled, and he rolled over onto his back, pulling her with him so that she straddled him. 'I want to see you,' he said softly. 'I want to see your face properly. I want to see your eyes light with pleasure, your skin glow. I want to see your beautiful breasts swinging proud and free in front of me.'

He lifted her slightly, easing his hand between their bodies and fitting the tip of his cock to the entrance of her sex. He let her slide very slowly down on to him. She gave a small gasp as his cock filled her, stretching her; and then Luke smiled up at her. 'Do you know how good you feel, Eunice? Like warm, wet silk wrapped round me.' He lifted his hands to her breasts, cupping them and pushing them up and together slightly to deepen her cleavage. 'You have the most beautiful breasts,' he said quietly. 'Soft and creamy skin, warm and delightful to the touch. You're beautiful, Eunice. This is a you that I bet hardly any man sees; but right now, you're all woman, sensual and soft. I want you so badly. Make love with me, Eunice.'

He squeezed her breasts gently and then stroked down to her midriff. He cupped her buttocks, massaging them gently and urging her to ride him. Hesitantly, Eunice began to move over him and Luke smiled at her. 'That feels fantastic. It's so good, when you move like that.'

Encouraged, she began to move with more confidence, circling her hips as she rode him to change the angle of his penetration. 'Oh yes, Eunice. That's it. That's perfect,'

Luke said, his voice growing husky. He let one hand drift between her thighs again, his fingers probing her curls delicately until he found her clitoris. He began to rub her rhythmically as she raised and lowered herself over him.

A mottled rosy flush stained her skin, spreading down from her throat and over her breasts; then he felt her quim rippling round his cock as she climaxed. It was enough to tip him into his own orgasm; he cried out softly as he came, and then she sank down on to his chest. Luke wrapped his arms round her, stroking her hair and whispering soft endearments.

When the aftershocks of her orgasm had died away, Luke gently withdrew from her and got to his feet, pulling her up next to him. 'Eunice.' He kissed her softly on the mouth. 'Thank you.' Tenderly, he dressed her again, but he didn't put her hair up. 'Leave it down,' he said. 'It makes you look so much prettier – the real you, not the face you hide behind.' She flushed, but she made no move to tie her hair back in the old unflattering way.

Luke dressed, then took the memo from the fax machine. 'I know how Leonard hates to have his office littered up,' he said. He smiled at her. 'Obviously I don't expect the university to pay for my fax. Is there anywhere that I can pay for the call?'

She shook her head. 'It doesn't matter. It's only one call and it was only one piece of paper.'

'Well.' Luke screwed the paper into a ball and handed it to her. 'Can you get rid of this, for me, please?' He grinned. 'Leonard did say that you were more efficient than anyone he knows.'

She dimpled at him. 'Did he really say that?'

'Yes,' he lied. 'Look, Eunice, I really do feel bad about sending that fax. Do you have a charity box or something like that, so I can ease my conscience?'

'Well – actually, there's one for the RSPCA on my desk. I've been putting my spare change into it.'

'If you don't mind, I'd like to do the same,' Luke said.

He emptied his pockets, giving her all his change. 'Is it all right if I wait here for Len?'

'Yes, of course,' Eunice said. 'Would you like me to get you a coffee while you're waiting?'

He shook his head. 'I'm trying to give it up.'

'I have some herbal tea in my desk. Camomile.'

He stroked her face. 'Oh, Eunice. I wonder if Leonard appreciates you as much as you deserve? Thanks, but I'll pass. I'll just wait for him to come back.'

'All right. Well, I'll be at my desk if you need me. I'm in the room round the corner.'

'Thank you.' He smiled at her as she unlocked the door and left the room. He waited just long enough for her to go back into her office and then left the room himself, closing the door behind him. He felt slightly guilty about what he'd just done; but maybe, in some odd way, he'd helped Eunice, made her realise that she wasn't the frumpy and dull secretary who slaved for Leonard Hollis. Maybe she was even carrying a torch for Hollis, and what they'd just done had given her the confidence to approach him. Luke's lips twisted. Though she didn't deserve a bastard like Hollis.

He left the library and headed for the coffee shop. Jennifer was waiting there, pretending to be absorbed in a magazine, but checking her watch every couple of minutes. As Luke walked through the door and joined her at the table, her face lit up. 'Luke, I was beginning to get worried about you.'

'Hey, I'm all right. No sign of Rachel, yet?'

'No.'

Luke looked thoughtful. 'Well, she shouldn't be too long now. While we're waiting, can I get you a coffee?'

'Love one. Espresso.'

Luke grinned. 'And a *pain au chocolat*, right?'

'I should have guessed that Rachel would have introduced you to them too,' Jennifer said.

'Mm, on our first meeting. After she'd drowned my notes in coffee.'

230

'How did you get on? You know, with the papers?'

'I'll tell you in a minute – I need coffee,' Luke said. He ordered two espressos and two *pains au chocolat*, and then went back to their table. 'I'll get Rachel's when she comes in.'

'So, did you find anything?'

'Better than that. I've faxed it to Max. Everything's in motion.' He paused. 'Jennifer, could I borrow your phone, please?'

'Of course.'

'I keep meaning to get one of these myself, but I never seem to have the time,' he said.

Jennifer switched on her phone, typed in her PIN number, and passed it to him.

'Digital. Very nice.' Luke smiled at her. 'Thanks, Jen.'

'Hey, I'm doing this for Rachel.'

'Funnily enough,' Luke said, 'although this started out as just another assignment, I'm doing it for Rachel, too. I want to see her reinstated and I want her bastard of a boss out of her way, so she gets to do what she's good at and what makes her happy.' He dialled Max's number and was relieved when Max answered immediately.

'Did you get my fax?'

'Yes,' Max said. 'Don't worry, everything's already in motion.'

'Thanks.'

'Is Rachel with you?'

'Not yet,' Luke said, 'but don't worry. I don't think she's in any danger.'

'She'd better not be,' Max said. 'I don't want her hurt in all this.'

'Trust me. I'll look after her, I promise. I'll talk to you later.' Luke cut the line, then switched off the phone and handed it back to Jennifer, who chuckled.

'Do I take it from that conversation that another of the Rachel Kemp fan-club just had a go at you?'

'Something like that. She's made a hit with Max.' Luke

231

shrugged. 'But that's not surprising. I think he's in love with her brain as much as her body.'

'Mm, she told me about the job offer. She said that it was too good to be true.'

'It's bona fide,' Luke said.

At that precise moment, the door of the café opened and Rachel walked in. She went over to the counter, ordered herself an espresso and a pastry, and then went to join Luke and Jennifer.

He leant over to kiss her. 'I'm glad you're all right. I was beginning to get worried – in case Hollis rumbled you.'

'Not a chance. Maybe I ought to take up acting.' Rachel held her hand out. 'Though I'm still shaking. There was one point when I didn't think that I could pull it off.'

'I'm sure you did brilliantly.'

'I owe you a new lipstick, Jen.'

'Hey, I can live without it. Call it my contribution,' Jennifer said.

Rachel nodded and turned to Luke. 'Well? Did you get it?'

'Yep. I faxed it to Max and I just rang him on Jennifer's phone. Everything's set in motion; all we have to do is wait.'

'How long?'

'Maybe today, maybe tomorrow. Either way, it's all over.' He stroked her face. 'I'm sorry that I had to put you through that, Rachel. But it was the only way.'

'As long as they're both caught, I don't care.' She swallowed. 'So what did you find?'

'A note. It was stuck to another piece of paper; I was surprised that he didn't notice.' Luke bit his lip. 'I don't think that it's a plant.'

'A plant? You mean others might be involved too?' Jennifer's eyes widened.

'I'm not sure. But those two are the main ones. We've

got enough on them.' He shrugged. 'It was close, though. I decided to fax it from his office.'

'You what?' Rachel was furious. 'Are you stupid? You could have been caught!'

'I could also have been caught leaving that office and searched,' Luke reminded her. 'It was a calculated risk.'

She caught the look on his face. 'What happened?'

'His secretary came in.'

'Oh, God,' Rachel said.

'It's all right, she was fine about it.'

Rachel grimaced. 'I've been at the university long enough to know that she's a dragon and she's completely devoted to him.'

'Everyone has a weak point,' Luke said, 'and dragons can always be tamed.'

Jennifer raised an eyebrow. 'I don't know if I dare ask what you did.'

'Something along the same lines as Rachel.' Luke's tone was dry.

'Then I think we'd better get out of here,' Jennifer said. 'And, to be honest, I don't think we should go back to either of your places. If she's that devoted to him, she's bound to tell him that there was someone in his room – no matter how good you are, Luke, you're not going to make her forget that – and if she describes you, he'll twig. He'll know that Rachel's involved, too, and that she was acting as a decoy. Supposing they send the heavies round?'

'Come off it,' Rachel said. 'This isn't gangster-land.'

'Jen has a point,' Luke said softly. 'There's a lot of money involved. Like enough to pay your salary until you retire.'

Jennifer whistled. 'For that sort of money, people don't give up easily. I think we ought to go to a hotel somewhere, at least until tomorrow morning.'

'You're forgetting something,' Rachel said. 'Some of us don't have a job.'

233

Luke took her hand, squeezing it. 'Ever heard of expenses? And I think that Jen's right.'

Rachel nodded. 'All right. If you two feel that strongly about it, let's go, now.'

Luke paid the bill, and they left the café. Their luck was in, as a taxi came towards them almost immediately; Luke hailed it and gave the driver the address of a hotel in Kensington. 'The last place they'll think of looking for us,' he explained, *sotto voce*, to Rachel.

# Chapter Seventeen

When they arrived at the hotel, Luke checked in. A discreet and smartly uniformed porter showed them up to the suite Luke had booked. 'All separate rooms,' Luke said with a grin, 'if you want to behave with decorum.'

Rachel laughed. 'To be honest, more than anything else, I could do with a very stiff gin and tonic.'

'I think there's something better than that in the fridge,' Luke said, 'bearing in mind that we have a suite.' He tipped the porter and ushered Rachel and Jennifer inside. 'We've just cracked quite an important case. I think that this deserves the best.' He walked over to the fridge; sure enough, as he'd predicted, there was a bottle of Bollinger inside and a box of Belgian chocolate truffles. 'The perfect combination,' Luke said, smiling. There was a silver salver containing six glasses on top of the fridge; Luke turned three of them the right way up, uncorked the champagne and poured out the wine. He handed a glass to Rachel and to Jennifer. 'To us,' he said.

'To us,' they echoed.

He took a sip, then turned to Jennifer. 'May I borrow your phone again, please?'

'Of course.'

'It's just that I'd rather trust a digital line. No one knows we're here – but even so, I'd feel safer not using a network,' he said soberly. She retrieved the phone from her handbag, tapped in her PIN number and handed it to Luke.

He dialled a number. 'I'd like to speak to Detective Inspector Forbes, please.' There was a pause. 'Mike? Yes, it's Luke. Yes, I thought that Max had probably called you by now. We're staying somewhere else tonight, just to be on the safe side.' He gave the name of the hotel. 'Yes, we'll stay here until you tell us that it's safe. Yes – I'd appreciate that. Thanks. I'll speak to you later then.'

'What was that all about?' Jennifer asked. 'Police protection?'

'Yes. The more I've been thinking about it, the more I think that you're right – they might turn nasty. Mike's going to have someone keeping an eye on us from outside.' He bit his lip. 'I only hope that Eunice doesn't get caught up in all this mess.'

'Eunice?' Rachel queried.

'Hollis's secretary.'

'Oh, you mean Miss Smith.' Rachel smiled wryly. 'No one's ever heard her first name. She's always insisted that we refer to her as Miss Smith. She's the only one of the secretaries who's so formal and I just assumed that it was Hollis's influence.'

'Yeah, well.' Luke handed the phone back to Jennifer, who replaced it in her handbag.

Rachel took a large gulp of champagne. 'That feels better.' She stretched. 'If you two don't mind, I think I'll take a bath. I don't feel particularly clean at the moment.'

'If you want someone to wash your back, just yell,' Luke said.

Jennifer groaned, raking her hair through her long dark curls. 'Why do I suddenly feel small, round, green and hairy?'

Luke took her hand, squeezing it. 'You're not a gooseberry, Jennifer. We couldn't have done this without you.'

'Of course you could.'

Luke shook his head. 'Without your back-up, Rachel and I would have been at much greater risk.' He smiled at her. 'Actually, this bath that Rachel fancies ... we have more than just an ordinary bath, in this suite.'

Rachel's eyes narrowed. 'What have you done?'

'I'm pretty sure that you'll like it.' He grinned. 'The best way to celebrate is in bubbles, don't you think?'

Jennifer frowned. 'That's what we are doing. Drinking champagne.'

His grin broadened. 'I mean literally in bubbles.'

Apart from the *pains au chocolat*, they hadn't eaten since breakfast. The champagne was beginning to go to Rachel's head. 'Are you suggesting that we have a bath together?' she asked, more amused than shocked.

'Not a bath,' Luke corrected. 'A jacuzzi. And, to preserve your modesty, I'll keep my eyes closed until you tell me that I can look.'

Jennifer chuckled. 'With an offer like that, how can we refuse?'

Luke topped up their glasses, grabbed the chocolates and led them into the bathroom. Rachel looked round, impressed. There was a large shower cubicle in one corner, a sunken circular jacuzzi in the middle and everywhere was in gleaming white, with a small discreet Greek key-line in gold. There were large thick fluffy bath-sheets, rather than towels, and there were a couple of thick white towelling robes hanging on the hook behind the door.

'Wow,' Rachel said. 'This is way beyond the sort of thing that a junior lecturer can usually afford. Pure luxury.'

'Mm.' Jennifer's lips twitched. 'I can feel a setting coming on. I'll have to start taking notes later.'

Rachel giggled. 'I won't ask what about!'

'Well, if you two will turn your backs,' Luke said, 'I'll strip off and get in the jacuzzi.' He pressed the switch at the side, and small bubbles began to rise to the surface

237

of the pool. By the time that he'd finished removing his clothes, the jacuzzi was ready. He stepped into the water and leant back against the wall, stretching his arms along the sides. 'OK,' he said. 'I'm closing my eyes now. Tell me when you're ready.'

Jennifer and Rachel smiled at each other and stripped swiftly. They slid into the jacuzzi, one either side of Luke.

'You can open your eyes now,' Rachel said.

Luke did so and smiled at her. 'There's only one problem.'

'What?'

'Our glasses, and the chocolates, are the other side of the room.'

Rachel groaned and climbed out of the jacuzzi. This time, she didn't bother covering herself with a towel; Luke had seen her in far more intimate moments, and she and Jennifer had gone swimming together before, in a place which only had a communal changing room, so she didn't feel self-conscious.

She brought the glasses and the chocolates back. She handed a glass each to Luke and Jennifer, balanced her own on the side of the bath and slid back into the water. 'Happy now?'

'Yes. This is the life,' Luke said in satisfaction. 'Drinking champagne, sitting in bubbles and being fed Belgian chocolates.'

'OK, OK, hint taken.' Rachel opened the box, taking a chocolate and holding it to Luke's mouth. He took a bite and she ate the other half, before offering the box to Jennifer.

Jennifer ate a chocolate and took another gulp of champagne. 'Rach, can I ask you something?'

'Yes, sure.'

'What did you actually do to Hollis?'

Rachel winced. 'Ah. I'd rather not talk about that. I've never made love to anyone as a decoy before, and it makes me feel a bit sleazy.'

Luke rested his hand on her thigh. 'I know one way to make you feel better,' he said softly.

'He's right,' Jennifer said. 'Who better to make you feel good, than close friends?'

Rachel licked her lips. What Jennifer was suggesting was way beyond her usual boundaries. The three of them, making love. She knew already that Jennifer found Luke attractive: and Jennifer herself was gorgeous enough for any man to want her. And then there was her, in the middle. Rachel was drunk enough for it to appeal to her; at the same time, she felt slightly nervous. Jennifer was her best friend. She didn't want anything to spoil that relationship.

'It won't,' Jennifer promised, and Rachel coloured as she realised that she'd spoken aloud.

'I . . .'

'Sh,' Jennifer said, sliding her hand on to Rachel's other thigh. 'It's all right.'

It reminded Rachel so much of the way that Luke and Max had made her come under the table in the restaurant that time, that she shivered. Luke and Jennifer took it as a sign of approval; slowly, Luke's hand moved up her thigh to cup her quim. Meanwhile, Jennifer moved slightly closer to Rachel and cupped her face in her hands.

As Luke's probing finger parted her labia and slid along Rachel's musky furrow, Jennifer kissed her lightly, her mouth soft and warm and gentle. Rachel gasped as Luke pushed his finger into her and Jennifer took advantage of the moment to deepen the kiss. Rachel found herself responding, sliding her hands round Jennifer's neck; Jennifer's hands moved to cup Rachel's breasts.

Rachel widened the gap between her thighs; Luke moved her slightly so that she was facing Jennifer and then lifted her on to his lap. She felt his cock pressing against the cleft of her buttocks, large and erect; she wriggled against him and he chuckled, kissing the back of her neck. 'Oh, Rachel. I can't resist you.' He manoeuvred her deftly, lifting her again, and she felt his cock push into her sex. She flexed her internal muscles round him as he lowered her on to his cock, and Luke nuzzled her shoulders, sliding one hand round her waist and settling the other one between her thighs.

Jennifer continued to caress Rachel's breasts as Luke rubbed her clitoris; Rachel moaned against Jennifer's mouth and began to move over Luke, lifting and lowering herself on to his cock. At last, she felt the rush of her orgasm fill her and cried out; Jennifer and Luke soothed her, holding her and caressing her until the sharp contractions had faded. Then, very gently, Luke lifted her from him, moving her so that she was sitting on the ledge of the jacuzzi again.

'Better?' he asked, stroking her face.

'Mm.' She smiled wryly. 'I certainly wasn't expecting that.'

'Neither was I,' Jennifer said. 'But if you think of the sort of day we've had, all the worry and the tension and the fear . . . Something like this was bound to happen.'

'No strings, no worries, no regrets,' Luke said softly. 'And I think we'd better get out of this, before we turn into prunes.'

He helped Rachel to her feet; she climbed out of the jacuzzi and grabbed three towels, handing one to Luke and Jennifer as they clambered out. Luke dried himself swiftly, then wrapped the towel round his waist. 'I don't know about you two,' he said, 'but I'm starving. How about I order us something from room service?'

'Sounds good to me,' Jennifer said. 'I'm hungry, too.'

A look passed between them: they both knew that they weren't just referring to food. Luke nodded. 'All right. Any requests or will you trust me?'

'We'll trust you,' Rachel said.

While she and Jennifer continued drying themselves, Luke padded out to the sitting room to order some food.

'Jen – what happened just now . . .'

240

'Was a one-off,' Jennifer said comfortingly. 'For today only, special offer.'

Rachel smiled. 'Now you're being silly.'

'Yes.' Jennifer kissed the tip of her nose. 'I think we all needed it though. Sex is the best release of tension I know.'

'But I was the only one who actually had any kind of release,' Rachel said thoughtfully.

'There's still the rest of the afternoon,' Jennifer said. 'Not to mention tonight.' She paused. 'If Luke and I . . . well, if we end up making love, would you mind? I mean, he's your man.'

'Mm. And friends share things, do they not?'

'Not everything. If you want me to back off, I will. Like he said, there are three bedrooms in this suite. I can always make myself scarce.'

Rachel shook her head. 'No – I think the attraction's mutual. And, like you said, today's a one-off.'

'OK.' Jennifer stroked her face. 'As long as you're sure.'

'I'm sure.'

When they'd finished towelling themselves and smoothing in the luxurious body cream which the hotel had thoughtfully provided, they dressed in the thick towelling robes. Jennifer took Rachel's hand. 'Come on.' They walked out into the sitting room; Luke smiled at them, and gestured to the table.

'Wow. That was fast,' Rachel said.

'I ordered cold things. Cheese, canapés, dips and fruit. I hope that's OK.'

'More than OK.'

They suddenly discovered just how ravenous they were; and although Luke had ordered plenty, there was virtually nothing left by the time that they'd finished. He'd also ordered a couple more bottles of champagne and kept their glasses topped up.

Rachel pushed her plate away and stretched. 'Mm. I feel a lot better now.'

'Me, too,' Jennifer said.

Rachel tipped her head on one side and looked at Luke. 'And now, I could just go to bed.'

'Curl up and go to sleep, hm?' he asked.

She shook her head. 'That's not what I meant.'

The air was suddenly electric. Luke swallowed. 'Then what did you mean, Rachel?'

'I mean,' she said, 'I feel like making love. Properly. Skin to skin.' She looked at Jennifer. 'Like we said earlier, we all need a release from tension: I'm the only one who's had that release so far. And even that wasn't enough.'

Luke licked his lower lip. 'Are you suggesting what I think you're suggesting?'

'You started it, with your idea of the bath,' Rachel said. She stood up and loosened the belt of her robe. 'So I think you should finish it too.' She shrugged the robe from her shoulders and sashayed over to the door of the main bedroom. As she'd hoped, it was a king-size bed. There was more than enough room for the three of them.

Rachel pulled the covers back from the bed and sat on the edge of the mattress. Luke and Jennifer had followed her into the room; she patted the mattress and smiled coquettishly at them.

Luke smiled back and came to lie beside her, sprawling on his side and propping his head up on his hand. 'So what did you have in mind, Rachel?' he asked softly.

She pushed him on to his back and unwrapped the towel from his waist. He was already erect, his cock springing up proudly from the cloud of dark hair at his groin. Rachel held out her hand to Jennifer. 'This.'

Jennifer gave her a look, as if to say, 'Are you sure?' Rachel nodded, and Jennifer shed her robe, climbing on to the bed next to Luke. She curled her fingers round his shaft and began to masturbate him, using long slow strokes which had him groaning and tipping his head back against the pillows.

Rachel leant over to kiss Luke, her lips moving gently

242

against his; he cupped her face in both hands, opening his mouth so that she could slide her tongue into his mouth, deepening the kiss.

Meanwhile, Jennifer shifted down the bed and lifted one of his feet, sucking his toes one by one, and kissed her way up his legs, licking the hollows of his ankles and the soft sensitive spot behind his knees. Luke moaned as she moved upwards, her dark wavy hair brushing against his inner thighs, but she didn't take him into her mouth; instead, she shifted to work on the other leg, starting with his thigh and moving down to his ankle.

Luke continued kissing Rachel, moving his hands down to caress her breasts and play with her nipples; Jennifer moved back to work on his thighs, kissing him and breathing tantalisingly on his cock. Luke's hips jerked and Jennifer curled her fingers round his cock again, bending her head and taking him deep into her mouth. Luke kissed Rachel more fiercely as Jennifer sucked him; Rachel felt his body tense, but then Jennifer stopped and squeezed gently just below the head of his cock to delay his orgasm.

Rachel broke the kiss. 'Luke.'

He groaned. 'Anything.'

She smiled and shifted slightly. Jennifer, too, shifted, moving to straddle him. She rested her quim against his cock so that he could feel how aroused she was, how hot and wet and ready for him; and then she lifted herself again, so that she could coax the tip of his cock to her sex, and pushed down hard.

Luke moaned, tipping his head back against the pillows, and Jennifer began to move over him, using her internal muscles to massage his cock and leaning back to increase the angle of his penetration.

'Rachel,' he said hoarsely. 'Rachel. I want to pleasure you too.'

She knew instinctively what he wanted, and moved so that she was kneeling astride his chest. Luke grasped her hips, urging her buttocks back towards her slightly, and nuzzled her skin, breathing on her and making her shiver. Then, at last, she felt the long slow stroke of his tongue against her quim.

Jennifer smiled at her friend, leaning forward, and slid her hands round Rachel's neck. She rubbed her nose affectionately against Rachel's, then kissed her lightly on the lips. Rachel could taste the muskiness from where Jennifer had sucked Luke's cock, and she slid her tongue into Jennifer's mouth, deepening the kiss.

Jennifer let her hands drift down to Rachel's breasts, cupping them and pushing them together slightly; her thumbs rubbed against Rachel's areolae, stimulating her nipples until they were hard as cherry-stones. Then she gently pulled on them, elongating them and making Rachel gasp. Rachel, in turn, touched Jennifer's breasts, stroking the soft undersides and then pinching her nipples gently, sensitising them.

'Please,' Jennifer said, breaking the kiss. 'Touch me.' She took Rachel's hand, squeezing her fingers and dragging her hand downwards. Rachel smiled and cupped Jennifer's delta, her middle finger parting Jennifer's labia.

Jennifer moaned in pleasure, arching back over Luke, and her movements became faster, pulling up rapidly and then slamming down hard. Rachel found her friend's clitoris and began to rub it gently, her fingertip gliding over the sensitive nub of flesh. 'Oh, yes,' Jennifer moaned. 'Yes. Yes.'

Luke continued to lick his lover, his tongue pushing deep inside her, and then flicking over her clitoris; he moved his hands so that he could stroke her thighs, and then move gradually upwards until he could touch her quim, rubbing her clitoris in the same way that she worked Jennifer's.

Jennifer licked her middle finger, then moved her hand behind her so that she could stroke Luke's perineum. His body jerked as she pressed the tip of her finger against his anus; then his muscles relaxed, allowing her the access she wanted. The three of them moved together in perfect harmony, rubbing and licking and kissing; at last Jennifer cried out, her eyes closed and her face contorting in pleasure.

Rachel leant forward to kiss her friend as she felt her own orgasm bubble through her; Luke's body jerked, and she felt him groan against her flesh as he, too, reached a climax. Finally, when their pulses had slowed down, Jennifer and Rachel climbed off Luke, shifting to lie either side of him and linking their hands across his waist. Luke kissed each of them lightly, in turn. 'That was incredible,' he said softly.

'For all of us,' Rachel replied.

He stroked her hair. 'I still can't believe this. I've dragged you into this mess and you've lost your job through it – but you can still be so generous towards me.'

'You've got one hell of a special woman there,' Jennifer said. 'And you'd better appreciate her – or you'll have me to answer to.'

Luke smiled at her. 'Oh, I appreciate her. Believe me.'

'So you should.' Jennifer winked at him. 'And now, I think – more champagne.'

The next morning, the three of them lay curled up together. They'd spent the rest of the previous day making love, and most of the night, too; then, finally, they'd fallen into a luxurious and satiating sleep.

They were rudely woken by the phone ringing. Luke groaned and sat up, picking up the receiver. 'Hello?'

'You sound like hell,' Max said, amused. 'I don't think I dare ask you what you've been doing.'

Luke groaned again. 'What do you want?'

'I'm downstairs, in the lobby. We're waiting for you to come down. But take your time.'

'Downstairs? What about – '

'Gilson and Hollis?' Max finished. 'They're in police custody. And I have a few things to talk to Rachel about.'

'Now?'

'Later.'

'Right. We'll be down in – say – half an hour.' Luke replaced the receiver. 'That was Max.'

'Max?' Rachel sat upright, instantly awake. 'What's happened?'

'Nothing to worry about,' Luke soothed. 'Gilson and Hollis are in custody.'

'Right. I take it we're needed, then?'

'Yes. I said we'd see Max downstairs in half an hour.'

Rachel climbed out of bed. 'I'll grab the shower first, then.'

'All right.'

As she left the room, Jennifer sat up and looked at Luke. 'So does that mean that Rachel's name is cleared and she gets her job back?'

'I don't know,' Luke answered honestly. 'Max said that he wanted to talk to her about a couple of things – so it could be the diaries, or it could be her job. Both, even.'

Jennifer nodded. 'She deserves the chance, Luke. She's worked bloody hard – and Gilson's held her back. Deliberately so.' She smiled wryly. 'There's a kind of poetic justice that she was the one to help bring him to book.'

'Yeah.'

Luke and Jennifer took their turns in the shower when Rachel returned; finally, the three of them left the suite. Max was waiting downstairs in reception; his eyes widened as he saw Jennifer. 'I didn't realise that you and Rachel had anyone with you.'

Rachel nodded. 'My best friend, Jennifer Clark. Also known as Jude Devereaux.'

'*The* Jude Devereaux?' Max's eyes flickered with interest.

246

'The one and only,' Rachel confirmed. 'Jen, this is Max Houghton, Luke's cousin.'

'Pleased to meet you,' Jennifer said, holding out her hand.

'So, what's the news?' Rachel asked. 'Luke said that Gilson and Hollis are in custody.'

'Yes – and they've made a full confession. They're both intelligent enough to realise that holding things back won't help them.' Max looked at her. 'I've some good and some bad news for you, though.'

'Bad first,' Rachel said immediately.

'I'm afraid that your place has been smashed up. Nothing's been stolen but it's a bit of a mess.' He winced. 'I think that Gilson sent some of his friends round to see you; when they couldn't find you, they decided to have a little fun with your belongings.'

'Bastard,' Rachel said. 'Hasn't he done enough?'

'I know,' Max soothed. 'I've already set the wheels in motion to clear everything up before you get home. Oh – and you'll need to testify in court.'

'That's no problem,' Rachel said. 'They deserve everything they get.'

'What about the good news?' Jennifer asked.

'The university's reinstating you,' Max said. 'Permanently.'

Rachel was surprised. 'I thought that they had to downscale, lose some staff?'

'Yes – but you're not one of them.' Max looked at her. 'Though if you have time, I'd still like you to work on those diaries.'

Rachel smiled. 'You bet.'

'Good.' Max smiled back. 'Now, I've already sorted the hotel bill. Rachel, while your place is being sorted out, you're very welcome to stay with me at Hilbury. You too, Jennifer.'

Luke coughed. 'What about me?'

Max rolled his eyes. 'You know you've got an open invitation.'

Luke grinned. 'Just testing.'

'Come on, then.' Max looked at him. 'Though I'm afraid that I brought the MG with me. There's really only enough room for one passenger – which I think should be Jennifer.'

Luke slid his arm round Rachel's shoulders. 'We'll catch the tube to Holborn, and I'll drive down later, then.'

'All right. See you in Norfolk.'

'I get the feeling,' Luke whispered in Rachel's ear, 'that Max has just got a new conquest in his sights.'

'And I get the feeling,' Rachel replied softly, 'that it's mutual . . .'

# *Epilogue*

$S$ ix months later, Jennifer and Rachel sat with their feet up in Rachel's kitchen, drinking coffee. 'Well, cheers, Dr Kemp,' Jennifer said, raising her mug. 'And congratulations on your PhD!'

'Thanks.' Rachel smiled at her. 'It's been quite a year, this year.'

'Mm. Getting a decent supervisor, finishing your PhD, being promoted out of the ranks of the junior lecturers and editing a best-selling edition of a racy diary about your favourite author. Not to mention gaining an extremely gorgeous live-in lover.' Jennifer ticked them off on her fingers. 'The best thing is, you deserve every bit of it. It's about time you had a run of luck, after Gilson.'

'Yeah, well. Gilson's in the past, now.' Rachel sipped her coffee. 'It looks like he churned a hell of a lot of documents – he and Hollis, between them. Though instead of boosting their pension funds, they've found themselves on the career scrap-heap, with a criminal record and a jail sentence to boot.'

'Serves them right.' Jennifer had no sympathy for either of them.

'Mind you, it hasn't been a bad year for you, either.

Rave reviews, the chance to be the first author in a new imprint and a certain financier in Norfolk lusting after you.'

Jennifer grinned. 'Max is really – quite special. You didn't warn me about that. Or about what Hilbury's really like.' Jennifer had spent several weekends at Max's place and had met Stella, Edmund and half a dozen of Max's more broad-minded friends.

'You didn't need warning,' Rachel teased. 'In fact, if anything, your imagination's even more inventive than his is!'

'True,' Jennifer acknowledged. 'So what time's Luke due home?'

Rachel glanced at her watch. 'Any time in the next hour. It depends on his current assignment, if there's a hold-up or anything.' She smiled. 'Though he's promised that next time he takes an undercover alias, he'll check it out with me first . . .'

# Visit the Black Lace website at
# www.blacklace-books.co.uk

# LOOK OUT FOR THE ALL-NEW BLACK LACE BOOKS – AVAILABLE NOW!

*All books priced £7.99 in the UK. Please note publication dates apply to the UK only. For other territories, please contact your retailer.*

## ENTERTAINING MR STONE
### *Portia da Costa*
ISBN 0 352 34029 0

When reforming bad girl Maria Lewis takes a drone job in local government back in her home town, the quiet life she was looking for is quickly disrupted by the enigmatic presence of her boss, Borough Director, Robert Stone. A dangerous and unlikely object of lust, Stone touches something deep in Maria's sensual psyche and attunes her to the erotic underworld that parallels life in the dusty offices of Borough Hall. But the charismatic Mr Stone isn't the only one interested in Maria – knowing lesbian Mel and cute young techno geek Greg both have designs on the newcomer, as does Human Resources Manager William Youngblood, who wants to prize the Borough's latest employee away from the arch-rival for whom he has ambiguous feelings.

## Coming in May

**CIRCUS EXCITE**
*Nikki Magennis*
ISBN 0 352 34033 9

Julia Spark is a professional dancer, newly graduated. Jobs are hard to find and after a curious audition she finds herself running away with the circus. It's not what she expected – the circus is an adult show full of bizarre performers forbidden from sex yet trained to turn people on. The ringmaster exerts a powerful influence over the performers, and seems to have taken a special interest in Julia. As the circus tours the UK, Julia plays the power games with Robert, finding herself drawn into his world of erotic fantasy. He dares her to experiment, playing with her desires and encouraging Julia to explore the darker side of her own sexuality.

**ELENA'S DESTINY**
*Lisette Allen*
ISBN 0 352 33218 2

The year is 1073. The gentle convent-bred Elena, awakened to the joys of forbidden passion by the masterful knight Aimery le Sabrenn, has been forcibly separated from her lover by war. She is haunted by the memory of him. Then fate brings her to William the Conqueror's dark stronghold of Rouen, and a reunion with Aimery. Although he still captivates Elena with his powerful masculinity, Aimery is no longer hers. As the King's formidable knights prepare for war, Elena discovers that she must fight a desperate battle for him against her two rivals; the scheming sensual Isobel and a wanton young heiress called Henriette, who has set her heart on becoming Aimery's bride. The backdrop of war tightens around them and dangerous games of love and lust are played out amidst the increasing tension of a merciless siege.

## Coming in June

### WILD CARD
*Madeline Moore*
ISBN 0 352 34038 X

When Victoria Ashe lures an ex-lover to her London hotel room, their passion is reignited with startling intensity. She's out to prove to Ray that intimacy can be just as exciting as the thrill of the chase. Ray Torrington might actually agree if it weren't for Kinky Bai Lon, a Hong Kong bombshell who doles herself out one delicate morsel at a time, always in public. And Penny, a champion poker player known as 'The Flame of London', also has her sights on the saucy jackpot. The scene is set for a high stakes, game of sexual exploration. When the wild card keeps changing it's difficult for even the most accomplished player to know who's bluffing and who is telling the truth. In this lusty tournament of champions, the winner takes all.

### SAUCE FOR THE GOOSE
*Mary Rose Maxwell*
ISBN 0 352 33492 4

Sauce for the goose is a riotous and sometimes humorous celebration of the rich variety of human sexuality. Imaginative and colourful, each story explores a different theme or fantasy, and the result is a fabulously bawdy melánge of cheeky sensuality and hot thrills. A lively array of characters display an uninhibited and lusty energy for boundary breaking pleasure. This is a decidedly x-rated collection of stories designed to be enjoyed and indulged in.

# Black Lace Booklist

Information is correct at time of printing. To avoid disappointment, check availability before ordering. Go to www.blacklace-books.co.uk. All books are priced £6.99 unless another price is given.

## BLACK LACE BOOKS WITH A CONTEMPORARY SETTING

To find out the latest information about Black Lace titles, check out the website: www.blacklace-books.co.uk or send for a booklist with complete synopses by writing to:

Black Lace Booklist, Virgin Books Ltd
Thames Wharf Studios
Rainville Road
London W6 9HA

Please include an SAE of decent size. Please note only British stamps are valid.

Our privacy policy
We will not disclose information you supply us to any other parties. We will not disclose any information which identifies you personally to any person without your express consent.

From time to time we may send out information about Black Lace books and special offers. Please tick here if you do <u>not</u> wish to receive Black Lace information. ❑

Please send me the books I have ticked above.

Name ...............................................................

Address ...........................................................

.......................................................................

.......................................................................

.......................................................................

Post Code .........................................................

**Send to:** Virgin Books Cash Sales, Thames Wharf Studios, Rainville Road, London W6 9HA.

**US customers:** for prices and details of how to order books for delivery by mail, call 888-330-8477.

Please enclose a cheque or postal order, made payable to Virgin Books Ltd, to the value of the books you have ordered plus postage and packing costs as follows:

UK and BFPO – £1.00 for the first book, 50p for each subsequent book.

Overseas (including Republic of Ireland) – £2.00 for the first book, £1.00 for each subsequent book.

If you would prefer to pay by VISA, ACCESS/MASTERCARD, DINERS CLUB, AMEX or SWITCH, please write your card number and expiry date here:

.......................................................................

Signature ..........................................................

Please allow up to 28 days for delivery.